"Hello. Thi   [barcode: 10364565]
calling. Is

His voice was low and resonant. Masculine. God help her.

"This is Erika."

"I thought we should talk on the phone." *Brilliant, brilliant, keep it up, Kal.*

Erika bit her lip. There was a bellows stuck in her throat, and it was opening and closing with each beat of her heart. *Talk,* she thought. *Say something that will make him…*

Oh, she wanted it. They could settle into permanence—permanent celibacy, permanent family—and her life would not change again. Safe.

"Your daughter's beautiful." The ensuing pause was so long that at last she asked, "Are you still there?"

"Yeah. I… Erika, I've thought a lot since I got your letter. Are you serious about this?"

This. As though he couldn't say it himself. Erika swallowed. She wanted a family—and an opportunity like this wouldn't come again. Normal people wanted sex. Kal and his grief were her only hope.

"Yes," she said. "Yes, I am."

Dear Reader,

I'm the youngest of eight children and have more than thirty first cousins. When I married my husband, I acquired even more family, not just my beloved spouse, but *his* family.

So let me tell you a story.

It was like something out of a romance novel. I was in distress, fleeing personal difficulties, taking my two-year-old son with me. My destination: Iowa. My husband-to-be's family were to meet me at the airport; though I had never met them, on the trust of *his* love for me, they had invited me to come to their home and stay.

My beautiful future sister-in-law met me at the airport with the words "Welcome to Iowa, Margot!" Just hours later my fiancé's parents encouraged me to call them "Mom" and "Dad"—a tradition unfamiliar to me, but which I found immediately comfortable and welcoming. In the coming days Mom would inspire me with her courage and love (especially her love for my son!), Dad with his profound generosity, and Grandma with her wisdom and her chocolate chip cookies. I had already conversed at length with my brother-in-law-to-be on the phone. An added bonus was my new sister's daughter, born the same day as my son. One couldn't wish for better in-laws!

Five years later, five years sprinkled with love and laughter during periodic visits with these delightful people, I found myself with them again while completing this novel. Perhaps that is why *Mr. Family* celebrates the Hawaiian concept of *ohana*—not just family, but extended family. Though the characters of *Mr. Family*—Kal, Erika (who first appeared in *The Third Christmas*), Hiialo and their *ohana*—are purely imaginary, perhaps you can feel in these pages the love I've been fortunate to know. I hope so. Wishing you and yours the same....

Sincerely,

Margot Early

P.S. I love hearing from readers. Please write to me at P.O. Box 611, Montrose, CO 81402-0611.

Margot Early

MR. FAMILY

Harlequin Books

TORONTO • NEW YORK • LONDON
AMSTERDAM • PARIS • SYDNEY • HAMBURG
STOCKHOLM • ATHENS • TOKYO • MILAN
MADRID • WARSAW • BUDAPEST • AUCKLAND

For my *ohana*

ISBN 0-373-70711-8

MR. FAMILY

ACKNOWLEDGMENTS

I would like to thank the following people, each of whom helped in some way with this book:

For enriching my appreciation and understanding of art, I'm grateful to Elaine Barnhart, Jan Carlile and Alan Fine.

To all my *ohana* who helped in large and small ways during the writing of this book, thank you.

Laura and Cecilia, your friendship and wisdom brighten my days.

And most of all, I thank the two closest to me, my husband and son, for your patience and love.

CHAPTER ONE

Santa Barbara, California
January

> WANTED: Woman to enter celibate marriage and be stepmother to four-year-old girl. Send child-rearing philosophies to Mr. Ohana, Box J, Haena, Kauai, HI.

"THAT'S THE WRONG page." Impatiently Adele reached over the butter plate with a long-nailed hand that seemed dwarfed by rings, onyx and jade in hand-crafted gold settings. She gestured for Erika to turn the magazine pages. "It's in the middle."

"Wait, wait. Look at this." Strangely excited—in the same way she became excited when a painting was going well—Erika Blade handed Adele the copy of *Island Voice,* open to the ad for a celibate marriage. In the last few months she had begun to pay attention to personal ads, to flyers for computer dating services, to bulletins for singles'-club activities. She never acted on any of them. Only desperate people did things like that, and she wasn't really even looking for a mate. Not exactly. She was simply...curious.

Celibate marriage. Send child-rearing philosophies...

If she was ever to answer a personal ad, this would be the one.

Erika and Adele sat at an ocean-view table in the Surf Room, the grand glass-enclosed breakfast room of the famed Montecito Palms Resort Hotel. The glass-topped table was graced with potted violets, fine bone china, heavy English silver, the remains of breakfast, and transparencies of several of Erika's latest watercolors of women by the sea. Momoy Publishing, owned by Adele and her husband Kurt, had published many of Erika's paintings as limited-edition prints. In fact, Adele had brought the copy of *Island Voice* because she'd purchased an ad in it for Erika's recent serigraphs. Her work sold well in Hawaiian galleries.

But Erika was less interested in the prints Adele had already published than in her verdict on the work shown in the transparencies. Nervous, she'd flipped past her publisher's advertisement, lost her place and stumbled upon the personal from Mr. Ohana.

As Adele squinted at the ad, Erika took stock of the changes in her publisher's appearance. Though Adele was only five foot three and tipped the scales at 140, she'd never let that turn her from the world of haute couture— an attitude Erika admired. She loved color, and Adele was an ever-changing palette. Her hair was cut in a severe bob that slanted from ear level on the left to chin level on the right. Its present hue was eggplant—Cobalt Violet, Payne's Gray and just a touch of Cadmium Orange, if Erika had wanted to mix it from paint—and her dangling purple-and-sapphire earrings matched. During their eight-year professional relationship, Erika had come to anticipate meetings with Adele as a time to vicariously enjoy nail polish, chic hairstyles and makeup.

And at fifty-one, fifteen years older than Erika, Adele was one of the very few people in the world with whom Erika felt comfortable exposing something of who she really was. Adele was her judge, support and promoter of the thing most intimate to her—her art.

"Tell me you're kidding," Adele said. "Not the personals, Erika."

Erika suddenly realized that she'd been injudiciously enthusiastic about the ad. Even Adele would think she was crazy.

"God, is it the biological clock?" exclaimed her publisher. "If it is, I've got a fifteen-year-old son you can *have.*"

Erika laughed, glancing nervously out the window at the sun-soaked Santa Barbara Channel and the islands beyond. Because it was Adele, she said, "Oh, I don't know. Having a kid underfoot doesn't sound half-bad." After this too-truthful admission, she rushed on, "I'm trying to picture this Mr. Ohana."

"Well, I doubt it's his real name. *Ohana* is the Hawaiian word for family. Actually it implies extended family," explained Adele, whose second passion, after art, was Hawaiiana. "A feeling of helping one another, of loyalty."

Erika leaned over the table to stare at the upside-down personal ad. "Mr. Family?" The pseudonym seemed tinged with self-mockery.

"Yeah. He's got a real sense of humor. 'Send child-rearing philosophies'?" Adele rolled her eyes, then gave Erika a dubious look plain as words. *Celibate? Surely it's not that bad.* Rather than dwelling on her artist's unnatural whims, she flipped through the magazine until she came to the advertisement for Erika's prints.

Erika took the magazine again and smiled at the ad for *Sand Castles.* "Can I take this?" Erika held Adele's copy of *Island Voice* questioningly above the straw carryall slung over the back of her chair.

"Sure. I brought it for you."

Erika slipped the magazine into her bag and met Adele's black-rimmed eyes.

Her publisher sighed. She gathered the transparencies, glanced at one of them under the light and put them in their envelope to return to Erika.

Erika's heart fell. But somehow she'd already known Adele wouldn't take a chance on them.

"Erika, these paintings just don't have your usual vigor—or depth. And they're very similar to things you've done before."

It was true. "Is it because I used Jean for a model in several of them? She's so gorgeous...." Her sister-in-law had posed for some of Erika's best work, including *Sand Castles*. "I'm having trouble making people look real."

"Well, in *Sand Castles* you certainly managed it."

Sand Castles was a watercolor of Jean with Erika's eight-year-old nephew, Christian. Erika knew her feelings for Chris had translated in paint. She had perceived and understood Jean's nurturing of her stepson. Because, of course, she'd played that role herself. It was Erika's best piece ever. But in her publisher's candid response, she saw the truth—that it was rare for her to capture so much feeling in her art.

She counted on that honesty from Adele, who went on, "No, I don't think Jean's the problem. I think you're afraid to take risks, and you're trying to stay on familiar ground."

The words tolled inside Erika like the bell of truth. *Afraid to take risks* ... Erika had her reaction, which was emotional. Visceral. It was hard to get up after a fall. Adele had watched; she should know.

"Look," said Adele. "I don't want you to feel bad about this. I know what you've been going through this past year. A lot of change. I think *Sand Castles* is going to sell very well, and if it does maybe we'll do a second series. In the meantime, you can work on some new projects." Scraping back her chair from the table, Adele drew an enameled cigarette case and matching lighter from her handbag.

Erika frowned. With soaring cholesterol and blood-pressure, her friend was a walking time bomb. "You know, I want to have you around for a few years, Adele."

"Trust me. I'm prolonging my life—using techniques from the Adele Henry school of stress reduction."

Cigarettes, cognac and French cuisine...

Adele changed the subject. "Speaking of Jean, did you say you're without her as a model for a while?"

Erika took the hint; she couldn't force Adele to take care of herself. "They're in Greenland. Studying walruses." Erika's father, Christopher Blade, had been a renowned undersea explorer, and her brother, David, had followed in his footsteps after his death. Now, David and his second wife, Jean, and his son were in the Arctic for a year. The expedition had followed closely on the heels of an overfishing study in Japan. In fact, they'd spent little time in Santa Barbara since David had married Jean a year before. The sea was their home. It had always been Erika's, too.

Adele contemplated the burning end of her cigarette. "Kurt and I are leaving for Hilo next week. Why don't you join us? Make it a painting trip?"

Erika smiled, shaking her head. She loved Hawaii; when she was nineteen, she'd spent three months there with her parents and David studying sharks. But she wouldn't intrude on her publisher's vacation time with her husband in their getaway on the Big Island. It occurred to her that Adele felt sorry for her. That was the last thing she wanted—from anyone. "Don't worry." She laughed. "I don't plan to answer any personal ads while you're gone." *Afraid to take risks.* She'd just confirmed it.

Adele drew on her cigarette with a wry smile. "Hawaii can be tough on *malihinis*—newcomers. Especially *haoles* like us."

Caucasians. Erika remembered the word.

"But, hey," said Adele, "Haena's a beautiful place. And all he wants is to know if you follow Dr. Spock or James Dobson." She rolled her eyes again. "Take my advice. Get a dog."

Erika's present living situation didn't allow for a dog. In fact, she'd never lived anywhere she could have one. Dogs were for people with homes. They implied permanence. Erika *wanted* permanence—if she could get it without more change. She'd known too much of that.

She contemplated the personal ad in *Island Voice*. Celibate marriage. She was probably one of the few people in the world who could see the appeal of that.

Mr. Family, she thought. Mr. Family.

Minutes later Adele paid the check with her gold card, and they stepped outside into a crisp winter breeze that made the palms chatter. Her faded carryall slung over her shoulder, her silk dress from Pier 1 Imports swishing against her legs, Erika accompanied Adele to her black Saab.

Erika walked with the slight limp that had become natural to her. Two years of rehab had made her strong and lean, but her legs would never be as they once were. She felt Adele's appraising glance.

"You look great," said Adele. "Really."

"Thanks." Adele had known her in the periods Erika thought of as Before, During and After. The present was After.

Something to remember, to be thankful for.

They paused beside the driver's door of the Saab and embraced. "Now take care," Adele told her, "and remember, the invitation to Hilo is open. Kurt would love to have you, too."

"Thank you, Adele." Erika released her. "Drive safely."

After Adele had backed the Saab out of its space and driven off, headed for an appointment with an artist in Solvang, Erika made her way under the palms to her own car, the sun-bleached, sea-foam green Karmann Ghia she had bought eleven months before, when she began driving again.

Sliding behind the wheel, she set her carryall on the passenger seat. The copy of *Island Voice* showed from the top, and Erika drew out the magazine, thumbing through, looking for the ad for *Sand Castles,* to convince herself that she really could paint.

But she couldn't find the right page, and instead, she turned to the classifieds in the back. Mr. Ohana...

Haena's a beautiful place. And all he wants is to know if you follow Dr. Spock or James Dobson.

Nothing else.

Not even sex.

Erika shut the magazine and started her car. *Afraid to take risks.*

No pain, no gain; no guts, no glory?

No risk... no fulfillment.

Ever since David had met Jean, ever since Erika had begun to feel superfluous to her brother and his son, she'd been lonely. She missed Chris.

She wanted a family of her own.

But the usual route to that place was not for her. She always met the same obstacle in the road. *No, really, it's not you. It's me. I'm just not ready for this.* Trying to sound normal, blaming it on her accident.

Yes, Adele, I'm afraid. You would be, too.

Mr. Ohana's personal ad, however... maybe this was a risk she could take. A child. A celibate marriage. Yes, she liked the idea.

But why did *he* want it?

*What's wrong with you, Mr. Ohana? she wondered.
What's your story?*

Pepeluali: February
Haena: the heat

On the island of Kauai... THE RAIN SHATTERED through
the Java plum trees and the ironwoods, drumming on the
roof of the bungalow hidden in the foliage. Wet tropical
blossoms gave off a heady aroma scarcely noticed by the
occupants of the house. On the porch, Hiialo was catching rainfall in a plastic cup to measure—a "science exper-
iment," she had told Kalahiki.

Kal was glad she was busy—and happy. Everyone knew
when she wasn't. He turned from the envelopes littering
the throw rug to the open front door and the barefoot little girl beyond. He could hear her voice under the rain,
talking to a lizard out on the porch.

"Aloha, Mr. Skink. My name is Hiialo. This is Eduardo..."

Eduardo was an imaginary friend of Hiialo's, a thirty-
foot *mo'o,* or magical black lizard. A fearsome sight for
Mr. Skink, thought Kal.

"Oh, don't run away," said Hiialo. "Eduardo won't
hurt you. He only eats shave ice."

Danny's voice drew Kal's eyes toward the floor where he
sat. "Spark dis." Pidgin for "Check this out."

Running a negligent hand through his short-cropped
hair, Kal moved to stand over the muscular brown shoulders of his Hawaiian brother-in-law. On the floor in front
of Danny lay a photo of a bottled blonde whose curves
belonged on a beer poster. She stood beside a sailboard,
smiling brightly at the camera.

Well, sort of brightly. Kal was choosy about smiles. A
smile wasn't a matter of orthodontic work or a pretty

mouth. A smile came from the soul and shone through the whole being. A good smile was contagious.

There was a sound from Kal's bedroom, the amplifier going on. Jakka, Danny's cousin, six foot four and 240 pounds, emerged from the hallway, carrying Kal's Fender Stratocaster guitar. He played a riff, and Kal's own fingers itched for the strings. They'd planned to practice today.

Besides being part of his *ohana*, Danny and Jakka were members of his old band, the three-man band they'd called Kai Nui—high tide. And his former band mates haunted Kal's house as though waiting for something to change, for that tide to come back in. But today's jam session had never gotten off the ground. Danny, the percussionist, had seen Kal's mail and wanted to read the replies to his ad. Now he was perusing the letter from the blonde with the sailboard. He grimaced. "She's from the mainland."

Jakka, whose fingers were master of the bass, slowly attempted the lead-guitar melody to "Pau Hana," the song that had helped make Kai Nui the favorite band on the Garden Island. Long time ago...

Playing the right chords at the right tempo in his mind, Kal tried to lose the nervousness that had been with him ever since he'd visited his post-office box that day. Seeing the letters filling the box—and the larger stack he'd had to stand in line at the counter to collect—had made it real. He *hadn't* been serious when he sent the ad to *Island Voice*. He wasn't that desperate. It had been Danny's idea. Nonetheless, Kal had written the ad. It had seemed barely possible to him that somehow it would all work out. He might find someone he could get along with, someone who would love Hiialo. Hiialo would have two parents again, instead of just a never-there father—him.

And he...well, maybe things would be better for him, as well.

He hadn't expected many answers. At most, two or three. But now he was getting replies from not just Hawaii but the mainland. There were dozens of envelopes on the floor.

Danny pored over another letter. "Did you really say a *celibate* marriage?"

"Yes."

Jakka stopped playing and frowned at the letters on the floor. "*Nobody* wants that." A line divided his brow from top to bottom.

Kal said nothing. His stomach hurt. Work tomorrow. *On your left is Kauai's stunning Na Pali Coast. "Pali" means cliff, and...* He reached into his shirt pocket and surreptitiously popped an antacid.

"You know," remarked Jakka, "if you marry some rich woman, you could quit baby-sitting tourists and play with us again."

Danny said, "That's the whole idea."

"No, it's not," said Kal, with a fighting-dog stare no one challenged.

Maybe someday he'd play professionally again, but that hadn't been the point of the ad. Hiialo was.

Smiling, bemused, Jakka toyed with the guitar strings again.

Kal wandered to the front door. Hiialo had filled two cups with rainwater and was busily filling a third. Her hair, a sun-lightened shade of brown that seemed the consummate mingling of his own genes with her mother's, swung lank around her face and bare shoulders as she moved about the porch, wearing only a pair of boy's surfing trunks.

She was just four, so Kal didn't mind her playing at being a boy, going without a shirt as he often did. Still, it nagged at him. *He* shouldn't be her role model. He wouldn't be, if only...

Scarcely aware of the leaden pall on his heart, the dead feeling, he turned back to the room. To the letters on the floor. It wasn't going to work. No way could he invite a stranger into his life or his home—or within a thousand miles of his daughter.

Danny tossed his wavy shoulder-length hair back from his face and sat up straight as he read the message inside one note card. "Hey, Kal. This one's not so bad."

Kal stepped over the stack of opened letters and crouched beside Danny, who handed him the card.

Danny glanced at his watch and began to stand. "Gotta work, brah. Good luck finding your picture bride."

Picture bride. At the turn of the century, most immigrant plantation workers in Hawaii were poor single men. A man who wished to find a mate from his own culture had one option—to choose a woman from a photograph sent by family members or a marriage broker in his homeland. Then the picture bride came to Hawaii....

Kal groaned as Danny used his shoulder for support to push himself to his feet, feigning aching bones. Danny was on his way to meet his hula group. Besides playing drums, he was a dancer, like—

"Hey, wait for me!" Jakka unplugged the Stratocaster, then hurried back to Kal's room.

Danny swept up his car keys. Nabbing Hiialo as she came inside, he swooped her up in his arms. "Gotcha. And Eduardo's not stopping me." Danny was always willing to enter Hiialo's make-believe world, to accept the existence of her imaginary giant lizard friend.

As Hiialo squealed in delight, presaging her uncle's turning her upside down, Kal examined the card Danny had handed him. On the front was a watercolor of a woman with long curly gold hair swimming underwater with a dolphin. Ordinarily Kal didn't care for sentimental artwork—and he'd been around enough art to form an opinion. But something about this image struck him as realistic, natural, as though the woman and dolphin *were* actually swimming together. He studied the watercolor for a moment before he opened the card and read the writing inside.

The script was small and lightly etched, the letters running almost straight up and down.

Dear Mr. Ohana,
As Kurt Vonnegut says, "There's only one rule that I know of—" It applies to child rearing as to anything. "Damn it, you've got to be kind."

Sincerely,
Ms. Aloha

"So what do you think?"

Kal hadn't known Danny was paying attention. Even now, he was swinging Hiialo back to an upright position, his eyes on his niece.

Kal stuffed the card back into its envelope—another mainland address—tossed it on the stack with the rest and stood up. Taking Hiialo from Danny and feeling the comfort of her small slender arms circling his neck, Kal told his brother-in-law, "I think this was a stupid idea."

"What was stupid?" asked Hiialo. Then, seeing Jakka emerge from the hallway, she said, "What was that song you were playing, Jakka?"

Danny burst out laughing, and Jakka approached Hiialo, threatening to tickle. "You didn't like my song?"

Hiialo grinned, and Jakka ruffled her hair affectionately. He met Kal's eyes, his own apologizing for his earlier remark. "I miss our band."

Kal thought, *I miss her.* He'd lost all his music in one bad night.

"Laydahs, yeah?" Jakka squeezed Kal's shoulder briefly, then wandered out onto the lanai, down the steps and into the rain.

As Jakka crossed the tiny lawn to stand beside the ze-
bra-striped door of his cousin's lavender-and-green VW
bus, Danny lingered on the porch. "You got to be kind,"
he mused. Swiftly he executed a *ka hola*, four bent-legged
steps to one side and back to the other, his hands and
muscular arms saying aloha. "I like Ms. Aloha." With a
last tug on Hiialo's hair, he turned and leapt down off the
porch and into the rain.

"Danny!" In Kal's arms, Hiialo perfectly and gracefully imitated her uncle's aloha, eliciting approving
laughter from Danny and Jakka. Stirring useless pangs in
Kal's heart.

Wish you could see her, Maka....

As his friends climbed into the Volkswagen and the bus
backed out and disappeared down the wet driveway, Hiialo
pulled the sleeve of Kal's T-shirt. "Can we go to the gas
station and get shave ice? Eduardo's hungry."

"That *mo'o* is going to eat up my last dollar on shave
ice."

"*Please?*" Hiialo smiled at him from her eyes, from ear
to ear, from her heart. "And can we stop and see Grandma
and Grandpa at the gallery? I have a picture for them."

Her grin made him grin, too. So much like someone
else's smile.... Kal asked, "You know who has the best
smile on this whole island?"

Hiialo kissed him. "My daddy." She slid down, starting for her bedroom, knowing they would go get shave ice.

"Put on a shirt," he called after her.

"I know," she said, as though he were so tiresome. "I
have to dress like a girl."

DAMN IT, YOU'VE GOT to be kind.

Kal turned again on his mattress, trying to quiet his
mind—and ease the burning in his gut. But the moon outside was too bright, and tonight he couldn't make his
breath match the rhythm of the waves hitting the shore just

two hundred yards away. He shifted his chest against the bottom sheet, wishing he could sleep. His fingers spread on the mattress, and he remembered touching something more.

But this bed, the captain's bed he'd built of koa just to fit his small room, this bed was only wide enough for him and then some—Hiialo when she bounced up beside him with a book in the mornings, wanting him to read to her.

Hiialo... Shave ice... His eyes closed, and his mind, drifting off, played music. His own. Chords. Finger-picking...

He opened his eyes and stared without focus at a groove in the paneling beside his bed. Sitting up, Kal grabbed a pair of loose cotton drawstring shorts beside the bed and pulled them on.

He put his bare feet on the floor and reached past his two packed bookshelves, filled with humidity-warped paperbacks, music books, lives of musicians. His fingers grasped the neck of the Gibson L-50, familiar as the limb of a lover, and he pulled it from its hanger on the wall. As he slipped out of the room, he passed the other instrument still hanging, the shiny chrome National etched with palms and plumeria, and those in cases on the floor, the Stratocaster and the Les Paul. The guitars saved him each night. Companions in the emptiness of forever. Loyal as dogs.

In the dark, he went into the narrow front room and pushed aside the hanging curtain to look in on Hiialo. She slept in one of his *puka* T-shirts—full of holes. Her mouth was open, her legs uncovered. Kal drew the quilt back over her.

"Thank you, Daddy," she murmured in her sleep.

"I love you, *keiki*." She made no response, and Kal headed out onto the lanai through the open front door.

He inhaled the ocean and the flowers, the jasmine crawling up the wood rails, and as he sank down on the tired porch swing and stared at the plants in the moonlight, he felt the water hanging everywhere in the air.

A sprawling blue house with an oriental roof, a vacation rental owned by his parents, stood between the bungalow and the beach. No view from his place, but Kal could hear the ocean and the insects, the bugs of the wet season. He saw the gray shape of a gecko doing pushups on the porch. Watching it, he reached for the unseen with his mind and his soul.

Nothing.

Where are you? he thought. *I need you.*

It was one of those nights.

She was dead.

He strummed his guitar, tuned up in the moonlight. A flat, F minor, B flat seven ... "The Giant was sleeping by the highway/winds called pangs of love brewed on the sea..." The words were symbols of Kauai and of his life—with her and without her. "Why didn't you wake up, Giant?/Why didn't you wake up and save me?"

He sang into the night, the act of singing easing tension in his abdomen, and he didn't hear the sound of feet. But he noticed the small body climbing up onto the swing beside him.

Fingers still, he stopped singing. "I'm sorry, Hiialo. Did I wake you?"

She shook her head, her lips closed tight, middle-of-the-night tears-for-no-reason nearby.

Kal rested the old archtop in the swing, the neck cradled in a scooped-out place in the arm. It was a system he often used—for holding a guitar so that he could hold Hiialo at the same time. He lifted her into his lap and cuddled her against him.

"I don't like that song," she said. "It's sad."

That was true. And the song was true. Mountains didn't rise up to stop fate. Kal hadn't been able to, either. Not the accident. Or Iniki, the hurricane.

It wasn't a truth for children.

"Want to hear 'Puff'?" Kal had played "Puff the Magic Dragon" too many times in bars in Hanalei to consider it anything but agonizing. Still, it was Hiialo's favorite, and maybe Puff could wipe that teary sound out of her voice.

But Hiialo shook her head, snuggling closer against his chest.

Five seconds, and she'd say, *Wait here,* and dash off to get her blanket and a stuffed thing called Pincushion that Kal couldn't remember where or when she'd gotten. Whenever she tried that trick, he'd get her back into bed, instead. If allowed, she would stay up all night.

Like him.

Hiialo whispered, "I wish you weren't sad."

Something shook in Kal's chest. He opened his mouth to say, *I'm not sad.* But he never lied to her.

He hadn't known he seemed sad.

"You make me happy, Hiialo. The best part of my day is seeing you after work and finding out what you've been doing."

Hiialo's little fingers touched the few dark golden hairs on his chest. "Will you tell me a story about my mommy?"

Kal winced.

"Tell me about when you were in the band in Waikiki and Mommy—"

"How about not?" He kept his voice light. "But I'll play 'Puff.'"

She shook her head. He took a breath and watched the trade winds make some nearby heliconia, silver under the full moon, wave back and forth like dancers. Maka had moved like that.

Gone.

In a weary tone of resignation, Hiialo said, "I'll hear 'Puff.'"

"What an enthusiastic audience we have tonight." Kal set her on the swing beside him, then picked up his guitar. As he started to play and sing about the dragon, he thought, *I'm not the only one who's sad.*

Hiialo couldn't remember. But she felt the void.

Later, after he'd tucked her in with Pincushion and the invisible Eduardo, Kal went to get his guitar and hang it up in his room, and on the way he noticed the paper grocery bag into which he'd stuffed the letters to Mr. Ohana.

Damn it, you've got to be kind.

Yes, he thought. Be kind to my daughter.

He put away the Gibson, and then returned to the front room that was kitchen and dining room and living room crammed into a hundred square feet. He grabbed the grocery sack, took it to the boat-size chamber where he slept, turned on his reading light and dumped out the letters on his bed.

He had to push them into a heap to make a place to sit, and then he read them and dropped them, one by one, back into the paper bag on the floor. He'd work up a form reply to the letters. *Thank you for responding to my ad in Island Voice... Good luck in life and love. Sincerely, Mr. Ohana.*

Only one note he laid aside, without taking the card from the envelope. He could cut out the picture of the girl and the dolphin and give it to Hiialo to tack on the wall of her room.

Damn it, you've got to be kind.

Finally he took an old spiral notebook and a pen from his desk drawer, and he lay on his bed and wrote a letter he didn't intend to send to a woman he'd never met. The bag of letters on the floor seemed pathetic—answers from a sad but hopeful world to an even more pitiable plea. But their collective refusal to despair gave *him* a fleeting, moonlight-made hope. And after he signed the letter, "Sincerely, Kalahiki Johnson," he got up and pulled open another drawer, the big bottom drawer, and drew out the shoe box full of photos.

Pushing aside the cassette case that lay on top, cached among things he loved, he flipped through the snapshots, careful of fingerprints. Careful of his own eyes. Pictures still hurt.

The photo Christmas card showing the three of them was near the top. It seemed right. Stealthily, not wanting to wake Hiialo, not wanting his actions to be known in the light of day, he went out to the kitchen to find scissors and finally picked up Hiialo's green-handled little-kid scissors from the floor by the couch. Biting closed his lips, his eyes blurring in the ghostly gray dark, he cut apart the photo.

Maka's arm still showed, stretched across his waist as she touched Hiialo, and for a moment Kal pondered how to remove it. But at last he left it, because then Ms. Aloha would understand what he'd tried to say with words.

CHAPTER TWO

Santa Barbara

ERIKA COMMITTED HERSELF to overcoming fear of risk. In the days after she answered Mr. Ohana's ad, she photographed scenes on the streets of Santa Barbara. A pink poodle outside Neiman-Marcus. Children giving away kittens in front of the supermarket. She spent as much time petting the poor dyed dog as photographing it, and she wanted to adopt a kitten. Instead, she developed the pictures and painted from them, telling herself this was the kind of gamble she'd promised to take. These were not women by the sea.

But what would Adele say? Would she say that Erika might lose her following? If her art stopped selling, if she had to get another job, she would die. Flower without water. Painting was all she had.

Erika's reaction to the possibility was detachment; she tried to feel equally aloof about the other risk she'd taken. Answering a personal ad.

So when she pulled bills and catalogs out of her post-office box and saw a number 10 envelope hand-addressed to Ms. Aloha, she muted her feelings. The response had come from K. Johnson, Box J, Haena, Kauai.

K. Johnson.

Mr. Ohana.

She didn't open the letter in the post office or when she reached the Karmann Ghia parked at the curb. Instead, she

set her mail in the seat beside her and drove down State
Street toward the harbor. She parked in the marina lot, in
Jake Donahue's space. Jake was her brother's business
partner and sometimes first mate on his ship. Jake was
going to be in Greenland with David until June, and Erika was boat-sitting his Chinese junk, the *Lien Hua*. It was
a usual sort of living arrangement for her.

Temporary.

Erika collected the mail and her shoulder bag and
crossed the boardwalk, pausing at a gate in the twenty-foot
chain link fence outside Marina C. She used Jake's key
card to open the lock and made her way down the creak-
ing dock. Erika was painfully familiar with the harbor. It
was where she had lived with her brother and his son on
David's old ship, the *Skye*. It was where she had lived
During.

That was over, she reminded herself again. This was
After.

Memories of that earlier time would always be with her.
Some things shouldn't be forgotten. Some things couldn't
be.

She reached the *Lien Hua*'s berth. Walking alongside
the junk to its stern, she caught her muted grayish reflec-
tion in the dingy glass windows. Tall. Rayon import dress.
Hair that fell several inches below her shoulders, neither
smooth nor curly, brown nor blond, but simply nonde-
script.

Erika unlocked the cabin of the junk and ducked
through the hatch, descending into the two-room space
that contained all her worldly goods and most of Jake
Donahue's. Her art supplies lay on the fold-out kitchen-
ette table. Unfinished watercolors covered the meager wall
space in places where the sunlight wouldn't fade them.

She tossed her mail on the narrow bunk where she slept.
K. Johnson's letter was on top, but Erika resisted picking

it up, tearing it open. Restraint was possible through routine.

She opened the overhead hatch, then dropped down a companionway to the unlit galley. In the gloom, the light on Jake's answering machine glowed steadily. No messages. From the small icebox run on dockside electricity, she took a bottle of fresh carrot juice. Erika removed the lid and sipped at it.

Suddenly she could wait no longer. She capped the juice, put it back in the refrigerator and returned to the salon and her mail.

She took K. Johnson's letter topside, where the air smelled of beach tar, and settled in a wooden deck chair in the shade of the mast. The closest sailboats were deserted, covered. Opening the letter, Erika was glad of the solitude, glad her brother was faraway across a continent and an ocean, glad Adele was across another, glad no one could know that she'd done this insane thing. That she, a thirty-six-year-old woman, had answered a personal ad involving a celibate marriage.

And a four-year-old girl.

As she withdrew the letter and unfolded it, something dropped into her lap. A photo, upside down. Erika didn't look. She put her hand against it, protecting it from the breeze, and turned to the page. The letter was written in black ballpoint pen on warped paper torn from a spiral notebook. Neat male handwriting.

Dear Ms. Aloha,
My name is Kalahiki Johnson, though you know me as Mr. Ohana, who placed a personal ad in *Island Voice*. I am thirty years old, and I was born and raised on the island of Kauai, where my father's family has lived for six generations and where I work as a tour guide on the Na Pali Coast.

My four-year-old daughter is named Hiialo, pronounced Hee-AH-lo, which means "a beloved child borne in the arms." Soon Hiialo will be too big to carry, but she will always be the most precious thing in my life.

Hiialo's mother was my wife, Maka. Maka was a hula dancer and chanter who won competitions in *hula kahiko,* traditional hula, and also in *hula auana,* modern hula, both of which tell stories. She was a kind and graceful human being in every way, and we loved each other deeply. Three years ago, driving back from a hotel where she'd been dancing, she was killed in a head-on collision.

Erika set down the letter, biting her lip, unable to read on.

She'd thought that he was some yogi who'd taken a vow of abstinence. Or maybe that he was impotent or burned out on relationships. She'd wondered about Mr. Ohana's reasons for wanting a celibate marriage, but she hadn't expected anything like this. Though she should have.

Why was it affecting her this way? And she *was* affected, her eyes hot and blurry, her heart racing with horror, as though she'd just learned of the death of someone *she* loved.

And he was only thirty.

Since then I have raised Hiialo alone, but I work long hours, and it's hard on her. I wish there was someone who could do what Maka would have done for our daughter and who would love Hiialo as she did.

If you are still interested in Hiialo and me, please write back. But understand that even if a permanent domestic arrangement is possible, your relationship with me would be platonic. Maka and I were married for seven years, and no one can replace her in my

heart. I want no other lover, and I would prefer to live
alone, if not for Hiialo. Please understand this, because, as you said, we all need to be kind.

                                    Sincerely,
                              Kalahiki Johnson

Erika put the heel of her hand against her mouth,
pressed her lips together. In her mind, she heard an echo
of the past, and she couldn't shut it out. One word repeated itself.

David.

Her brother.

For the three years after his first wife's death, Erika had
lived with him. For three years, she had been a mother
figure to his son, Christian. That had been the best experience of her life, though it had begun out of duty. There
had been much entangled pain—David's and her own,
both caused by the same woman..

But this situation was different. So different.

Talk about risk.

The winter breeze pushed at her hair, and Erika reached
for the photo in her lap, so that it wouldn't blow away. She
turned it over, and her breath caught when she saw him.

He was a beautiful man.

Light brown hair, still damp from a swim, stood out in
short uncombed spikes, as though he'd just come out of
the water and shaken it. His lean muscular chest and arms
were tanned the color of oak. The child's skin, the skin of
the almost-toddler in his arms, was a shade darker. And
darker yet was the rounded well-toned female arm brushing his body, the hand touching the baby.

Maka. He'd cropped her from the shot, all but her arm.

Erika absorbed every detail of the picture. The sea. The
man's smile. His grin came from sensuous lips and slitted
dark-lashed eyes of uncertain color and, clearly, from his
heart. Anyone could see he held the baby often. Erika saw

gentleness and love between the child in her green swim-suit and the man who held her in front of him, feet out to face the camera. Somehow the baby had been coaxed into a dimply laugh, and Erika wondered if her father's fingers cupped under one small bare foot were responsible.

The picture was like a book, and when she read it she cried.

Erika heard the dock creak and saw a couple who owned a sloop two berths down approaching. Not wanting to talk, she stood up and limped to the cabin door, slipped inside. The junk rocked gently. She listened to the lapping of water, to some wind chimes outside. The monotonous music of solitude.

Her heart felt simultaneously fearful and excited.

He had answered her letter. From however many replies he'd received, Kalahiki Johnson had chosen hers. His answer had contained no proposal of marriage, no promises. Just an invitation to write back.

She lay down on her bunk and read it again.

Twice.

Three times.

The light faded outside, and she turned on the lamp over the bunk and studied the photograph and the letter, memorizing the words, especially the last paragraph.

A sensible part of her, the part that was the older sister of a man who'd lost his wife, wanted to step back and say, "Oh, Kalahiki, you're young. You'll fall in love again."

But the photograph won a debate words would have lost. And Erika resisted admitting even to herself that he did not seem a man destined to live out his life in celibacy.

I have to tell him.

She would have to tell him about herself. Reveal her past to a stranger and hazard rejection because of it. It would be unconscionable not to tell him, but the prospect was horrible.

Erika found comfort where she could.
I don't have to tell him everything.

Haena, Kauai

KAL PEDALED HARD through the rain to the post office to
collect his mail. The transmission on his car had given out,
so that morning he'd cycled to the office of Na Pali Sea
Adventures in Hanalei in the rain. He would get home the
same way, in the dark, on one-lane roads and bridges,
veering into the brush and mud when headlights approached. Raindrops clattered against the wide green
leaves all around him as he pulled up outside the small
building of the Haena post office. It was after five, so the
counter was closed, but Kal could still go inside and open
box J.

"*Please, Mr. Postman...*" He thought in music all his
waking hours. He dreamed music in his sleep.

Rain dripped from him onto the stack of bills and flyers he drew from the box. The letter from Santa Barbara
was on top. The return address sticker read "Erika Blade"
and had a logo of an artist's palette beside it. Alone in the
office, he tossed the rest of his mail on a bench, sat down
and opened the envelope, his curiosity stronger than his
embarrassment over the letter he should never have mailed.

To Ms. Aloha.

Erika Blade.

She had sent another card. Same artist, different picture. A very old woman sitting in the sand, gazing out to
sea. The ocean really looked like the ocean.

As Kal opened the card, the photo dropped out faceup.

A good-looking brunette in cutoffs and a faded T-shirt
sat against the side of a weathered wooden building with
a drawing board against her knees and a paintbrush in her
hand. She had long muscular legs and a laughing smile.

A good smile.

But sunglasses hid her eyes.

Reflexively fishing for an antacid from a bottle in his pack, Kal studied every detail, down to the shape of her toes, before he turned to her small delicate handwriting, which covered the whole inside of the card and continued on the back. She had a lot to say, and as he chewed on a tablet, he read with curiosity, not with hope.

Dear Kalahiki,

Thank you for answering my note. Reading of your terrible loss made my heart ache. I am so sorry about your wife's death, and I wish there were something I could do to ease your grief.

My conscience dictates that I precede this whole reply with the advice that you not marry anyone at this time. Despite the things you said in your letter, I believe there is more love in store for you. You should find it before marrying again—for your daughter's sake and your own.

This is what I believe, but I can't know your heart. Leaving your choices to you, I'll introduce myself.

My name is Erika Blade. I am thirty-six years old and a watercolor artist. But probably, if my last name is familiar, it's because my father was the undersea explorer Christopher Blade. My brother, David, and I grew up on his ship, the *Siren,* and accompanied him and my mother all over the world on scientific expeditions until I entered art school in Australia and began to make art my career. While I was at school, the *Siren* sank and my parents were killed. My brother continued my father's work, and I have helped him some.

About five years ago, I was seriously injured in an automobile accident. Though luckier than your Maka, I was temporarily paralyzed.

During the three years I spent in a wheelchair, I lived on my brother's ship with him and his son, Christian. Chris was three at the time of my accident; he lost his mother soon afterward. For three years, I helped my brother look after him, and this experience shaped who I am today. I love children.

Eventually I decided to move off David's ship and into a place of my own. Shortly afterward, I regained feeling in my legs. With the help of therapy, I have been walking for about eighteen months, but because of knee injuries in the accident I still walk with a limp.

Because my parents are dead, my family consists of my brother, his wife, Jean, and my nephew, Chris. However, they are seldom in Santa Barbara anymore; David's work takes them all over the world. In any case, I want a family of my own. And, like you, I prefer celibacy. The arrangement you have suggested appeals to me very much. I think it would be good for me. I'm less sure it would be best for you and your daughter.

So, Kalahiki, I leave you to your thoughts. I would always be glad to hear from you again.

                                        In friendship,
                                        Erika Blade

The last line was her phone number.

On the front of the card, Kal found her name. No wonder she could paint the sea. Christopher Blade's daughter. Did his parents have her prints in their gallery?

Erika . . .

When he'd placed the ad, it was with the hope that there was someone like her out there. Someone who wasn't interested in sex—but who still seemed capable of a meaningful relationship. Someone who loved children and would love Hiialo.

But Erika Blade didn't know Hiialo. And he didn't know Erika.

Can't do this.

Kal replaced the photo and the card in the envelope, put them in his day pack with the other mail and stood up. Pushing open the glass door of the post office, he went out into the rain and the scent of wetness and grabbed his ancient three-speed Indian Scout from where he'd leaned it against the siding.

The downpour pelting him, Kal flicked on the headlight on the handlebars and pedaled out to the road, his T-shirt and shorts immediately drenched anew. He crossed a long stone bridge, riding as though he could escape the rain, and his heart raced. His mind replayed the contents of the letter, and he knew he would read it again that night when Hiialo was in bed.

Christopher Blade's daughter. Three years in a wheelchair.

He could hear his tires on the wet pavement and the sound of the violent winter surf just a block away, a sound that once would have called him to the breaks at Hanalei Point, to Waikoko or Hideaways. Freedom...

Don't even think about bringing her here, Kal. You never really planned to do it. It just seemed better than having your daughter in day care.

To temper tantrums and moodiness.

To trying to do it alone.

To messing up.

But he couldn't go through with this. It wouldn't be right.

Why not? Riding through the rain, Kal tried to remember exactly what Erika Blade had said about sex. Hardly anything.

Painful thoughts came.

Loneliness.

The glow of headlights cast a long shadow of his body and bicycle ahead of him on the water-running pavement. Kal steered into a roadside ditch, springing off his bike when the front wheel stuck in the mud. As rain streamed down his face, a red 1996 Land Rover whipped past. Kal recognized the vehicle. It belonged to a movie star who used his fifth home, in Haena, two weekends of every year.

Reminding himself to buy a helmet, Kal yanked his bike out of the mud and back to the road before he realized the front wheel wouldn't turn and the forks were bent. He stood in the rain, and it drowned his voice as he yelled after the long-vanished car, "I hate your guts, *malihini!* You killed my wife!" He knew it wasn't really the driver of this car who'd hit Maka—just someone like him. Someone who would never belong.

Kal leaned his arms on the handlebars, his head in his hands.

Erika Blade would be a *malihini,* a newcomer, too.

He wouldn't write to her again. He'd said personal things to her. She'd said personal things to him. They were even.

And her advice was sane. Wait for love.

Wait...

He'd waited three years, dated women. They'd made him miss Maka even more.

Kal picked up his bike, slung it over his shoulder and began walking home through the rain. There was nothing to wait for.

She would never come back.

THE OKIKA GALLERY in Hanalei was a renovated plantation-style house with white porch posts and verandas. Next door, separated from the gallery by a wide walk bordered with heliconia, anthurium, spider lilies and ginger, a similar building housed the office of Na Pali Sea Adventures, the outfitter for whom Kal worked. The two buildings shared a courtyard away from the street.

The morning after he received Erika's letter, there were no Zodiac trips going out, so Kal's job was to shuttle sea kayaks to the Hanalei River for the tourists who had rented them. At ten-thirty, when he returned from that errand, he slipped out for his break.

It was raining, but the espresso stand in the courtyard was still doing business as he dashed through the downpour to the steps of the gallery. He entered through the open French doors, and Jin, his mother's champion Akita bitch, stood up and came over to greet him.

"Hi, Jin. Hi, girl." Kal crouched to pet the dog's thick red-and-white coat, to rub her back and behind her ears, to look into her eyes in the black-masked face. As Jin licked his cheek, Mary Helen, his mother, abandoned a mat-cutting project at the counter to join him.

Kal had gotten his height from his father. With her neat tennis-player's body and no-nonsense short blond hair, Mary Helen stood barely five foot two. She always looked at home in shorts, polo shirts and slippers—elsewhere known as thongs—the footwear of the islands. Born and raised in Kansas City, Missouri, Mary Helen had first visited Oahu in 1960 and met King Johnson at a dog show, where their Akitas had fallen in love and played matchmakers like something out of *One Hundred and One Dalmatians*. Or so Kal had been told. His mother had left the Midwest and moved to Hawaii to marry King. Gamely she'd faced the challenges of island life, slowly exploring her new world, learning the social subtleties and embracing the cultural richness of Hawaii. Hawaiian quilting, Japanese *bon* dancing, foods as unfamiliar as *poi* and *kim chee*— Mary Helen loved them all. When she and King had children, they had given them Hawaiian names. Now, in the critical eyes of the locals, Kal's mother was considered a *kamaaina*, a child of the land.

Could Erika Blade do that?

"Hi, sweetheart," said Mary Helen. "No trips today?"

"No. I'm going to go get Hiialo in a minute." When Kal had no trips to guide, his boss, Kroner, let Hiialo work with him at the Sea Adventures office, doing small tasks her four-year-old hands could manage. Despite her tantrums, Hiialo had a knack for winning friends.

"She can come over here," his mother said. "I'll be here all day. I'm changing some prints on the wall."

Kal had come to look at prints, but his taking a sudden interest in the family obsession—art—would make his mother suspicious. "I'll bring her over to say hi. I'm going to clean the equipment room next door, so I thought she could help." His parents gave enough to Hiialo; she spent every Tuesday with them at the gallery.

"Oh, that's good for her." His mother smiled approvingly. "And she'll have fun."

Kal straightened up from petting Jin, who walked away to keep watch out the front door. Why had he placed that ad, anyhow? It wasn't as though Hiialo had no female influence in her life. She had his mother and his sister, Niau.

"Your dad took Kumi to the vet," his mother told him. "And Niau went to Honolulu. She took Leo some prints. Did you know he's remodeling? He wanted you to help."

"I know. He called me."

Kal's oldest brother—Lay-oh, not Lee-oh—ran a gallery on Oahu. Keale, the next oldest, was a park ranger on the Big Island. Uncles and aunts. What didn't Hiialo have? If he wanted, they could even get a dog, one of his folks' Akita puppies. Though he wasn't home enough...

He wasn't home enough.

He needed a partner.

Kal sensed his mother looking him over, and he knew she was wondering if he'd wind up in the hospital again, receiving a blood transfusion. Apparently deciding he was going to make it, she smiled and said, "Come tell me what you think of this oil painting. A man from Kapaa painted it, and I think he's good."

Where usually he would have begged off, Kal followed her to the counter, surreptitiously scanning the walls. He didn't need to look that far. When he reached the counter, he saw that one of the prints his mother was putting up or taking down was by Erika Blade.

He tried not to stare, but he recognized the model as the same woman in the dolphin card Erika had sent. In this print, the woman was building a sand castle with a boy.

It was the best of her work he'd seen. The interaction between the woman and child, their absorption in their construction project, conveyed a lot. Motherhood. Happiness. Friendship. Nurturing. Fun.

If Erika Blade had a lot of prints out, she was probably doing well. What Jakka had said weeks before needled him. *Marry a rich woman.*

Not a pretty notion, but practical. Kal *wasn't* looking for a woman to support him so he could play professionally again. But he worked six days a week. Needed to. *At least she can support herself.*

He dutifully assessed the oil landscape by the Kapaa artist. "It's nice." But his eyes drifted back to the print.

Jin left the door, wandered over to them and sat down by the counter. The Akita looked at Kal and so did his mother.

"Isn't that lovely?" Mary Helen asked, noticing his interest in Erika's print.

"Yes." Kal turned away, chewing on unasked questions.

"That's hers, too, up there," said his mother. "The girl sailing. We sell a lot of her work actually. Her name is Erika Blade. I think she's disabled."

"Oh."

Mary Helen's head was tilted sideways, as though she was listening for the *akua,* the island spirits, to give up secrets. She was staring curiously at Kal, picking up on the anomaly of his looking twice at a piece of art.

"Well, I'm going to get Hiialo," he said. "I'll see you later."

Then he left, before the *akua* could tell their tales.

CHAPTER THREE

Malaki: March

TO ERIKA'S DISAPPOINTMENT, Adele expressed misgivings about *Poofie* and *Free Kittens*. Good work, she said gently, but not enough universal appeal for a print series. How about something with *people* in it?

Erika was painting people now, but nothing she could sell: Six similar paintings, not just in watercolor but also in acrylic and oil. Two of the subjects had come from an incomplete photograph. The third eluded her and stood ghostlike on the side.

Maka, she thought, *who are you?*

She had shaped each different Maka using pictures of hula dancers from Hawaiian travel magazines, which now lay all about her studio. She had used no one model but had combined different characteristics.

What had Maka been doing? Was her other arm behind Kalahiki, holding him? Was her face turned up to his? What was she wearing? How tall was she? Her right arm was medium-size and well-toned—

The phone rang.

Erika had trained her heart not to leap at that sound, and now she debated letting the machine pick it up to prove her self-control. Ever since she'd received Kalahiki's letter—and answered it—she'd been unsteady. She shouldn't care so much. But she did. About a broken-hearted man she didn't know. Twenty times a day, Erika laid those feelings aside, put them in the place where she put her reaction to his picture, a reaction that was all wrong.

Kal's grief was his business, not hers.

That he looked like an engraved invitation to come to Hawaii and fall in love was irrelevant.

A celibate marriage was exactly what she wanted. A husband. A child. And no physical complications, no difficult intimacy.

She could keep her head, not get involved. It was easy when she remembered what doing otherwise could mean. Sex.

Yuck.

So he was hung up on his dead wife. Good. He could have his hang-ups; she'd keep hers.

The telephone rang again. She should answer. Adele was back from Hawaii. This might be something about work. *Like what? She's already rejected all my paintings.*

The phone rang a third time. Erika set down her brush, dropped down to the shadows of the galley and picked up the receiver. "Hello?"

There was a silence, like a punctuation mark. Then, "Hello. This is Kal Johnson calling. Is Erika there?"

She sank down on the steps of the companionway. With a slight breeze from the open hatches blowing her oversize T-shirt against her back, she clutched the receiver. His voice was low and resonant. Masculine. Unique.

God help her.

Sexy.

"This is Erika." She was in a vacuum and her insides were being sucked out of her. She heard the engine of a cabin cruiser crawling past in the harbor, and a slow wake rocked the junk at its berth.

"I'm not sure if you know who I am, but—"

"I know who you are. You're Kalahiki."

Across the Pacific, in the sun-dappled morning shadows inside the bungalow, Kal heard her say his name for the first time. At the same moment he saw Hiialo outside beating Pincushion against the porch. "Bad Pincushion! Bad! No talk stink!"

What had Pincushion said?

"I thought we should talk on the phone." *Brilliant, brilliant, keep it up, Kal.*

Erika bit her lip. There was a bellows stuck in her throat, and it was opening and closing with each beat of her heart. *Talk,* she thought. *Say something that will make him . . .*

Oh, she wanted it. They could settle into permanence— permanent celibacy, permanent family—and her life would not change again. Safe.

"Your daughter's beautiful." The ensuing pause was so long that at last she asked, "Are you still there?"

"Yeah. I . . . Erika . . ."

Silence surrounded her name. Silence . . . and feeling. It was so dark in the galley she didn't know why her eyes burned that way, why she felt so—

"I just wanted to tell you some things," he said. "I've thought a lot since I got your letter. Are you serious about this?"

Erika swallowed. *This.* As though he couldn't say it himself.

"Yes."

"My house is small. It's a bungalow. I could fix it so we'd have our own rooms, but it's still cozy. It's not right on the beach, either. Close, though."

Erika tightened her fingers on the phone. *Was he saying he wanted her to come?*

"I don't make a lot of money. I'm buying the house from my folks. They have a gallery, by the way. Actually they have three. I went into the one in Hanalei and looked for your prints. They have some."

Parents. Did his parents live near him? The thought was reassuring. *Mr. Family.*

She asked, "What's the name of their gallery?"

"The Okika. It means 'orchid.'"

His voice was both warm and sandpaper rough. It made her want to hear him talk more.

But he was quiet.

Erika asked, "What does Hiialo do while you work?"

"Um...she goes to a day-care center." Actually, she'd been to a few. One in a church basement with forty other kids. One with an elderly woman who had made the mistake of saying Hiialo needed a firm hand. The latest situation was a home with an unhappy dog tied up outside.

"My nephew used to be with me while I worked, when he was Hiialo's age." As soon as she'd said it, Erika wished she hadn't. She sounded too eager. *Desperate.*

But an opportunity like this wouldn't come again. Normal people wanted sex. Kal and his grief were her only hope.

"Hiialo is..." His voice startled her. "Well, she's moody. In fact, she can be a bugger sometimes."

"All kids can." The dock made its endless aching cries.

"I'd like to..." On the lanai, Hiialo was making Pincushion and her stuffed lion, Purr, shake hands. Kal remembered proposing to Maka. At Waimea Beach. Kissing. *I love you....* "You could come over here," he said. "I'll buy your ticket. If it doesn't work out, I'll buy you a ticket home, too."

"I'll buy my own ticket." *Somehow.* Her hand was deep in her hair, tearing at it. She felt like crying. What if he didn't like her? What if he didn't think she'd be a good stepmother for Hiialo? What if... "When do you want me to come?"

"Not right away. I have to figure out some things. About the house." About how to tell his parents.

How to tell Hiialo.

"I'll call you again, yeah?" he said. "And I'll send pictures of the house. Maybe you could come in June?"

"That sounds great. I'm boat-sitting for my brother's business partner. He'll be back in June." Oh, she sounded flaky. Practically homeless.

"Good," said Kal.

Her worries evaporated. She was wanted—by a stranger. *Why was he doing this?*

He said, "Let's get off the phone for now. I'll call you again soon. Do you have any questions before we hang up?"

"Yes." With a presence of mind that astonished her, she asked, "What's your phone number?"

Moments later she set the receiver back in its cradle. Still sitting weakly on the steps, she leaned against the side of the counter and wept.

"DADDY, PINCUSHION'S stuffing is falling out." As Kal hung up the phone, Hiialo appeared before him, bringing everything into immediate and demanding focus.

"You beat the stuffing out of him. That's why it's falling out."

Hiialo started to look tearful, and Kal reached for Pincushion, who was made from a faded gray-blue sock and wore a turban. In addition to a split seam on the side, one of his felt eyes was coming off. Repair time.

"I'll fix him." Sewing up Pincushion would calm him.

A picture bride. Danny's analogy was accurate, and since the night he'd said it, Kal had stumbled upon two accounts of Japanese picture brides from the turn of the century. One was in the newspaper, the other in a book sold in the office of Na Pali Sea Adventures. And he'd remembered that his parents' next-door neighbor, June Akana, who had taught Japanese *bon* dances to him and his sister and brothers when they were kids, had been a picture bride, too. She and her husband were in their nineties, still going strong. Best friends. People could be happy.

But the picture brides of old hadn't come to Hawaii for celibate marriage.

Oh, shit, what were his friends going to say? They all knew what he'd advertised for. He'd told them why, because of Hiialo, because he was never home and she needed someone who could be. *He* needed someone who would be. He killed a useless yearning. Not for love—for life. His own.

The Stratocaster in his hands. Playing...

But he was doing this for Hiialo.

"You'll be all right, Pincushion," said Hiialo, patting the toy in Kal's hand. She trailed after him as he went to the kitchen drawer where he kept needles, thread, extra guitar picks, junk. The scissors were missing, as usual.

"Hiialo, I need your scissors. Could you please get them for me?"

"Yes, Daddy. Thank you for fixing Pincushion." She went over to the couch and looked underneath it, then went to her room to find the scissors.

Sunshine. Hiialo was like sunshine now, but she was changeable as the north-shore weather. And sometimes as wild.

Would Erika Blade, a thirty-six-year-old childless woman, really be able to handle it?

Dear Erika,
I'm glad you're coming to Hawaii. I'll try to call you once a week. Here are the pictures I promised you of my house. You can see what Hiialo looks like now. She is holding Pincushion, who is her favorite toy....

I mentioned my family on the phone. My folks live in Haena, and my sister, Niau, lives in Poipu, on the south side of the island. My brother Leo...

MIDAFTERNOON sunlight shone through the open hatch
and the windows of the *Lien Hua*. Lying in her berth, Erika read Kal's second letter and studied the photographs
he'd sent. At four, Hiialo was sturdy, with thick, wavy,
medium brown hair cut in a pageboy. Even in the photograph, in which she was crouched on the lanai of the green
bungalow with the thing called Pincushion, she seemed full
of energy, ready to leap to her feet and race away. Not like
Chris...

   That's okay, thought Erika. *I know I can love her.*

If she was certain of anything, it was her ability to love
and care for children. Chris had been exceptionally good,
exceptionally bright. Exceptionally quiet. But she could
love Hiialo. It would be easy.

Another photo showed Kal with his brothers and sister
and parents and their three dogs, all Akitas. His father—
King, said the corresponding name on the back of the
photo—was tall and white-haired. His mother, Mary Hel-
en, seemed compact and athletic. And Kal and his sib-
lings all had a look of radiant good health and of energy
and power—not unlike the dogs. One brother was
bearded, the other clean-shaven. His sister had shoulder-
length light brown hair. They were a handsome family. Kal
was the youngest.

The photo and letter, the proof that he really was a
family man in every sense, reassured Erika. Since his
phone call, she'd had doubts. Kal was a stranger. With
David so far away, no one would really know if she got into
trouble.

She ought to write to him, tell him.

She ought to tell *someone* what she was doing.

But she knew what her brother would say: *Kal will get
over Maka's death.*

For the hundredth time, Erika tried to quiet her qualms
about that. She *had* advised him to wait—for someone
else, someone he could love.

She should send him photos of her and David and Chris and Jean to give him the same kind of reassurance he'd given her. But she had no photos of herself with them, only with Chris, when she was in a wheelchair.

Not an option.

She looked back to the letter.

...I haven't told anyone our plans. June is a long way off. Before you come, I'll explain to my folks and Hiialo. Also, my in-laws. Maka's folks live on Molo-kai, but her brother and her cousin live in Hanalei and they're like family. In Hawaii, *ohana*, or family, means more than just your immediate relatives. It can extend to all your loved ones—

The telephone rang, and she went down into the galley to answer. It was Adele, calling to ask how the painting was going. Did she have anything else yet? Had she tried placing those "other pieces" in a gallery?

"Ah...I'm just experimenting right now." Erika thought it through at light speed. "Actually a friend has invited me to Hawaii in June. I'm going to do some work there."

"Oh, great! Which island?"

"Kauai." Belatedly Erika recalled that Adele had seen Kal's ad. But surely it wouldn't occur to her that Erika had *answered* the ad.

It didn't. "Wonderful. I think it's recovered a lot since Iniki. The hurricane in '92? Try to get up to the north shore...."

Erika listened to Adele's suggestions and chewed on her bottom lip.

Yes, it was good that David was in Greenland and no one really had to know what she was doing. She would write to her brother and tell him who she was staying with and where. But why say more? If it turned out that Kal didn't like her, no one would have to know the truth.

"Erika? Are you there?"

"Oh, yes, I'm sorry. I'm spaced out today, Adele. What is it?"

"There are some galleries on Kauai that carry your prints. I'll send you their names. I know they'd love it if you stopped in."

The Okika Gallery, Erika remembered. Kal's parents owned three galleries. It seemed like destiny. She longed to tell Adele everything. But if she did, Adele would worry. Anyone would worry, would question her judgment. Erika hated that. Better to say nothing, just leave Adele her new address and stick to her story. "All right."

After they'd hung up, Erika climbed back up to the main cabin, where the paintings of Kal and Hiialo and Maka confronted her. She *needed* someone to ease her anxiety, to believe with her in this risk she was taking, believe that it would work out.

There was really only one person who could help with that, and Erika wished the phone would ring again.

He had promised to call.

Apelila: April

Dear Kal,
    Thanks for your letter and the photographs and your phone calls. I painted the enclosed picture for Hiialo. I did it using the photos you sent. I hope she can recognize who it's supposed to be....

The watercolor was of Pincushion. Kal loved it, had wanted to keep it himself. He'd considered taking it down to the gallery to get it framed, but then... Questions. How come he had an Erika Blade original. Of Pincushion.
    I stole it, Mom.

Instead, he'd put the watercolor in a cheap document frame, replacing a photo of the great blues guitarist Robert Johnson, and he'd given it to Hiialo, as Erika had wanted, saying it was from a pen pal. After explaining what a pen pal was, he'd added, "Sometimes I talk to her on the phone, too."

Soon he'd have to explain more. To everyone. Erika was coming to live in his house, maybe for good.

Sitting on the porch swing while Hiialo played in her room, Kal remembered his phone conversation with Erika just that morning. He had asked if she'd told her brother what they were doing. "I wrote to him," she'd said, and Kal had wondered if she knew she wasn't answering the question. He was pretty sure she did.

He was pretty sure she'd told her brother almost nothing.

Kal talked to her once a week, always calling Thursday at seven in the morning. It was his day off, Hiialo usually wasn't up by then, and it was around ten in Santa Barbara. Making the call was agonizing every time. The cultural gap between them was bigger than Waimea Canyon. But Kal wanted to know all he could about Erika Blade before she arrived, before he brought her into Hiialo's life.

She was hard to know. She turned conversations away from herself and tuned into him, perceiving his difficulties as a single father almost as though she'd been one herself. Or had known one, which she had.

Her brother.

He left the swing and went inside. It was already one o'clock, and he had things to do. He'd recently enclosed the back lanai, creating a new room—for Erika. It still needed finishing touches. But Danny and Jakka had stopped by that morning, and a jam session had eaten half the day. "Hiialo, let's go to Hanalei. I need something from the hardware store."

Kal heard a rustling from his room and took a step down the hallway, pushed aside the beads in his doorway and looked in. Hiialo peered up from where she crouched beside his open desk drawer, photos spread out around her. The portrait of a naughty girl.

Kal saw a photograph of Maka under the leg of his folding metal desk chair. Entering the room, he picked up the chair. The surface of the photo was marred, across Maka's face.

"What are you doing, Hiialo? Those aren't yours."

She began a cry he knew would rise to a full-throated wail. She looked at a photograph in her hands, a snapshot of her mother, and ripped it in half.

"*Hiialo.*" Kal scooped her up, and she hit him with her fists and kicked him, screaming. "Don't hit. I don't hit you."

Her small arms and legs struck a few more times, to prove that she didn't care what he said, before she subsided to screams. He carried her through the beads and out into the main room and then through the curtain door of her room. Her voice had reached a high continuous sob, and she cried, "It's your day off! You're supposed to spend it with me! You're supposed to spend Thursday with me!"

Kal couldn't speak. Even as he left her on her bed, kicking the wall and crying, he wondered what he'd done that had made her that way.

Not enough time at home.

He should have skipped the music, told Danny and Jakka it was his day with Hiialo.

Listening to her shrieking, he wondered if all parents felt trapped. Guilty for wanting their own time. For wanting...

Music spun inside him, trying to soothe. "*Rock Me on the Water...*"

He went back into his room and saw the photos scattered on the floor, including the one that had been ripped in half. In the next room, Hiialo's cries reached a crescendo, and Kal crouched down to pick up all the Makas from the throw rug.

HIS FATHER CAME BY late that afternoon to look at some bad siding on his rental property, the blue oriental house in front of the bungalow. Kal was caretaker of the vacation home. He cut the grass and cared for the plants and cleaned after tenants left. The blue house had been rebuilt after Iniki; he'd just discovered that the siding was poorly installed.

Leading Raiden, one of the Akitas, up to the porch, King asked Kal, "Where's the *keiki?*"

"Taking a nap." They stood together under the porch awning with the rain pounding the roof and the garden, and at last Kal said, "Yeah, it's been a great day." He told his father about the photos.

King shook his head. He'd seen Hiialo in a temper, too. They all accepted her moods as part of her nature, but everyone hated the sulks and the screaming.

Together the two men toured the back-porch room, scrutinizing the construction. King had never asked the reason for the project; the house was small. When they'd examined the new room, Kal offered him some juice—he seldom bought beer, which he liked but which made him sick—and they sat on the veranda with Raiden exploring the yard nearby.

The Akita had a pure white coat and double-curled tail, and Kal studied the dog with admiration and envy. His parents' stud was immaculately bred, intensively trained, utterly trustworthy. Kal knew the time that went into raising an animal like that.

He didn't even have time for his daughter.

Watching Raiden lift his leg against the heliconia, Kal said, "I've made friends with an artist in Santa Barbara. Erika Blade. We write letters. Talk on the phone."

His father tipped back his cup of guava juice. "She's a big artist. How'd you meet her?"

"I placed a personal ad. She's coming to Kauai this summer. She's going to stay here."

Lazily King stretched out his legs and rocked the porch swing. "With you?"

On the top porch step, Kal shrugged. "Here." His house, not his bed.

The rain drizzled, creating waterfall sounds all around the lanai, and Raiden came over to lie at his master's feet.

"Is this romance?"

No, thought Kal. *It's practical.* "Something like that."

The rain poured from the gutter and splattered on the ground at the corner of the house. As Kal stared out at it, his father said at last, "Well, we'll look forward to meeting her." He stood up and so did Raiden. "I'm going to take a look at that siding."

Kal glanced toward his own house. All was quiet indoors, Hurricane Hiialo sleeping. Watching the Akita follow his father down the steps into the rain, he drew a quiet breath. King hadn't criticized, hadn't shown any disapproval at all. Kal knew that when his father had said they'd look forward to meeting Erika, he meant it.

His parents always kept things in perspective. They'd survived Hurricanes Iwa and Iniki.

And Kal had cried in his dad's arms after Maka died.

CHAPTER FOUR

Iune: June

HIIALO KICKED HER SEAT in the Datsun. Thud, thud, thud, in a mindless rhythm. Her lips were tightly sealed, her eyes nervous. In her lap was a plastic bag containing a braided *lei hala lei,* made of flowers of the pandanus tree, and a second *lei* made of braided red ti leaves.

"Stop kicking the seat, Hiialo." He ate a Tums. "You okay?"

She nodded.

She'd been up half the night, coming out of her room every five minutes for another drink of water. Must have picked up on his mood. All he'd told Hiialo was that he'd placed a want ad to meet a woman; he was lonely without her mom. His daughter had reacted as though what he'd done was sensible. But did she suspect the truth about Erika? That if all went well she would stay for good, as Hiialo's stepmother?

Kal saw the sign for the airport and manually worked the Datsun's broken turn indicator, flipping it back and forth as an Aloha Airlines plane flew in over the sea, descending to the terminal.

"Is your pen pal on that plane?" asked Hiialo.

"I think so."

Her lips clamped shut again.

Kal parked in the visitors' lot and came around to Hiialo's side of the car to lift her into his arms. "I love

you, Ti-leaf." It was his special name for her. Ti leaves
were a symbol of luck; she was all of his. Everything he
had.

Hiialo kissed his face and rested her head against his
shoulder. "I love you, Daddy."

Kal carried her toward the terminal, thinking, *Hiialo B.
Goode*...

LOW GREEN SHRUBS—Hooker's Green Dark, thought Erika—lined the shore, and white caps dotted the ocean beyond. Her carryall was tucked under the seat in front of
her, and she resisted reaching for it to open her compact.
She looked fine—especially for a woman who hadn't slept
in a week. She'd been too excited to sleep.

Absently Erika touched her hair. Days earlier she'd gone
to the beauty college in Santa Barbara for a free haircut.
The result was that her hair hung at one length, just
brushing her shoulders. Nothing dramatic, but she was
glad she'd done *something*. She wore a silk sheath of
aquamarine—shin-length, with slits partway up both sides.
Sandals, no stockings.

She hoped Hiialo would think she was pretty, would like
her. That was everything. Meeting Kal was just...

Well, okay, it was natural to want him to like her, too.
In fact, it was necessary. She couldn't afford to go back to
the mainland. Adele hadn't wanted to publish prints from
any of her recent watercolors. Erika didn't know what she
was doing wrong, but it was months since she'd sold anything. Until she received royalties from *Sand Castles,* she
had four hundred and fifty dollars to her name, not even
enough for a ticket home. She was going to have to get a
job.

But if she had a job, she couldn't watch Hiialo during
the day.

I have to sell some art.

As the plane touched down, the captain welcomed everyone to Kauai. "The temperature in Lihue is eighty-five degrees..."

The plane taxied interminably before it stopped and the seat-belt signs went off with a quiet *ding*. Erika remained in her seat, letting the other passengers go first. She'd be slow on the stairs. Beside her was a diminutive local beauty in a beach cover-up and flip-flops. She jostled Erika with her bag, then turned and said in charming apology, "Oh, I'm so sorry!" Her voice was musical, her manner sweet. Had Maka been like that?

A graceful human being in every way...

Suddenly Erika felt about a hundred years old.

When the other passengers had passed, she stood up, ducked under the overhead and limped to the door. Slowly, holding the railings, she descended the stairs to the humid airfield and made her way to the small utilitarian terminal. As soon as she stepped inside, she smelled flowers.

He was there, conspicuous for his height and his looks and the little girl beside him, who wore turquoise shorts and a tank top silk-screened with the image of a surfer and the slogan "Breaks to da max!" She was peering intently into a nearby planter bigger than herself.

Kal spotted her and waved, and Erika walked toward him, conscious of her limp, of him watching her. Three yards away, she thought, *Your eyes are blue.*

Teal, so fine a shade that Erika was surprised she hadn't always known the color. A teal she could mix from Turquoise and Hooker's Green Dark. He wore off-white, slightly wrinkled cotton pants and an aloha shirt in navy blue, black and yellow, covered with trumpet vines and ukuleles. Despite the flip-flops on his feet, Erika knew he had dressed up for her coming, but in contrast to the men she knew in Santa Barbara, he seemed casual. Unpretentious. No designer labels, no cologne. Yes, red meat, yes, domestic beer. *Shaka.* Hang loose.

Mr. Family?

Like a daddy wolf. His wolf's expression was on her, assessing her, sniffing the air. Alert.

Mutely Erika submitted to the examination.

It was brief, though Kal found her face hard to absorb in one take. Brown eyes. Olive complexion. Smooth skin. She was tall and slender, with the honed limbs of an athlete.

And a slight limp.

He draped the *lei hala lei* around her neck, and her thick hair reached out and wisped against his fingers, clinging to them with static electricity. "Aloha," he said and touched his lips to her cool cheek. Strands of hair seemed to leap against his face, and he drew back.

Still feeling the kiss and his hands brushing her as he'd put the *lei* around her neck, Erika recalled the word for thank you. "*Mahalo.* What a beautiful *lei.*"

Well, she'd figured out that *mahalo* wasn't Hawaiian for airport trash can, reflected Kal. When she clued into the fact that the word was used mostly by poolside entertainers and interisland flight attendants, she'd be all right.

She was fingering the *lei,* examining it as though she found it wondrous, which he had to admit it was.

In truth, the *lei* gave Erika an excuse not to look at Kal. A slanted half-inch white scar crossed the indentation above his upper lip. Its effect was to make her want to stare at his mouth, at his straight white teeth and the faintest gap between the front two.

Instinct distracted her from the flowers, made her glance down, and there was Hiialo, her arms reaching up with another *lei.* Erika crouched in front of her, and the little girl put the braid of reddish leaves around her neck.

"Aloha, Erika. I'm Hiialo."

"Aloha to you, Hiialo."

"My uncle Danny's hula group made these for you."

Had that been Maka's hula group, too? No wonder the *leis* seemed so intricate, so special. An unexpected welcome from people she had never met. People who loved Kal and Hiialo enough to reach out to her, too. The depth of generosity, the level of hospitality and courtesy, seemed foreign—and beautiful.

No wonder Adele's so crazy about Hawaii, thought Erika, looking forward to sharing stories about her trip. Then she remembered it wasn't just a vacation. She might stay here.

Kal said, "Let's go get your bags."

AS THEY DROVE NORTH, Erika tried to adjust to riding in a car with two strangers who might become the most important part of her life. Luckily there was a lot on the road to occupy her. Sugarcane grew in fields between the road and the sea. Outside a shopping mall, men harvested coconuts from royal palms that reached skyward like Jack's beanstalk.

When the businesses and houses of Wailua were behind them, Kal nodded toward the inland hills. "That's Nounou Ridge. We call it the Sleeping Giant. Can you see him lying on his back?"

"Yes." Erika knew from studying a map that they were on Kauai's main highway. It almost circled the island, stopping only for the impassable mountains of the Na Pali Coast. *Was Maka killed on this road?* How did it happen? Who was at fault?

Kal was thinking of Maka, too. The road was narrowing. They drove past the place where her heart had stopped beating. If Hiialo hadn't been in the back seat, he would have shown Erika where the cars collided.

He ran out of words until they neared the next town. "This is Kapaa. My folks have a gallery here. It's right there." He pointed out the Kapaa Okika Gallery.

Beyond the reflections in the windows, Erika caught a glimpse of paintings hanging against a light background. Then the gallery was out of sight, and the car trawled past shops full of tropical-print silks, colorful beach totes, surfboards and various trinkets. In a blink they left Kapaa, and the highway opened out with a view of the sea.

Miles farther on, as the road curved around the north shore, Kal indicated a lighthouse on a promontory. "Kilauea Lighthouse. You surf?"

"Not anymore." Not well enough for Hawaii's waves. Erika stole a glance at Kal. She'd seen in his photographs that he was attractive. But a photo couldn't carry a man's smell or his voice. She'd thought she was used to the low warm gravelly quality of the latter from talking to him on the phone. But hearing him speak and seeing his face, his body, all at once was a different matter.

The Pacific shifted colors under her eyes, like a quilt being shaken out.

We'll be fine, she told herself. *I'll get used to him, and he won't seem so sexy.*

The countryside became lush, and Erika could feel the dampness in the air as the Datsun passed valleys planted in taro. Blossoms spilled from tree branches, and the roadside flowers held as many shades as her paint box. In a tree whose limbs stretched out on sweeping horizontal planes, like a bonsai, sat dozens of white birds with exotic plumage on their heads. They reminded Erika of tropical ports of her childhood, and she thought of her parents, especially her mother, who had loved flowers.

What a place to paint.

She subdued the now familiar doubts... that she'd never sell another watercolor.

"Daddy, Eduardo's hungry."

Erika glanced into the back seat. Hiialo had one toy with her in the car, the thing Erika had thought was called Pincushion. A watercolor subject. But she must have been mistaken about its name. "Is that Eduardo?"

"No," said Hiialo. "This is Pincushion." She frowned, as though puzzled that Erika had asked. "Eduardo is a *mo'o.*"

"What's that?"

Hiialo seemed at a loss. "Daddy..."

"Mo'os," said Kal, "are giant magical black lizards of Hawaiian legend."

"Giant?"

"Thirty feet long." The topic was a good icebreaker. "The ancient Hawaiians worshiped their ancestors, who they believed could be powerful allies after death. Actually some people still depend on their *aumakua,* deified ancestral spirits, to help them out of trouble. In the old days, a *kahuna,* an expert in magic, would help people transform their deceased relatives into sharks or *mo'os* or whatever. *Mo'os* lived in ponds and were supposed to be fierce fighters, protective of their families."

"Except Eduardo lives in our house," said Hiialo.

Erika briefly entertained the notion that Maka had become a *mo'o* after death. It was a silly idea, but it seemed less cruel than death's stealing her, leaving her husband and baby alone.

There was only a shade of humor in her next thought: *I should make friends with Eduardo.*

With Maka's memory.

"We're coming up on Princeville," Kal said. "In a minute you can see Hanalei Bay."

The terrain was changing again. The green hillocks inland had become mountains, rich forested green and draped in billowing shifting mist. Banyan trees grew alongside the road, their roots stretching twenty feet down the earthen embankment to the asphalt. Erika understood why Kauai was called the Garden Island. Everywhere, everything was verdant; plants with sprawling leaves caught the mist and the first raindrops.

A moment later a shower came in a clattering torrent. Through the rain streaming down the windshield, Erika caught her first glimpse of Hanalei Bay. A Zodiac motored across the water, and then the bay was obscured again by a tangle of foliage, trumpet vines, bottlebrush trees, amaryllis blossoms.

In another few minutes they reached Hanalei.

"That's the gallery," said Kal, identifying a white building with a wraparound porch.

Hanalei was not the tourist trap Erika had half expected. Despite its galleries and T-shirt shops, surf shops and boutiques, the community had an unpolished small-town atmosphere. Leaving the shopping area, they passed a soccer field set against the backdrop of mist-cloaked mountains. Beside the field was a green clapboard church with dramatic Gothic stained glass, a bell on the roof peak and a side tower with a pointed pagoda roof. In the doorway two women in identical *holoku* gowns and *leis* corralled some small children. Other people emerged, and Erika realized it was a wedding.

Somberly she looked away.

Kal was silent.

As they left Hanalei and continued driving west, the road narrowed. Vines and blooms overhung the road, which was broken by one-lane stone bridges. To Erika, it seemed a fairy-tale place—enchanted. They passed the sign for Haena, and soon Kal turned right, toward the ocean, on a gravel road. At its end, amid a jungle of flora—plants with pointed Cadmium Red leaves resembling lobster claws, trees with frilled and lacy hanging blossoms—stood a Private Property sign. Kal turned down the dirt drive.

A stand of mixed tropical trees to the left hid a tiny one-story green house. The dwelling would have blended in with its background if not for its white porch pillars and railing, a faded wind sock hanging from the roof of the lanai and a child's bright plastic tricycle in the road. Erika recognized the bungalow from the photos Kal had sent.

But he didn't stop there.

"Where are you going, Daddy?" asked Hiialo.

The Datsun continued down the gravel drive. "I thought Erika would like to see the beach."

Separated from the bungalow by a forest of trees and shrubs was a vast lawn and a low slate blue house with an oriental roof. Palm trees shaded the beach. The calm summer sea was every shade of blue and green. It took Erika's breath. When Kal parked beside the beachfront house and she got out, she could only stand and hold her arms about herself as the trade winds cooled her body.

"This house is a rental property owned by my parents," said Kal, as Hiialo climbed between the seats and out his door. "It's occupied off and on. When my aunt and uncle from the mainland visit, they stay here. I take care of the place."

Erika stared at the sea. "I didn't imagine you were this close to the ocean."

No longer having to concentrate on driving, Kal studied her face. Prominent bones, smooth planes, a straight nose. He'd already noticed that with different expressions the whole arrangement of her features seemed to change— and that she had a way of looking at things with deep concentration, as though planning to paint them someday. Erika's was not a boring face.

"Daddy , I want to go home."

"*Bumbye,* Hiialo." In a while.

"We can go," said Erika. "I can walk back here anytime. This is just beautiful." *I want to stay....* She spotted a boat covered by a canvas tarp, lying on some vines under what seemed to be a pine tree. "Is that yours?"

"That's the outrigger," said Hiialo. "It was my dad's wedding present from my mom. She and Uncle Danny made it."

Maka. "It must be a very special boat," Erika said. Hiialo was sweet. This would be easy.

Kal moved toward the car. Erika would have preferred to walk to the bungalow, but they all climbed into the Datsun, instead, and he backed up the driveway, spun the wheel and reversed into a gravel space beside a wobbly green gardening shed.

He parked, switched off the ignition and stared straight ahead, out the windshield. Then he looked at Erika. "We're here." He lifted his eyebrows slightly, then turned away, reached for the door handle and got out.

He and Erika carried her belongings up to the lanai. Seeing Kal and Hiialo kick off their flip-flops beside the door, Erika bent down to remove her sandals. When she straightened, she saw a gentle smiling expression in Kal's eyes. He held open the screen door. *"E komo mai.* Welcome."

Stepping into the shadows, onto a warped hardwood floor covered with irregular remnants of gold-and-green carpet, Erika surveyed the small front room. The walls were cheap paneling. On the right side was the kitchen, on the left a couch, an old end table and a throw rug. Over the couch hung a framed print of a schooner, a Hawaiian chief in the bow. A hanging lamp with a plastic tiffany shade advertising Coca-Cola dangled above the coffee table, and two pieces of batiked cloth blocked a doorway opposite the porch.

Erika peered down a hall and spotted a threshold obscured by bamboo beads. At the hallway's end was a real door, a solid door.

She glanced at the kitchen, the sink, the gas stove. Crayon drawings on the refrigerator. The baseboards looked streaky—perhaps hurriedly swept after a long dust buildup. For some reason, the sight touched her.

This place might become her home. Kal might become her husband—though not her lover—and Hiialo her child. It seemed hard to imagine, but she said sincerely, "I like this."

Kal swallowed, relieved. Surprised. "Thanks." He set down her duffel, garment bag and a blue suitcase she'd said contained art supplies and ankle weights. "Let me give you a tour."

"I want to show you my room," said Hiialo.

"Okay."

Hiialo went to the batiked curtains and pushed them apart. Ducking between them, Erika found herself in a tiny chamber with a single koa captain's bed. The wood was familiar; there had been a lot of koa on the *Skye*. Hiialo's closet was built into one wall, and a window looked out on a yellow-blossomed tree beside the driveway.

The watercolor of Pincushion hung over the nightstand, in a plastic frame, no mat. The cheap frame affected Erika much as the hastily dusted baseboards had. "This is a wonderful room, Hiialo."

Hiialo pointed to a turquoise-and-green ginger pattern quilt on her bed. "This is the quilt Tutu made for me. She gave it to me when I was born." Her gaze drifted up to Kal, behind Erika in the doorway.

Turning, Erika caught him with a finger to his lips. He and Hiialo must have a secret.

Tutu. "Is that your grandmother?" Maka's mother?

Hiialo nodded. "My *tutu* on Molokai. Not Grandma." She sat on her bed and turned on a lamp with a friendly-looking dragon at its base. "Would you like to see my Barbie dolls? I have Cinderella, too."

Kal tried to remember the last time Hiialo had shown an interest in dolls. The change seemed to confirm everything he'd suspected: a woman in the house could make all the difference.

But he said, "Let's let Erika settle in first, Hiialo." He stepped around the bed and opened the door to the re-modeled porch. "This is your room."

Erika followed him. The narrow room ran two-thirds the length of the house. Windows stretched along two sides, bamboo blinds rolled near the tops of the frames. The sashes were raised, bringing in heady floral scents, and by the window nearest the driveway, new track lights shone down on an art table.

When Erika saw, her eyes felt hot. He didn't even know her, and he had done all this. He'd made a place for her to work.

What if I can't sell another painting?

She had to. She'd lower her prices. She'd paint women by the sea again.

Then she remembered something else—the things she hadn't told him. About her accident and her paralysis. It wasn't his business, but the untold facts made her feel sneaky.

Kal flicked the light switch. "It's hard to get natural light in this house. Too many trees. Tell me if you need more light for your work. The table's an old one my folks had in their Poipu gallery."

It was hard to get out the words. "Thank you."

"You're welcome."

Erika crossed the koa floor to the captain's bed. It was wider than Hiialo's—full-size—and covered with a slightly faded yellow-and-red handmade quilt. The pattern was tropical, Hawaiian, with vines and blossoms radiating out from the center. Where had it come from?

"Do you like it?" burst out Hiialo. "My great-grandmother made it for my daddy for when he was born. And my daddy built your bed."

She had to stop this feeling—like she was going to cry. He'd made everything so homey. He must want her to stay. Of course he did. He'd invested a lot in her coming.

Kal's bare feet moved over the polished hardwood until he stood beside her. He, too, examined the quilt, which his mother had brought over. It had been packed away in a box during the remodeling of his parents' home twenty years before, and he'd forgotten it existed. His mother hadn't. *You know, I looked and looked for this when you and Maka were married. You know where I found it? In the shed behind the kennels. Your dad and I were clearing it out the other day to make the new whelping room....*

Erika studied the quilt, wanting to soak up its history—and Kal's. "Which of your grandmothers?"

"My dad's mom. She grew up here. Hiialo is the sixth generation of my dad's family to be born and raised in Hawaii."

"I remember."

There were four doors in the room, one that opened to the outside, toward the mountains. Kal opened the nearest, the original door to the porch, and went into his room.

Hiialo scooted in front of Erika into her father's bedroom, then huddled close to Kal. Erika followed more slowly.

Inside, her eyes were drawn toward the light from the open window. The quilt on his bed was purple and lavender and well-worn. It was folded over double, and it took a moment for Erika to realize why.

He slept in a single bed.

Erika looked away from the piece of furniture, as though she'd caught him there naked. He really *didn't* want a lover.

On one wall was a stereo and a rack of tapes and CDs that stretched to the ceiling. Bookshelves and two guitars hung nearby. One instrument was chrome, etched with Hawaiian designs, the other an old archtop. On the floor beneath them were an amplifier and two cases Erika suspected held electric guitars.

She was startled. Kal had never mentioned music to her. "You play?"

He nodded, without humble disclaimers.

"You never said anything."

Kal touched the Gibson, drawing sound from the strings. "No."

Erika decided he wasn't as simple an equation as she'd first thought.

The bathroom was across the hall. Thin strips of black mold grew on the tub caulking—difficult to prevent in watery climates. For a single father who worked six days a week and cared for a rental property as well, he kept a clean house. *You do good, Kal,* she thought.

"There's a gecko, Daddy," said Hiialo.

An orange lizard scaled the wall above the towel rack.

"Oh, cool!" Erika peered closer.

The lizard scurried away.

"They eat cockroaches," Hiialo told her.

Erika glanced at Kal.

He shrugged. "It's Hawaii. We get some." He stepped out into the hall, Hiialo one pace behind him. "You probably want to unpack, relax."

"Actually I brought some gifts for you."

Hiialo's eyes grew large.

In her own room, Erika crouched beside the bed, opened her tote and removed a gift bag. "This is for you, Hiialo."

As Kal entered the room, bearing Erika's other luggage and a large flat box containing watercolor paper, Hiialo peeked in the bag. "Oh, look! Oh, Daddy, he's cute! He looks like an Akita puppy."

Erika's gift was a small stuffed roly-poly dog. It was cinnamon-colored with a black muzzle and fluffy curled-up tail.

Smiling, Kal squatted beside Hiialo to look at the stuffed animal. "Sure does. Hiialo—"

Erika watched him mouth, *What do you say?*

"Thank you, Erika." Her grin was toothy, dimply.

Erika said, "There's something else in the bag."

Hiialo reached down to the bottom and pulled out a tin of felt-tip pens. Her face fell. She met Erika's eyes. "I already have these."

A blush burned Kal's face. "But some of yours are drying out."

Erika wished she'd chosen something Hiialo didn't have.

Hiialo put the pens back in the gift bag and hugged her stuffed puppy. "Thank you, anyhow, Erika."

"You're welcome, sweetie. I hope you enjoy them."

"I'm going to go make a little bed for my dog." A moment later she disappeared into her room.

Kal shrugged, an apology. "She's only four."

"She's darling," Erika replied politely. She lifted out another gift sack, this one heavier and decorated with suns and moons, and handed it to Kal. When he took it, she saw the veins in his sun-browned forearms and the calluses on his hands. He had nice hands.

Kal opened the bag and pulled out a thick navy blue T-shirt with a primitive design in black, white and rust on the front. The figure of a whale was circled by a field of white dots.

"It's a design of the Chumash Indians of Santa Barbara," said Erika.

"Thanks. I'll wear it now."

He set the bag, not yet empty, on the bed and started to unbutton his aloha shirt with the eagerness of a man who hated to dress up.

As he took it off, Erika had an impression of a lean muscular chest and roped abdominal muscles. Trying to ignore him, she memorized the colors in the flowers outside the window. When she sensed that he'd put on the new shirt, she glanced back at him.

He was holding out the hem, checking the fit, which was good. "Thanks," he said again.

"There's more."

Kal picked up the sack and withdrew a quart of beer from a micro-brewery in Santa Barbara. She saw him hesitate before he said, "Thank you. We'll have to share it tonight."

"Thank *you*, Kal. This bed..." It was bigger than his.

Wide enough for two.

"The drawers came off an old dresser. The rest was easy." He edged toward the window, touching the frame.

His legs, Erika noticed, were long. Even covered by the loose twill of his drawstring-waist pants, they suggested muscle. Though his skin was golden brown from the sun, it was also smooth, the kind of skin that made her want to touch the area around his lips and his mouth, touch that tiny scar. And the bare abdomen, the chest, the shoulders she had glimpsed when he changed his shirt. He was powerfully built. *Six years younger than me.*

The thought was not unappealing. He was certainly a grown man.

But her observation was distant. Uninvolved. She assessed him as she thought another woman might.

When he turned from the window, Kal found her staring. Shot by a feeling he hadn't expected—something sexual—he hurried to end the moment. "You probably want to rest. Are you hungry?"

"The food on the plane was good. I'd just as soon spend some time with Hiialo."

"Look, I don't expect you to baby-sit. That wasn't the idea." Not exactly.

Good. Maybe he wouldn't mind if she had to get a job. "Well, she's why I came," she said, suddenly needing to make that clear. *He could have changed his shirt in the other room.*

"Mmm," Kal agreed. Hiialo's door was opened just a crack, but he could hear her playing in her room, talking make-believe with her stuffed friends. He leaned against the wall he had framed. "So...you probably want to make sure you like us before we go any further with this."

Erika felt the quilt beneath her—and the bed. Things had gone pretty far. "I don't see anything likely to make me run away."

You haven't seen my daughter throw a tantrum.

But Erika Blade struck him as a woman who wouldn't flee difficulty.

"We can give ourselves as much time as we need," he said. "I was thinking of about six weeks."

Panic stricken, Erika thought she might break into hysterical laughter. *Six weeks* to decide if she wanted to spend the rest of her life in a celibate marriage to a man with more sex appeal than Brad Pitt?

But even making contributions to household expenses, she should be able to make her money last six weeks. And surely she could produce some marketable art in that length of time. "Six weeks sounds reasonable."

Kal nodded. The air in the room felt oppressive, stuffy, and he knew it was because of the topic, the future he'd planned, the prison of a marriage without touch, a marriage to a stranger.

He said, "I'll leave you alone. Maybe we can go swimming later."

She nodded and so did he. Kal hurried out of the room, then the house. Moments later as he stood on the lanai quaffing the air, he realized he hadn't been fleeing the awkwardness. He'd been getting away from Erika Blade's tawny arms and legs, her narrow bare feet, her brown hair and eyes. He was fleeing the woman herself.

Because he found her very beautiful, which was the last thing he'd expected.

CHAPTER FIVE

THEY AGREED ON A SWIM before dinner.

At five Kal threw on some faded red surfing trunks and went into Hiialo's room to tell her to put on her swimsuit. She was playing with her new stuffed puppy, whom she'd named Fluff. Kal wondered if Erika liked dogs.

"Hiialo, want to go swimming?"

"Yes! Hooray!" She tucked Fluff in a shoe box she'd lined with doll blankets, and then hurried to her closet, which looked about like his, a pit, and began throwing her clothes around, looking for a swimsuit.

Kal went out into the front room.

Erika was on the lanai, dressed in a coral swimsuit, a sarong around her waist. He could see the muscles in her suntanned back. *Strong.* Unaware of him, she crouched to touch a Mexican creeper growing beside the veranda. She studied it with the intense concentration he'd noticed before, as though she had to take a test on it later. He saw her eyes drop slightly, her lids brush her cheeks, and she swallowed.

Emotional... Whatever she felt, Kal understood. She'd just moved in with a stranger she'd met through a want ad.

He walked out onto the lanai and Erika straightened. He said, "You've got a towel. I was going to ask if you needed one."

"No, I—I brought everything."

"Literally?"

Erika met his eyes, and her heart moved from her chest to her throat. "Yes." She'd even sold the Karmann Ghia. "I don't own much. I've always lived on boats."

The way she said it made him wonder. She must have traveled all the time as a kid. No neighborhood. No best friend, unless it was her brother. Kal had never known anyone who could put all her worldly goods in four pieces of luggage and a cardboard box. "This house is kind of like a boat," he said, "that stays in one place."

His half smile, combined with the sober look in his eyes, made Erika feel he knew things she'd never told him.

Hiialo bounded out of the house, clutching her Pocahontas beach towel. "Let's go. Come on, Eduardo." She shouted, "Can we go in the outrigger, Daddy?"

Erika made the kind of involuntary wince someone does when the music comes on too loud. *Because of Hiialo?* Kal wondered. That would be bad. If his daughter was an amplifier, she would go up to eleven. Higher than high, louder than loud. "Not today."

Barefoot, Erika stepped down to the soft green lawn. The thatch was short and dense, different grass than she knew on the mainland. The warm earth invited her to sink in roots. She wanted to. She could be happy surrounded by so much color.

As Kal grabbed a faded towel from the clothesline, Hiialo bounded ahead toward the drive. Erika peered after her, then back at Kal. Her eyes were caught by a tree with white flowers and round waxy leaves. On one of the leaves, someone had etched a picture, a childish drawing of a girl in a dress.

Erika touched the leaf.

"That's an autograph tree," said Kal. "You can scratch something on the leaves when they're young, and the image grows with the leaves. Here." He picked up a twig from the ground and pulled an autograph leaf toward him.

With the twig he wrote, "ALOHA, ERIKA," then let the leaf spring away.

Erika had been watching his hands. "Thanks."

They both turned toward the sea.

As they followed Hiialo down the drive, Erika again noticed the evergreens shading the beach. "Are those pine trees?"

"They're ironwoods. Some people call them Australian pines, but they're not true pines. They were introduced as windbreaks."

"Oh."

By the time the adults reached the beach, Hiialo had splashed into the surf. Erika glanced at Kal, but he seemed unconcerned.

He shouldn't let her go in alone like that. A sea-dweller all her life, Erika had strong feelings about children and water.

She dropped her towel in the sand near the high-tide line, and so did Kal. Casting her a quick smile, he turned toward the ocean and was soon wading after Hiialo. He dove into the breakers and came up with his skin glistening wet, his hair suddenly darker, yet still tinseled with blondish highlights.

Hiialo swam to him. "Let me dive off your shoulders!"

Erika limped into the foam. Small fish darted about on a reef under the surface. She waded over the wet rocks, then lowered her body into the sea and swam away from the shore, away from the reef. The water was cellophane clear. From the surface, she spotted a stingray and a dogfish. Unafraid of the ocean or its inhabitants, she swam out to Kal and Hiialo as Hiialo dove off his shoulders, then emerged, sputtering and small. Wiping hair from her eyes, she dog-paddled to her father's waiting arms.

As Hiialo wrapped herself around him like a koala on a eucalyptus branch, Erika watched Kal's face. His eyelashes were thick dark triangles, drawn to points by the salt water, and his eyebrows were black against his skin and his fairer hair. His face was not so much rugged and craggy as sensual, his lips one commanding feature, his eyes another. A straight well-shaped nose. The muscles in his arms and back shifted in the reflected light from the water as he lifted Hiialo, helping her stand on his shoulders again.

Her throat closing, Erika gave herself some quick advice.

Whatever happened, she mustn't fall in love with Kal.

KAL HAD SPENT a year as prep cook at the Hanalei Grind and watched the chef every chance he had. In honor of Erika's arrival, he prepared shrimp with a spicy Cajun sauce. He'd been surprised months before to learn that red peppers and garlic wouldn't irritate his stomach, could in fact be beneficial. Which was good. Giving up beer was hard enough.

While he cooked, with Nirvana playing from the front room speakers wired to the stereo in his room, Hiialo showed Erika her Barbie collection. Leaving the sauce simmering, Kal went into the bathroom, and before he turned on the shower he heard them talking.

"Oh, can I put that dress on her, Hiialo?"

Kal turned on the water, drowning the voice that, until today, he'd heard only on the phone—the voice that now had become one of the sounds of his house. He rinsed off the salt, soaped down, squirted shampoo on his hair. He was out in three minutes, and he shaved, then slipped into his room and pulled on a pair of baggy cotton shorts and the new shirt Erika had given him. After checking on dinner, he moved toward Hiialo's room. As he started to part the curtains and look in, he heard Erika say, "Who's this?"

"That's my mother and me."

Kal closed his eyes, listening.

"She's pretty, Hiialo."

"Daddy says I look like her. But mostly like me."

Erika had a low rich laugh. A kind laugh.

Kal stood in the shadows of the front room, not noticing that the sun was down and he hadn't yet turned on a lamp.

Sitting on the edge of Hiialo's bed, Erika examined the face in the photograph, the woman whose image was missing from the first photo Kal had mailed her. The woman he'd loved so much.

Maka was strongly built, with long wavy black hair and an infectious grin somehow made more attractive by the fact that her small teeth were fairly crooked. She looked like...fun. Clearly she was enjoying the baby she bounced in her lap. *A hula dancer...*

Erika remembered Kal's single bed and felt something too much like jealousy. But that was ridiculous.

The curtain on the door moved and he stuck his head in. "Dinner's ready."

Erika stood up while Hiialo turned off the dragon lamp, leaving her Barbies on the bed.

In the other room Kal switched on a light over the stove. "Hiialo and I usually sit out on the porch when the weather's nice." Taking plates from the cabinet, he started as Erika came up beside him.

"Oh, sorry. Let me help." She took the plates from him. "Silverware?"

"I'll get it!" Hiialo sprinted across the room and opened the drawer. It came out, and all the jar lids and silverware and knives with chipped blades crashed to the floor.

There was a silence. Seeing Hiialo's face begin to fall, Kal said, "It's okay."

But she was going to cry. *No. Don't, Hiialo.*

Erika set the plates on the counter and stooped to help gather the utensils.

Hiialo bit her lip, tears brimming, and Kal didn't breathe. Erika helped her pick up the things from the drawer, and he could see she was trying not to look at his daughter, not to make the four-year-old cry. It made him like her.

Kal scooped up Hiialo, held her against him, kissed her. "Find us some napkins, Ti-leaf, yeah?"

She nodded, blinking back her tears, and then she shimmied down out of his arms. "I'll pick up everything, Erika. You just relax on the porch."

Kal bit down a smile. She sounded like her grand-mother. On the *haole* side, the Caucasian side. His mom.

Erika lifted her eyes and smiled at Hiialo. "Are you sure I can't help?"

Hiialo worked her mouth as she did when she was thinking. At last she said, "Okay." She squatted in her bare feet and bare legs beside Erika and collected some silverware. "Should we wash it, Daddy?"

"Yes."

Kal watched Erika's hair tumble in front of her, show-ing her bare shoulders. She was wearing a plain pale yel-low dress with narrow straps, and as she bent over he could see the tops of her breasts, high smallish breasts he had noticed in her wet swimsuit.

He turned back to the food, trying to remember what had been happening before Hiialo pulled out the drawer.

The phone rang.

Erika tensed.

The telephone hung on the wall next to the refrigerator, beside the hallway. Kal lifted the receiver. "Hello?"

Erika thought she heard a woman's voice on the line.

"Hi, Mom.... Yes.... Yes." He pressed the mute but-ton and addressed Erika, who was taking silverware to the sink. Her dress brushed his leg. "Want to have dinner at my parents' house Wednesday? It's my birthday."

A birthday. He'd be thirty-one. When she was thirty-one, she'd been in a car accident. And after that... Thirty-one had been a bad year. "Sure. If you do," she added, taking more silverware from Hiialo's small hands.

Kal put the phone to his ear again. "Okay. Thank you. We'll come. What should we bring?"

"Can we see the puppies?" demanded Hiialo.

Kal ignored her.

Erika whispered, "Do your grandparents have puppies?"

"They have two litters," said Hiialo. "I can't play with the new puppies yet, but the other ones might be big enough. They look just like my puppy you gave me. But we can't have a dog," she added, sounding resigned. "Daddy has to work too much. So I have Eduardo."

The *mo'o*. Erika found Hiialo's attitude surprisingly mature—and a little sad. Children should be able to have pets, but she knew Kal was being responsible. He didn't have time for a dog. If she was there...

But how likely was that—really?

Ten minutes later Kal sat on the porch steps while Hiialo and Erika shared the swing. The shrimp was messy, and they needed the dish towels Hiialo had brought from the linen cupboard—makeshift napkins.

Hiialo talked, and Kal hardly had to think, only eat and stare across the dark yard at the rusted white Datsun, which burned a quart of oil a week and needed new tires. New everything. The night was damp and fragrant.

"My uncle Danny—I just call him Danny, but he's my uncle," said Hiialo. "He's a hula dancer, and he teaches me hula sometimes...."

Kal picked up another shrimp.

"This is great, Kal."

Erika had spoken, and he glanced up in surprise. "Thanks."

"My dad is a mugician, too," said Hiialo. "He plays the guitar."

In the glow from the light at the end of the porch, Erika smiled. "I know. Will you play something for us, Kal?"

Hiialo set aside her plate and jumped down from the porch swing, knocking her fork to the ground. "I'll get his guitar."

"Hiialo."

She stopped.

Kal raised his eyebrows at the fork, then at her plate. "Grandma made chocolate-chip macadamia-nut cookies. Don't you want some?"

"Cookies!" she exclaimed.

He wondered how she'd planned to get down a guitar. They both hung high on the wall, and the National was too heavy for her to lift.

Hiialo took her plate inside, ending conversation on the lanai.

The tension eased from Erika's body.

The trade winds breathed on them.

By and by Kal said, "I've arranged to take an extra day off tomorrow. I thought you and Hiialo and I could do something together. Picnic. Sight-seeing. Also, you may as well know, my mom's not going to be satisfied to wait until Wednesday night to get a look at you."

Erika didn't smile. "How are your parents reacting to this?"

He was bringing a piece of shrimp to his mouth. He put it back on his plate. "Um . . . they know I . . ." He slowed down. There was no reason to tell her that his parents knew how much he missed Maka. "It's okay with them. They don't know . . . I don't talk to them about my sex life." Taking a breath, he retreated to a point of safety. "Anyhow, you're an artist. Art is their main thing, besides their dogs. They're prepared for the best."

That thought made Erika more nervous than if he'd said his parents were disapproving.

Kal stood up, picked up his own plate, then reached for hers. "Let's have some cookies."

Inside, Hiialo was standing on a chair washing her plate at the sink. He said, "You're a good girl, Hiialo. You want to wash these plates too?"

"Okay."

Twenty minutes later, they had finished the cookies, and he brought out the chrome resonator guitar. When she saw the instrument, Erika exclaimed, "How beautiful! Do you play Hawaiian music? What do you call it—slack-key?"

"Sure." He played everything. He sat down on the steps.

On the swing beside Erika, Hiialo looked sleepy and dissatisfied. The other guitar, the Gibson, was the guitar for playing "Puff." But she liked Hawaiian music, too, and when he began to play "Ua Kea O Hana," she made no complaint.

Even the opening notes were magical popular Hawaii. But when Kal began to sing, Erika's body hummed in response. His voice was powerful, rough and earthy, raking her heart.

When the song ended, she said, "You're great."

"My dad has perfect pitch," Hiialo informed her.

"I believe it." Such a voice. And he was good with that guitar. "Play something else."

"Puff," said Hiialo, not quite under her breath.

It was almost her bedtime. Kal told her, "Brush your teeth while I play another for Erika. After that I'll play 'Puff.'"

Once Hiialo had gone inside, he tuned the guitar to open G and played blues—Robert Johnson's "Come on in My Kitchen." Then he went inside for the Gibson, played "Puff the Magic Dragon" for Hiialo, and afterward he put her to bed.

Erika went into Hiialo's room to say good-night to her. It felt a little like baby-sitting, and it made her think of Chris, her nephew. Of three dark and difficult years. During. Maneuvering her wheelchair in the narrow confines of the *Skye*. Accidents and private struggles. Emotional exchanges between her and David. *Look, if you fall, don't just lie there. Call for me.* Silent nights full of taunting ghosts.

"Good night, Hiialo."

"Good night, Erika." Hiialo hugged her new puppy. "I love Fluff."

Erika hoped Hiialo would love her as easily—and that Kal would accept her. She slipped past his tall body, unable to escape brushing his warmth, and pushed between the curtains in the doorway. Behind her, she heard the soft tones of him saying good-night to Hiialo and imagined him hugging her, tucking her in.

When he emerged, he went to the refrigerator and took out the bottle of beer Erika had brought from the mainland. "Want some?"

"Sure."

His back to her, he grabbed a plastic bottle from the counter, shook out a couple of tablets and popped them in his mouth. He noticed Erika watching. "Ulcer."

You're pretty young to have an ulcer. But what did she know about it?

He divided the bottle of beer between two mugs, and they went outside. There was room for three or four people on the porch swing, but he let Erika have it to herself and sank down on the steps against a post.

They tried the beer before she asked, "Have you ever played professionally?"

"Oh . . . sure." He didn't want to get into it. It could make him bitter in a hurry. He watched the night, the leaves lifting with a breath of wind. He heard the ocean, saw the quality of light change as the high beam of a full moon rose in the trees on the other side of the driveway.

On the swing, she waited.

Music. "Before Hiialo was born, Maka and I lived in Honolulu. We actually worked together for a while. I was in a *hapa haole* band. We played Waikiki hotels. Maka's hula group danced with us."

Erika had leaned forward. Her chin was in her hand. Listening.

"Then I had another band, Kai Nui. We're...we were kind of...I guess now they'd call us 'alternative.' We played a lot of rock and roll, but a little bit of everything. Our own songs were hard to classify, I guess." Hard to classify, but good enough to win the favor of the biggest island label—and the attention of the biggest of the late-night talk-show hosts. Later that hadn't mattered. Except to rub him raw inside. "We moved back here when Maka got pregnant. To be near our families. We had a place down in Waimea. Then Maka died, and Iniki leveled our house." And changed his plans. Bad luck. He changed the subject. "Are you afraid of hurricanes?"

Erika considered. When she was a child, the *Siren*, her father's ship, had been near hurricanes, but they'd never been caught in one. "Not especially."

"These houses—" his glance included the stretch to the beach, the whole neighborhood "—they've all been rebuilt in the last three years."

"Were you here during the hurricane?"

"Yeah." Living in a daze without Maka. Drinking rum every night after Hiialo was in bed. Staying up for hours trying to get her to drink goat's milk and formula from a bottle. Crying while she cried—and not just for Maka. "When we knew it was going to hit, I took Hiialo and came up here to be with my folks and my sister. It was pretty bad. The waves were coming up over the telephone poles. My folks' house is *mauka*." The inclination of his head indicated the direction inland. "But they lost their roof, too."

"*Mauka?*"

"Inland, toward the mountains. *Makai* is toward the sea. Forget compass points." Kal remembered his fears that having a *malihini* in the house would be annoying. What he felt now was different. He wanted to help her, so that she wouldn't say something wrong and be hurt by people reacting the way they could.

He returned to the weather. "It's hurricane season now. A few times a year they say there's one headed this way. It can get to you."

"You love this place." To have stayed through such mayhem.

"It's my home."

She saw the bright white in the trees. "There's the moon. I forgot it was full."

Kal looked over his shoulder.

"I guess it comes from living on ships," said Erika. "I always think home is where the people I love are."

"Yeah, well, mine—they're here." Kal took a drink. In the moonlight, he surveyed the garden, remembering devastation. Wondering why Erika wasn't with the people she loved.

But her brother had remarried. The child she'd helped raise had a new stepmother. Kal wanted to ask her if she missed the kid, but he thought he knew the answer. He thought it had been there, in her letter. Unsaid.

The beer didn't last long.

They went inside, and Erika washed the pots and pans while he put the food away and wiped off the chipped Formica counter. When the last pot was in the drying rack, she said, "I think I'll turn in."

"Sure." Kal was squeezing out the sponge, wondering how long he could keep the house clean. He glanced at Erika. "Good night."

"Good night."

Erika knew she shouldn't feel deflated when he turned his back.

In her room, by the full-moon glow that stole through the windows, she found the wall lamp above her bed and switched it on. She shut the blinds and checked that the outside door was locked. Then she undressed, donned an oversize Blade Institute T-shirt and folded back the covers of the bed.

The sheets were soft, clean, new. The mattress was firm. Turning out the light and pulling the covers over her, she felt alone and faraway from anyone who really cared about her. *And low on money...*

Her fingers clutched the edge of the quilt, Kal's birth quilt made by his grandmother, and she tried not to think about his face or the scar above his lip or his shoulders wet in the ocean.

Why had he never said the word "music" to her?

Closing her eyes, she saw him in her mind and wondered things she knew she shouldn't, things that could hurt her in the end. What it would be like to be wanted by him. To be touched by him.

To be loved by him.

CHAPTER SIX

IN THE MORNING, his mother called and invited them over for breakfast.

Kal didn't answer at once.

He'd awoken in the middle of the night, and like always, Maka was dead. But knowing Erika was in the room next door had made it worse. More real. Another sign that he had to go on without his wife. *I can't do this.*

"Kal?" said his mother. "If you have other plans, it's okay."

Erika came down the hall in cutoffs and a white crop top. There were surgical scars on her left knee. Kal had glimpsed them the day before, when they went swimming. Now he wanted to take a good look, but instead, he met her eyes. Remembered her face, so new to him that he'd lost the recollection in sleep.

The future that had seemed gruesome by night suddenly looked salvageable. Erika was a project, someone to learn about. The decision he'd made, asking her to come, was good.

Good to have someone for Hiialo.

He told his mother they'd be over at nine, and he got off the phone and asked Erika if she drank coffee and how she wanted it.

KAL'S PARENTS LIVED in a two-story plantation home set on a hillside above Haena. As Kal reached the foot of their drive, he spotted an elderly Japanese-American couple walking out of the driveway next door. He waved to them, and they waved back, smiling.

"That's Mr. and Mrs. Akana. She was a picture bride, too."

"Picture bride?" asked Erika.

Turning up the driveway, a narrow corridor of green, he smiled a little. "This is actually a very Hawaiian thing we're doing." He explained about picture brides.

Erika thought, *How silly I was last night, feeling alone.* What if she had never been anywhere before in her life and she had come to Hawaii from Japan to meet her new husband? What if she'd never spoken with him on the phone first? What if all she'd had, all he'd had, was a picture? She twisted around in her seat, trying to see the older couple, but the vegetation hid them from sight. After a moment Erika said, "It does sound a little like us." Though surely the Akanas shared a bed.

The wide second-floor veranda of the Johnsons' house appeared through the foliage. At the end of the drive was a patio with a red Subaru station wagon and a white-and-red Ford Ranger parked nearby. On the *mauka* side of the house, a volleyball net divided a lawn ringed with tropical flowers. On the *makai* side, facing the sea a half mile away, were the kennel runs.

As Erika got out of the car, carrying two jars of Java plum jam that Kal had handed to her before they left the bungalow, she heard dogs barking, and a giant with a fluffy white coat came snuffling up to her side.

"*Raiden,*" Kal said, a hint of sternness in his voice. The Akita took his wagging tail toward him. "Good boy."

Hiialo clambered out of the car on Erika's side just as the front door opened and a woman came out. Erika recognized Mary Helen Johnson from the pictures Kal had sent. She tried to quiet her nerves as the woman moved toward them, her eyes on Erika with an expression of pleasure.

Kal abandoned Raiden and joined Erika. He couldn't remember the first time his folks had met Maka. Now he was introducing them to Erika, who might become his wife but would never be what Maka had been to him. "Mom, this is Erika Blade. Erika, Mary Helen Johnson, my mom."

"Hi, Erika. I'm so glad you're here." Mary Helen tossed highlighted blond bangs back from her eyes. "Oh, look, you brought us some jam! Kal buys this at the Haena Store. There's an old man who sells it outside. Come on in." She peered about the gardens and kennels. "I thought your dad was out here somewhere, Kal."

As they stepped through a generous foyer into a spacious family room, King Johnson came through the sliding glass doors, his white hair damp with sweat from some exertion. He shut the screen before he turned to face the others.

Mary Helen was saying to Erika and Kal, "You have to see the puppies."

"I want to see them now," said Hiialo.

King caught her up. "Even before you say hello to your old Grandpa?"

"Hi, Grandpa." Hiialo hugged him. Grinning in his arms, she said, "Can I see the puppies? Erika brought me a stuffed puppy, and it looks just like an Akita."

"Well, did she now. Hello, Erika. I'm King."

"It's nice to meet you." It *was* nice. She hadn't counted on their being so ready to welcome her, to like her.

But then she thought of Kal's single bed.

Erika felt like a fraud. She hoped they weren't anticipating more grandchildren.

Mary Helen showed them into a living room with a ceramic-tile floor. Erika sat with Kal on a blue-and-white plaid sofa while King brought one of the Akita puppies inside for Hiialo to play with.

It was cute, a deep rust fluff-ball with a black muzzle, and resembled nothing so much as a teddy bear—or the stuffed animal she'd given Hiialo.

"This is one of Kumi's puppies," King told Kal.

"How old is he?" asked Erika.

"Six weeks. We have another litter outside that's just a week old."

Kal watched Hiialo take the puppy in her lap. A moment later Erika left the couch and knelt beside her. She stroked the dog with her graceful artist's hands. Long fingers, practical nails with no polish. They showed her age. Her hair fell in front of her as she and Hiialo petted the Akita.

King brought in another puppy and set it down in front of Erika. This one had a much paler coat. "Want one?"

She said with appreciation and, Kal thought, tact, "Who wouldn't want one?"

"Daddy, can we get one this time?" asked Hiialo. *"Please."*

Kal shook his head.

Her mouth twisted, but for once she didn't beg.

Erika stroked the lighter-colored puppy. "Hi, you." The puppy licked her hands, and she made up her mind that if she did return to the mainland, she would find a place to live that allowed pets. But the thought reminded her of her financial situation, and she grew worried. What was she going to do? David would help her, of course, but she would never ask. He'd done enough for her.

Kal left the couch and sat down on the floor beside her, and Erika handed him the puppy. "Here."

Accepting the ball of fur, Kal lay back on the tile floor. "Hey, you little monster." As the puppy crawled on him, he felt Erika watching. But when he looked at her, her color deepened and she turned away.

Hiialo abandoned her puppy and came and sat on his stomach.

Kal groaned.

King corralled the deserted puppy and took him outside, and Kal let the other puppy lick his neck while Hiialo
tried to grab the animal. Then Raiden's big head appeared above him, and a full-grown Akita-size tongue
slurped across his face.

Kal sat up, not wanting to be belly-up to anything that
big.

His father scooped up the remaining puppy, six hundred dollars' worth of purebred dog. "Raiden. Go lie
down."

The giant obeyed.

Erika kept her eyes away from Kal. She should have
guessed that he was a man who would lie on the floor and
let children and dogs climb all over him. She liked men like
that. And she already liked Kal too much.

Not that she'd want to have sex with him or anything.

Yuck, she reminded herself.

She stood up, and Kal, beside her, wondered how she'd
respond if he began nibbling on her calf. Or licking her. He
restrained the uncivilized urge. She didn't seem like she was
even used to being around dogs, let alone people who
sometimes forgot they weren't dogs themselves. She
jumped whenever Hiialo talked loudly or ran in the house.

When King had taken both puppies outside, Mary Hel-
en offered everyone passion fruit or guava juice, kona
coffee, bagels, mangoes and mango bread. "Mango season," explained Kal.

They ate in the living room. Hiialo knelt on the tile floor
beside the coffee table, and no one bothered her about
crumbs or dripping mangoes. Mary Helen turned the
conversation to art and suggested places Erika might enjoy painting. "The Hanalei Bridge is a great landscape
scene. Of course, I know you have your niche."

"Actually," said Erika, "I'm trying to go a little
broader. I want to try something new in Hawaii." *Like*

selling something. Kal's parents seemed interested, but Erika again felt her fraudulence. She had to talk to Kal about money. She'd try to paint again first, but—

"Do you have any new prints coming out?" asked Mary Helen.

"Just *Sand Castles.*" Erika looked at Kal. *Change the subject.*

Kal saw the silent plea in her eyes, but he wasn't sure what she wanted. Finally he put his arm around her and drew her against his side.

Erika shuddered.

Kal's stomach went warm. When his penis stirred, he shifted slightly. Less surprised than disturbed.

Mary Helen broke the silence. "You know, Erika, it would be fun if we could talk you into coming in and working at the gallery someday. Just sitting in a corner painting. An artist in residence." She added, "We sell mainly prints, but we do have some original pieces, as well."

Erika could feel Kal's heartbeat. His hand was stroking her arm, almost absently. "I'd love to." Her voice cracked. "Let me know what day." Work at the gallery. Maybe Mary Helen and King would give her a job. Oh, no, she couldn't ask. They were absolutely the last people who should know she was destitute.

"Can I come?" asked Hiialo, settling onto the couch beside her and spilling crumbs between the cushions.

Erika hesitated, turning to Kal. He was oblivious. Taking his arm from around her, he picked up an embroidered pillow. He set it in his lap and explored the floral design with his fingers.

"Hiialo spends each Tuesday at the gallery with us, anyway," said King. "It's up to Erika, Hiialo."

"Of course you can come," Erika told her.

The teakettle whistled in the kitchen, and King and Mary Helen both leapt up. Erika wondered if they were going to

talk about her over the stove. Leaning forward, she
reached for a glass of passion-fruit juice on the glass-
topped coffee table. When she sat back, Kal's hand came
up to touch the side of her mouth. His thumb wiped
something away.

"Mango pulp," he said.

Erika sank deeper into the cushions. The right side of
her body pressed against his left, but neither of them
moved. When she dared a glance at him, he was watching
her with his lips slightly parted, his eyes sweeping over her.

Her own face got hot, and she drank her juice, trying
not to think.

THEY STAYED at his parents' house for an hour, and before they left they went out to the kennel runs to see the
younger puppies. King slipped into the whelping shed with
Jin, the mother, and he held the puppies up one by one so
that Erika and Hiialo and Kal could see them.

One of the pups had markings almost identical to his
mother's. A sharply defined white patch began midway on
his chest and stretched down his legs and all along his belly.
The rest of him was rust-colored except for his black ears
and mask. He didn't protest being picked up by King, and
Jin allowed it with the calm of a madonna.

"You've got an all-white one, Dad." Kal peered over the
waist-high door of the shed.

"She's sold."

Erika was smiling at the puppy he held. "I like that
one."

"Yeah. He looks like Jin." Jin was Kal's favorite of his
parents' dogs, in looks, temperament and brains.

Hiialo lost interest in the puppies. Squatting in the
gravel, she began to draw a picture with a stick.

"I've always thought of Akitas as aggressive," Erika
said. "Your dogs are so nice."

"Well, all the spitz breeds are independent," admitted King, returning the puppy to its mother and letting himself out of the shed. "But you won't find a more loyal animal. You probably haven't heard the story of Hachiko."

"I'll tell her in the car, Dad," said Kal. "We've got to go." The day off was rare, and he and Erika and Hiialo had a lot of getting to know one another to do.

They said goodbye to Kal's mother, who surprised Erika with a quick embrace.

When they were buckled into the Datsun again, Kal reversed the car and started down the driveway.

Erika said, "So... the dog story."

"Oh, yeah." Kal was grateful to his father for giving them something to talk about. He wouldn't have to examine what had happened during breakfast. "Okay. Hachiko was born in Akita, Japan, in 1923."

"You're good with dates," said Erika.

"Tour guide."

"Tell about the train station!" Hiialo shouted.

Erika wanted to tell her to keep her voice down, but Kal obviously didn't care. She wondered if he was a little deaf. Sometimes musicians were.

"Okay," he was saying, "so Hachiko lived in Tokyo with a Mr. Uyeno, who was his owner. Every day Hachiko accompanied him to the train station and waited there for him to come home in the afternoon. Then, one day, Mr. Uyeno became ill at work and died before he could get home. Hachiko was only sixteen months old, but he never forgot his master. He went to the station every day to look for Mr. Uyeno, and sometimes he would stay there several days without returning home."

Erika felt warmth behind her nose and eyes and wished she had a tissue.

"He did that for nine years, and as people saw the dog waiting and growing old, they were so moved that when he died they decided to erect a statue in his memory. There's still a statue of Hachiko at that train station."

"No wonder your folks love that breed," Erika said, blinking hard.

"Loyalty is a good trait. Hey, you're crying."

Loyalty. Erika thought how loyal he was—to Maka's memory. That single bed. Would never sleep with another woman.

They had turned onto the main road. "Are we going back to the house?" she asked.

"I thought we'd do some sight-seeing. A couple of waterfalls. The Hanalei pier. We'll go down Waimea side another day. You have to visit Barking Sands Beach. The sand barks when you walk on it."

"Let's take Erika to the *heiau*," said Hiialo from the back seat.

She meant the old hula platform near Keʻe Beach, on the north shore at the end of the Kuhio Highway, the main road, the only road. There were actually two sites of interest there, a *heiau* and a *halau hula*, the site of an old hula school dedicated to the hula goddess, Laka. It was a place no visitor should miss, but Kal didn't want to go there with Erika. For him, it was Maka's place.

"What's a *heiau?*" asked Erika.

"A temple ruin. After Kamehameha the Great died in 1819, Kamehameha II, who was a Christian, ordered all the temple buildings and altars destroyed. Only the rock platforms are left. Hiialo's talking about a place near Keʻe Beach. There will be a lot of tourists there today. I thought this evening we'd go to Keʻe in the outrigger, though."

"And visit the *heiau?*" asked Hiialo.

"No."

They drove to a waterfall, walked through a wildlife refuge, then went into Hanalei and ate at a deli there and bought ice-cream cones for dessert. On the way home, Kal saw some little kids with a flower stand beside the old

Hanalei Bridge. He pulled over and got out in the liquid sunshine, rain under the sun. Minutes later he was back with two floral bouquets that would have cost a mint on the mainland.

He handed one between the seats to Hiialo, the other to Erika. In the sun, her eyes were the color of mahogany. "Aloha. Don't cry, eh?"

She smiled. *Good* smile.

"These are beautiful. Do you know the names, Kal?" She touched a waxy red heart-shaped flower with a long yellow spadix.

"That's an anthurium. I forget the Hawaiian name." His suntanned callused hand fingered another with red bracts reaching upward in a pinecone shape. "This is red ginger, *awapuhi*. This big pointy thing is heliconia. It comes from Mount Helicon in Greece. We've got some at home with more pink in them. Also, red lobsters and hanging heliconia. And these are *okikas*." Beneath the bouquet, her nearest thigh was thick with muscle and, at the knee, crisscrossed with surgical scars. The woman who'd survived a car crash.

He wished Maka had.

Easing away from Erika, he started the Datsun and drove home to the drenched garden outside the bungalow.

Before they could get out of the car, Hiialo asked, "Erika, will you paint with me?"

"Erika might want some time to herself, Hiialo." *Or time with me.*

Erika turned around in the car. "Do you like to paint?" Her knee brushed the warmth of Kal's thigh, and she moved it abruptly. *Too much touching...*

"I'm going to be an artist when I grow up," said Hiialo. "Or maybe a hula dancer."

Erika didn't look at Kal, but she wanted to. A hula dancer...

They got out of the car. Hiialo ran through the rain to the porch and kicked off her shoes, but Kal walked more slowly, with Erika. Holding her flowers against her small body, Hiialo opened the door they had left unlocked and padded barefoot into the house. "I'll get you a vase, too, Erika. We use juice pitchers."

Erika climbed to the porch, two steps for each stair. Climb, pull the other leg up.

"Do these steps bother you?" asked Kal. "I could make a ramp."

Erika hugged the flowers in her arms. Her thick rain-dampened hair hung loose around her brandy-colored eyes. "No. I'm fine."

No ramps, she thought.

Kal wished he could read her mind. She'd survived a major accident. Had her injuries affected her sexuality? Why *did* she want a celibate marriage? On the porch beside her, he said, "You and I need to talk story."

"Talk story?" Why was she breathless?

"Shoot the breeze. Get to know each other."

Erika felt she had to sit down.

Hiialo came out to the porch carrying a cumbersome pitcher filled with water. A welcome third party.

Kal took both the pitcher and Erika's flowers. "*Mahalo,* Hiialo." Father and daughter grinned at each other at the rhyme. Kal put the bouquet in the vase, spilling water as the stems displaced it, and handed the pitcher back to Hiialo. "Can you take that to Erika's room?"

"Yes, Daddy."

"Thank you, Hiialo," said Erika.

"You're welcome." She marched back into the house.

Erika sank on the porch swing, and so did Kal. Draping his arms across the back, one hand almost touching Erika's hair, he gently rocked the glider.

His body, Erika estimated, was eighteen inches from hers, and his arm and his hand were behind her. The

swing's slow rhythm reminded her of the gentle movement of a boat in its berth. Water splattered from the
eaves.

Kal said, "You like to go hiking?"

"Yes."

He nodded slowly, staring out at the rain, his legs
stretched out before him. Big. Relaxed.

"I'll have to take you to Waikapalae Cave sometime.
You'll like it. You can swim down this tunnel and when
you get to the end there's a place called the Blue Room.
The light's all blue."

"I'd like that. I need to go painting, too." And how.

She felt something on the ends of her hair and realized
Kal was touching her. The moment she discovered it, he
stopped.

"Erika, how much of your body was paralyzed?"

Her breath froze. The question was intimate, like his
hand on her hair. "Below the waist."

Where sex happens. Kal withdrew his arm from behind
her. He couldn't keep his fingers out of her hair. Leaning
forward, he tried to see her face. Her head was bowed,
hiding her expression. But after a moment she lifted it and
met his eyes.

His heart beat off time, and he felt the earth move....

It was just the swing, that he, with his feet on the
ground, was rocking. He stilled it. "So...you couldn't feel
anything?"

Better explain. But she couldn't; she barely knew him.
"Right."

"Did you have someone to help you?"

"At first. Later I learned to do almost everything
alone." What she could not do alone she hadn't done.

Kal sensed her withdrawing, shrinking like some kinds
of insects did when touched by people. He didn't want to
do that to her.

He stood up. "I think I'll play guitar for a while."

"Okay."

He left, and soon Erika heard him turn on the amp. She sat silent, keeping her eyes shut, recovering from his questions, revisiting the past. Wishing she could hide.

You should have told him.

The sounds of the electric guitar filled the house, and she heard running feet inside, Hiialo yelling, "Daddy, play 'Pau Hana'!"

How was she ever going to paint?

But if Kal was playing his guitar, maybe she could go down to the beach. As she got up to walk inside, she heard the guitar break into a beautiful melody with a joyous rock-and-roll tempo. In the hallway Hiialo was dancing. "C'mon, Erika. It's 'Pau Hana.' Let's dance!"

Erika limped over to the refrigerator. "I'd rather watch you." She didn't dance. Would Kal be offended if she asked him to turn down the amp? It couldn't be good for Hiialo's ears—or his. Maybe they were both going deaf.

But then the music paused, and the amp went off. Kal stepped through the beads in the doorway of his room. "Are we kind of loud for you?"

Erika teethed her bottom lip. "I'm not used to an amplifier. But the music's good. I've never heard that song."

"My dad wrote it!"

"Hiialo," said Kal. She was really wound up.

Erika said, "I thought I'd go down to the beach and sketch."

"Can I come?" exclaimed Hiialo.

Erika remembered telling Kal that Chris had come with her when she painted. Oh, what an ill-advised remark. She'd forgotten the fundamental way Chris had been different from other children. For three years after he'd seen his mother fall from the bow of the *Skye,* he had not spoken.

"Maybe Erika would like some space, Hiialo."

She did want space, but this would be a chance to spend time with Hiialo alone. "Hiialo, I'd love for you to come, but I have to explain something. When I draw or paint, I use the same side of my brain that works for language and talking. I can't have a conversation and paint at the same time. Can you bring some toys to the beach and play quietly while I paint?"

Her lips sealed shut, as though no word would escape them, Hiialo nodded.

"Then you may come."

"HOORAY!" She shot off toward her room, muttering to herself, "Whoops, not supposed to talk."

In the unlit hallway Kal asked Erika, "Want me to come, too?"

She shook her head. "We should give this a try alone."

"Good luck." He sounded as though he meant it.

ERIKA ACCOMPLISHED nothing at the beach—nothing worth keeping. Hiialo wasn't the problem; *she* was. She couldn't draw. She couldn't see a picture in her mind.

She had lost her confidence.

After about fifteen minutes Hiialo appeared beside her and said, "I'm going home."

Erika glanced toward the private road. It seemed a long walk for a four-year-old. She gathered her sketch pad, pencil and eraser and stood.

Hiialo said, "Why do you walk that way?"

"Oh." Erika managed a smile. "I was in a car accident. It hurt my knee."

"My mommy died in a car accident."

"I know." Erika wanted to pick her up, but she had too much to carry, so she began trudging through the deep sand up to the drive.

Hiialo, who had demonstrated that she could run like a greyhound, slowed her steps and walked beside her. And after they had gone a few steps, Erika felt a small hand slide into hers.

Immediately she felt the change in perspective a child could bring, the perspective that Chris had given her, that had helped change her from the self-involved person she'd been before her accident. In the past year, she'd lost that perspective, that appreciation for innocence and trust and a child's love. In the past year, she'd become self-centered again.

Her heart solemn, she held tightly to Hiialo's little hand and the comfort it brought.

THEY HAD DINNER early—stir-fry and rice with blackened tofu. While Kal cooked, Erika swept out the front room. Hiialo played make-believe with her stuffed friends on the couch. She was pretending to be Cinderella, being kind to the animals. A few minutes later she asked Erika if she could sweep, and Erika surrendered the broom.

Kal knew the serenity was temporary. Erika had been in his house for twenty-four hours, and Hiialo had been good the whole time. How long could it last?

After dinner on the porch they left the dishes, put on their swimsuits and walked back down to the beach to take a ride in the outrigger. At the edge of Kal's garden, Erika pointed to a tree with hundreds of slender aerial roots and fronds that formed one great pompom. "What's that called?"

"*Lauhala*. We call them walking trees, too. It's an ancient tree. People used the leaves for sandals and baskets and mats."

Hiialo skipped ahead, the skirt of her neon green swimsuit bouncing with each step.

"I like learning the names of plants."

"Yeah?" Kal paused, ignoring the fact that his daughter had gone around the blue house and out of sight.

"Okay, this one's a tropical almond, a *kamani haole.* You know '*haole*'?"

Erika peered down the driveway toward the crashing breakers. Where was Hiialo?

"You and I are *haoles.* Hiialo is *hapa haole,* part white. What's wrong?"

"We should catch up with Hiialo."

"She's all right." Kal crossed the driveway to touch a cluster of orange hibiscuslike blossoms. "This is a *hou* tree, not to be confused with the *hau* tree outside Hiialo's window."

"Kal, is that a private beach?" She was still staring after Hiialo.

Kal ran his tongue over his teeth. Mainland parenting. He saw it all the time on tours. "Okay, we'll go." He smiled and headed toward the sea, and soon they saw Hiialo crouched on the beach near the high-tide line, poking something with a stick.

She saw Kal and Erika and stood up. To the blob on the beach, she said, "Aloha, jellyfish."

Reaching her with Kal, Erika saw the blue bubble, the twenty-foot tentacles stretching down into the water, then swishing up with the incoming tide. Instinctively she grasped Hiialo's nearest shoulder, pulling her back. "That's a Portuguese man-of-war."

"Yeah," Kal agreed. "You usually see them over on the windward side, east side." He scanned the beach to make sure it wasn't a jellyfish invasion.

Erika said, "Those tentacles sting, Hiialo."

"I know." Hiialo lifted her face. "My daddy's been stung by one."

"You get box jellyfish here, too, don't you?" Erika asked Kal. Box jellyfish were related to the deadly sea wasp of Australia. Like the man-of-war, they presented a more serious danger to children than adults.

Kal kept his tongue in his cheek and his mouth shut. A week or two, and Erika would relax. Peaceably he said, "Let's take our canoe ride."

As Hiialo had told Erika, the outrigger had been his wedding present from Maka. Danny had found her a deal on the fiberglass canoe, and Maka herself had sanded and varnished the koa arms that attached the outrigger. With bicycle inner tubes, Danny had lashed the arms to the hull.

On the beach Kal uncovered the boat and dragged it down to the water. As he held it in the shallows, Hiialo scrambled in.

"Should I get in, too?" asked Erika.

He nodded. In the deep red glow of the sinking sun, her thighs shone amber against her coral tank suit. When she turned to climb into the canoe, Kal couldn't avert his eyes from the muscular backs of her legs, from the edges of her suit curving over her bottom. He wondered where her tan lines ended. He wondered...a lot of things. Why she'd answered his letter.

Why she wanted a celibate marriage.

If she liked sex.

He pushed the outrigger out into the sea and climbed aboard.

There were two paddles, and Erika took one. Kal divided his attention between speculative admiration of her body and the water turning purple and orange with the sunset. God, the spray felt good. The sea felt good, and the emerald cliffs rising beyond Ke'e Beach were steaming with mist. "Hiialo, what are you doing?"

"There's a crab in the canoe," she answered. "He's alive, but he's afraid of Eduardo."

Kal stopped paddling and bent forward, peering under the seats. Hermit crab. Hiialo was trying to catch him with a bailing cup.

"Kal, do you see that wave? Hiialo, sit down. You'll fall out." Erika had already figured out how she was going to grab her by her life vest if she went in. She was relieved when they reached Ke'e Beach.

As Erika helped Kal pull the canoe up on the sand, he saw a woman walking down the hiking trail that led to the *heiau*. A family was finishing a picnic at the far end of the beach, and a couple lay on towels under the ironwood trees drinking beer.

Hiialo stripped off her life vest and ran toward the water, yelling, "Watch me bodysurf!"

Erika called, "Hiialo, wait!"

"She's all right," said Kal. "Relax."

Erika held her breath as Hiialo caught a wave and surfed into the beach on her stomach. Standing up in the wet sand, she looked for Kal, who came to join her in the low foam.

"Good ride, Ti-leaf."

"I'm going to build a sand castle, Daddy."

Erika watched her sprint across the sand to the outrigger, her feet slipping, to get her toys. Kal wasn't cautious with her. Someone should tell him—

Just go in the water. It's his kid.

Her conscience preaching a different message, Erika waded into the ocean and swam out over the first low breakers, then turned to look back at the beach. Kal was behind her, coming up for air, sparkling wet.

Erika searched until she found Hiialo alone on the shore over by the outrigger. "Are you sure you should let her bodysurf?"

Kal blinked, stood up, tossed water from his hair. "What?"

Hiialo pulled a green bucket and a blue cup out of the canoe and hurried purposefully down to the water. She was so small. "There are a lot of spinal injuries associated with bodysurfing."

As they floated over a wave together, he threw her a look. "So, you worry a lot, yeah?"

A remarkable comment from a man with an ulcer. "No, I don't." She hesitated only a moment, recalling Hiialo running down to the beach ahead of them—and out of sight. Then that jellyfish. "It's just that accidents are the greatest danger children face. I mean, literally, the leading cause of death to children." Time to stop. She'd said plenty.

Kal stared *mauka* at his daughter. Erika was afraid she'd made him angry. But all he said was, "You can't stop accidents."

Erika knew where that had come from. She couldn't let it go unchallenged. "Sometimes you can."

Kal swallowed. He'd had enough of the topic. "I have to work tomorrow." His stomach burned.

Erika took the hint. "Do you want me to watch Hiialo?"

"I'd like it." Kal tried to forget her ominous warnings. Jellyfish, bodysurfing... He couldn't stand the thought of something happening to Hiialo. Why did people do that to themselves, worry like that?

The frightening possibilities at which Erika had hinted had the power to make him cry, and he ducked under the water, clearing his eyes. When he came up, she was still there, vigilantly eyeing the shore. Her beautiful profile was in shadow. It made him angry that she'd upset him—and that she could excite him, too.

Disliking the combination, he turned away and looked for a wave to ride in to his daughter.

CHAPTER SEVEN

HE SHOULD HAVE GOTTEN Hiialo to bed sooner.

"I ruined it," she was saying now.

Kal stopped playing, his fingers poised on the guitar strings. He was sitting on the bed in Erika's room while she and Hiialo painted at the art table. Hiialo sat on books stacked on a chair to reach the table. For the past hour, she had been working on a picture of a whale and Kal's outrigger.

"You can fix that," said Erika. "Here, let me show you how."

"No."

Kal laid down the Gibson as he saw Hiialo's lower lip go out. Kilauea preparing to erupt.

She reached for a new piece of the inexpensive art paper Erika had provided.

"No, Hiialo," Erika said. "Would you like to fix your mistake?"

"No!"

Kal stood up.

Hiialo snatched up her painting and ripped it in two, then crumpled the pieces.

Kal breathed her name. "Hiialo—"

"Why did you do that, Hiialo?" asked Erika. "It was just a little mistake. You put a lot of time into that."

Starting to cry, Hiialo turned away from the table and lifted her arms to Kal.

He didn't pick her up, but the anger he felt was at Erika. Would it have killed her to let Hiialo have another piece of paper?

Hiialo rubbed her eyes, sobbing. Tired. Kal glanced toward the window, then at the digital clock beside Erika's bed. Nine-fifteen. Forty-five minutes past bedtime. "Hiialo, why don't you say good-night to Erika and thank her for the painting lesson?"

Hiialo slid down off the books, and Kal caught her as she stumbled in her bare feet. She was wiping her eyes, still crying. "Good night, Erika. Thank you."

"You're welcome, sweetheart." Erika kept her own feelings inside. Kids acted out sometimes. And Hiialo was probably up too late. Ripping up the painting had been a bratty move, but it was her own picture, after all.

Chris would never have done anything like that, though.

Chagrined, Erika recalled her own certainty that she could be a good mother, that she could love Hiialo. And she remembered Hiialo's hand in hers on the beach.

"Daddy, pick me up."

"Please."

"Please," whimpered Hiialo.

Kal lifted her and pushed open the door to her room.

"Shall I run a bath for her?" asked Erika. Hiialo had already smudged her dad's shirt with blue paint.

Kal shook his head. "In the morning." He'd have to get her up early—or let Erika do it. He could feel Hiialo's sleepy head on his shoulder. She sniffled, her tears abating. For the moment.

As she cleaned up the paints and gathered the brushes, Erika heard Kal in Hiialo's room. "No. You have to brush your teeth."

"I'm too tired."

"In the bathroom."

"I'm too tired!" Hiialo screamed.

Erika took the brushes to the kitchen to wash them. As Hiialo's screams echoed through the bungalow, two figures appeared behind the screen door. "Aloha!"

Danny. Kal was carrying Hiialo into the bathroom. Though her cries mellowed, she barely looked toward the door. Very tired, thought Kal, if she wasn't wriggling out of his arms to run and greet her uncle.

Danny and Jakka pushed open the screen door and stepped inside, holding two six-packs.

"Whaddascoops, Hiialo?" said Danny.

She turned her head away.

Kal gestured toward the bathroom. "*Pau.* Bedtime. This is Erika. Erika, Danny Kekahuna. Jakka Bennee. They're cousins." He grinned and reminded her of the Hawaiian concept of *ohana.* "We're all cousins." He shrugged at Danny. "Brothers."

Maka's brother. Erika wiped her hands. "Hi, Danny. Hi, Jakka." Her nerves were raw, her thoughts uncharitable. *If Hiialo was an angel, Kal wouldn't have had to advertise…*

Getting a handle on her emotions, Erika focused on Kal's friends. Danny was a handsome Hawaiian, not quite as tall as Kal but probably about his age. Long-haired, strong. Jakka was large, amiable, friendly.

Hiialo's bedtime dragged. Fussing about brushing her teeth. Then wanting to learn hula from Danny. Erika's annoyance grew. Chris had never thrown tantrums, and David would never have stood for it the way Kal did. In a tone without conviction, he said, "No hula. Get in bed."

Erika could see the child collecting about twenty stuffed animals from the floor while Kal lounged in the doorway, on Hawaiian time.

His friends put the beer in the refrigerator and wandered into his room. One of them plugged in his guitar and amplifier, turned it up, turned it down and began playing something that sounded like "White Rabbit."

The noise and the late hour shifted Erika's sympathies to Hiialo. A child needed peace at night. And a regular bedtime. The night before, she'd gotten the impression Hiialo at least had that.

When Kal emerged from Hiialo's room after kissing her good-night, he glanced at Erika, then went to his own room to join his friends. She couldn't make out what they said, only a warm sound of shared laughter. The amplifier went off, the latches on the guitar case snapped closed, the beads rustled.

The men returned to the front room. With a smile at Erika, Danny opened the refrigerator and took out a beer. He held it up, offering it to her. She shook her head, and Kal didn't take one, either.

Ulcer. Yes, she could see it.

Danny and Jakka sat down near the coffee table, Danny in the torn overstuffed brown chair, Jakka on the couch.

Kal lingered in the kitchen. Erika was washing a couple of glasses.

He said, "Why don't you leave those?"

She didn't stop. "I grew up on boats. It's habit—the way I do things."

"Want to sit down with us?"

Erika turned off the water and followed him to the couch.

Danny said, "So your name is Blade, like the undersea explorer? Christopher Blade! I used to watch him all the time on TV."

"He was my dad."

Danny grinned, his teeth lighting up his face. "You're famous. So wait. That means your brother's the guy who—" He stopped, then waved his hand, brushing away his blunder. "Forget it."

Erika tried. But she could tell that Danny's unfinished remark had made Kal curious. He was glancing between

the two of them. *You knew it would come up, Erika.*
Skye's death had made national news.

Dammit. The guilt came, and she knew it would spend
the night. Along with what-ifs she sometimes thought were
behind her.

Danny drained his beer, changed the subject. "So, Kal,
your folks have Akita puppies. I'm going to get one this
time, already told them. Your dad, he's the best. He
promised me a deal."

"We saw them today. Both litters." Kal remembered the
puppy who looked like Jin, the puppy Erika had liked. It
would be gone in a week. Sold. Unless he said something
to his dad.

Jakka intruded on Erika's thoughts. "So now that
you're here, Kal can play music again, yeah?"

Play music again? Her heart beat hard. She'd missed
something.

Like maybe the reason he'd advertised for a wife?
Someone to watch his daughter while he stayed out till two
in the morning, playing in nightclubs? Erika didn't want
to believe it. From what she knew of his schedule, he didn't
see enough of Hiialo as it was. Then again, Hiialo wasn't
awake at two in the morning.

Yes, in that context, a celibate marriage made perfect
sense.

Erika suddenly felt hollow inside.

Kal stared at the coffee table as though lost in thought.

Danny said, "Hey, Kal, I got a new CD player."

The conversation turned, and after a few minutes Erika
excused herself to go to bed.

Kal waited until he'd heard all the end-of-the-day
sounds—water running in the bathroom, bedroom door
shutting—before he asked Danny, "What were you saying about her brother?"

"Oh!" Danny slapped his forehead. "Didn't mean to embarrass her." He looked from Jakka to Kal and whispered, "I think he killed his wife."

"Honest kine?" Incredulous, Jakka leaned forward, listening.

"She was rich. He got *twenty million dollars*, maybe more."

Kal's head was spinning.

Danny saw his dismay. He tipped back his beer. "You got to read the paper."

Jakka said, "We should get some gigs again."

Talk switched to pidgin, the language of locals, and for a while Kal let himself dream with his friends. The way it used to be. Playing wherever they wanted, recording... His stomach hurt. He didn't have time for music. Anyhow, if they were going to play for money again...

He eyed his brother-in-law. Ever since Kai Nui had nominally disbanded, Danny had been devoting his energy to hula. Kal knew everything that meant, and ulcer pain made him want to pick a fight.

Jakka and Danny were talking about a new club in Hanalei, the Hunakai, which in the past two years had become the music hub of the north shore. The others were daydreaming about playing there, but Kal, feeling trapped and mean, said, "We can't have a band again."

Both friends sat back. Blinked at him.

Jakka cracked a smile. "We still got a band, Kal. We got a tape out there."

It was four years old, like Hiialo. People had forgotten Kai Nui. Kal said, "Danny has too many obligations to his *halau*." He knew from living with Maka the allegiance a dancer felt to his or her school. Danny had moved on from the band, placed his loyalties elsewhere.

Danny's face seemed to pale slightly, the muscles to become rock-like. His stare was as unwavering as Kal's. But he said nothing.

That's what I thought. They couldn't go back to the way things had been. Kal knew he should go to sleep—before his bitterness found more words.

Jakka turned to Danny. "So, yeah, how is it, brah? Say, we get the band together again. Are you a drummer or a hula dancer?"

Kal felt sick. Suddenly afraid of the loss of friendship—more than friendship, because Danny was family—he said, "We're not getting the band together. Just drop it." He stood up and went to the sink for some water, wishing they would leave. He couldn't stand thinking about Kai Nui. Or about driving into Hanalei to work the next day.

The others stood up, too, and followed. Kal felt Danny beside him. His brother-in-law said in a mock-British accent, "'Where are we going, fellas?'"

Kal smiled, the pangs inside him intensifying at the familiar quote. Beatles trivia. They used to do this a lot, though in the past he'd been the one leading them. "'To the top, Johnny!'" Pretending he still believed it.

Leaning against the counter on his other side, Jakka said, "'Where's that, fellas?'"

Kal forced a smile, not wanting to make his friends feel as shitty as he did. He and Danny said in unison, "'To the toppermost of the poppermost!'"

They all stood there together in reverent silence for a moment. Then Kal looked at Jakka and at his brother-in-law, and Danny's brown eyes were looking right back at him. Yes, if Kai Nui became a band again, Danny would be with him all the way. Danny was not Maka, and for him hula was an expression of his fealty to rhythm. And to music.

Standing between his two best friends, Kal tried to ease the tension in his abdomen, tried not to think of the weeks and months and years ahead, guiding Zodiac trips. Nor of Erika Blade and what Jakka had said she could do for him.

For all of them.

Allow them to play again.

HE KNOCKED ON HER DOOR in the morning, and after a few seconds she answered, wearing gym shorts and a white men's tank top. Face flushed, breathing hard. Her ankle weights lay on the floor.

Kal curbed his curiosity. "I'm going to work. Hiialo needs a bath."

"Okay."

"You want the car? I can hitch a ride."

As in hitchhike? The day before, she'd been shocked to see boys hitchhiking in Hanalei. "I don't need the car."

When Hiialo woke up, she wanted mangoes for breakfast. All those in the house and on the tree in the yard were green, but Hiialo said they should cut them up and dip the slices in shoyu—which Erika learned was soy sauce—and vinegar. The result was edible.

After breakfast, Hiialo took a bath, playing with toys in the tub, and then she asked to paint again.

Erika asked, "Are you going to be good?"

"Yes."

"Then, okay. That would be fun."

Hiialo painted a scene of palm trees and an outrigger and herself on the beach. It was, she said, for her dad's birthday. As Erika sketched her and wondered what *she* could give Kal—and also how she was ever going to get some painting done with Hiialo around—Hiialo stopped painting and stared at Erika's art supplies, on another part of the table.

She reached for a bottle. "What's this paint?"

"Oh, honey, that's masking fluid. Actually it's pretty cool. You want to see?" Erika set aside her sketch pad and picked up an old brush she used for masking fluid. She grabbed a test strip of paper, opened the small jar and dabbed the brush in. Hiialo watched her paint it on the paper. "Okay, then we let it dry, and we paint over it."

When the paint was dry, Erika let Hiialo peel off the dried mask, revealing the white beneath.

"I want to try it! I want white space on my picture!" said Hiialo.

"Okay, but I only use this special old brush, because masking fluid can wreck the other brushes." Some of the brushes she'd given Hiialo were old, also, but too fine to be ruined with the fluid. "If we put a little soap on the brush first, it keeps it even nicer. I should have done that this time."

Hiialo masked a sun for her picture's blue sky. When she'd finished her painting, they let it dry, then hid it in one of the drawers in Erika's bed. After that, Erika insisted they clean Hiialo's closet. They played Mary Poppins while they did it, and when Kal came home that night, smelling of gasoline and salt water and sweat, she told him the day had gone well.

Kal showered first thing and shaved and was glad Erika had offered to make dinner. They put Hiialo to bed on time, and he took the Gibson and went out on the lanai.

Erika followed with her sketch pad. The lamp shining from inside the windows and the early-rising moon would provide enough light for her to do a rough drawing.

Kal was tuning up when she joined him. He saw her sketch pad. "I can turn on the porch light, but it'll draw bugs."

"I don't need it." Erika sat on the top step, using a post for a backrest.

He began to play and soon seemed oblivious to her presence, though Erika could hardly take her eyes off him to track her pencil on the page. He started with a song she'd never heard, a beautiful pop melody with Hawaiian overtones, and his voice was a soft rough serenade, a melodious crawl along the scales. Had he written the song? The lyrics were poignant, reflecting the intensity of youth. It made her think about what Jakka had said the night before. Danny and Jakka had been Kal's band mates. Strange that after so many years they wanted to get together again....

But the music drifted away from her ears, leaving just the man, who became sketched lines on the paper. She'd drawn him before, from the photo with Maka missing. But maybe *this* would work as a watercolor, something she could sell. She didn't notice he'd stopped playing until he rested the guitar in the swing and joined her on the top step to look at her sketch.

She let him see. *I need to sell something.* And she and Kal needed to talk about money. "Kal, I'd like to contribute to your household expenses."

The comment seemed to have come from nowhere. Erika wanted to chip in financially. In the long run, that was a great idea. If he married Erika, maybe he could work five days a week like a normal man. But now... "You're my guest. I don't want your money."

"Please."

"No. Don't say it again."

They both fell silent.

The leaves shifted around them, and Erika took a deep breath just as Kal said, "So, what's this about your brother?"

"Oh." The word came out in two syllables. No need to ask what he meant. "David's first wife committed suicide. She threw herself off the bow of his ship and was killed by the screws. Skye was a very wealthy woman—a publishing heiress—so David inherited a lot of money. People said he pushed her, but no one else was there. Just David and...and his son." She paused. "Chris was three."

She didn't mean to say more, but a motor inside her refused to stop running. "He's married again. The first time wasn't a good marriage. Actually Skye was the driver of the car that hit me. I was driving David's car. She thought

I was him, and she hit me on purpose." *Stop, Erika. Stop, now.*

Hit her on purpose? Kal's first reaction was disbelief. No one would do something like that. Maybe Erika was one of those people who liked to dramatize, who made things up....

His instincts said no. Telling him had upset her, he could see. The way she was trembling, yet seemed unaware of trembling, struck him as honest. He wanted to touch her, to soothe her, but she was holding herself, locking herself up. *I need to know more. Tell me everything, Erika.* He encouraged with a statement that was a question, a question to which he already knew the answer. "Your injury was temporary."

Erika had known he was bound to ask sooner or later. She turned off her emotions. The shame was too painful to feel. "There was a temporary injury, but I also developed something called a conversion disorder. The reason I stayed...paralyzed was psychological."

A stillness went over him. Kal slipped into his thoughts for a while.

Erika needed to explain. *I'm not unbalanced. I'm fine.* "The accident was quite traumatic."

He could buy that. But... "You really couldn't feel anything?"

"No."

She was defensive now. Backing away from him on the step.

Kal said carefully, "I just want to understand. Stay with me a minute, okay?" He tried to catch her eye. She wouldn't meet his. "How did this...psychological thing work?"

She drew a breath. It had been a long time since she'd put herself through these kinds of explanations. It hadn't gotten easier. "It's called a conversion disorder. It works like avoidance. Say, hypothetically, that a person has made a lot of sacrifices to take care of people. Then, suddenly, she gets sick, and when she's in bed she realizes that if she stays there she doesn't have to take care of people."

Kal's eyelids dropped to half-mast. In the moonlight, Erika was blue-black. "So, what were you avoiding?"

Her mouth opened slightly. Averting her eyes, she wet her dry bottom lip with her tongue. She looked back at him.

Beyond the trees, beyond the blue beach house, the ocean crashed.

"I'm not sure. There was some suggestion it might be..."

Kal lifted his eyebrows, inviting her to continue.

She murmured, "Sex."

Talkin' story bin get interesting. "Why's that?"

Erika hugged her calves, pulling her knees up to her chest. "Oh, I was engaged when I had the accident. My fiancé, René... He was French, but I met him in Australia. We lived together for three years before we were engaged, and he..." A quick, almost silent exhalation as she picked her words. "He was used to my diving with him and... doing physical things..."

Like sex, thought Kal.

"He latched right onto the doctors' saying it might be temporary. He kept talking about when I'd walk again. And then he slept with my sister-in-law. Skye."

"The one who killed herself?"

"Yes."

Again Erika felt the anger, an anger related to what she knew was appropriate guilt. She would not accept responsibility for what Skye had done. *I was angry. What did she expect me to say? "I know you didn't mean to hit me—you thought it was David...." "Oh, the incident with René? Yes, I understand. Sure, sleep with my fiancé."*

She sponged clean her conscience. But streaks remained.

"So," he said slowly, "does this have anything to do with why you answered my ad?" He wanted to be more direct.

Erika wished she'd brought a sweater outside. It was too cool for just cutoffs and a faded pink tank top. "Not exactly."

"Your accident?"

"No."

"Why don't you want a sex life?"

His eyes, midnight blue as the sky, gazed right into her, as though trying to see all her secrets.

Why not tell him? thought Erika. Who was more entitled to know? "I don't like it."

Kal drew in a breath, shifted. *Doesn't like sex...*

The chatter of the leaves filled their silence until he spoke. "Were you raped?"

"No." How awful he'd wondered. "Nothing like that." Rushing, before he could leap to other wrong conclusions, she said, "Look. With this guy... Skye wasn't the first. But that's not it, either. In fact, that has nothing to do with it."

Kal lined up his spine against the porch post opposite hers. Forearms across his knees, he waited. Burning with curiosity. Thinking she was pretty.

Erika saw no reason to say more.

Was it right to grill her? Kal didn't think so. She didn't like sex. End of story, as per their agreement.

He wanted to kiss her, but he only watched her until she looked at him.

Once she met his eyes, Erika found it wasn't hard to keep hers there. His expression was intelligent, direct and sensitive, and reminded her for no reason of her brother, David. A fact that calmed her.

He's different.

She shook inside and didn't look away.

Kal said, in that low sandpaper voice, "Just for the record, Erika Blade, I think sex is beautiful. If you love each other."

Later it occurred to her that the comment should have made her jealous of Maka, who had known his love. It didn't. Because he was speaking to *her*, and he was sharing something. Like a friend. A very good friend.

But not long after he'd said it, he got up and retrieved his guitar and went inside.

When the screen door swung shut behind him, Erika shivered under a trade-wind gust. Her head felt suddenly feverish. What had they been saying to each other? Why had the subject come up?

The prospect of a celibate marriage should have erected barriers between them. Instead, it had opened dialogue.

On a subject she discussed with no one.

The discussion had just begun, but it had already taught her some things about Kal. That he wasn't going to tell her she hadn't made love with the right man. That he didn't believe in Band-Aids for wounds of the spirit.

And that he had the potential to be what he'd seemed in those moments when he looked into her eyes and told her he thought sex was beautiful.

Her very good friend.

WHEN ERIKA GOT HOME from a predawn walk on the beach the next morning, Kal was on the swing eating cooked plantains and something that looked like library paste.

"What's that?" She peered into the bowl before going inside.

"*Poi*. Mashed taro root."

He seemed tense. Hurried. Dressed for work, shaved, already eating. Though he didn't have to be in Hanalei for forty-five minutes.

"Can I taste it?" asked Erika

He dipped his spoon into the *poi* and held it up.

Erika leaned over the swing. She tasted and swallowed. Bland, she decided, but quite edible. "Thanks."

"There's more inside. Hiialo loves it." He shifted on the swing, feeling only half-present, trying to look forward to the day on the water. It was a good job. He was lucky. And he didn't have to take Hiialo to day-care. She and Erika were going to the gallery.

He ate some more *poi*.

"Want coffee?" Erika looked at him.

"No, thanks."

She hesitated. He'd asked her about sex the night before. She could ask this. "What do you have to do for your ulcer?"

Change my life. He couldn't—any more than he already had. He'd actually felt good when he went to sleep the night before. The alarm clock had ended that. "Eat right. Take antacids. It's a stomach ulcer. I'll live." His smile glanced off her.

"Are you seeing a doctor?"

"Yeah."

Erika nodded. She'd asked enough, but when she went inside, she put on water for tea, instead of coffee. Kal liked kona. She wouldn't tease him with the smell.

His day pack was on the counter, a lunch bag and a cheap plastic thermos on top of it. Thursday was his day off. The rest of the week—and the weekends—he belonged to Na Pali Sea Adventures.

Stressful.

And then, of course, he had a new housemate. A stranger.

Erika could see his back through the window as he sat on the swing. He was still eating. Still tense. Plantains and *poi* and antacids for breakfast.

She wanted to help and realized she could.

She'd answered Kal's ad because of what she wanted. To mother a child. But he must have placed it because of something he needed. Erika saw now that it was something more complicated than a stepmother for Hiialo.

Kal was in desperate need of a partner.

That, she could be.

SHE AND HIIALO TOOK HIM to work, then drove home, played with Barbies, and returned to Hanalei and the gallery at eleven.

"I thought you could work over here," said Mary Helen when they arrived. She showed Erika to a corner created by a wall partition. An artist's table and stool were already set up under a skylight beside French doors opening onto a veranda and the courtyard beyond. Across from the gallery, the back door of Na Pali Sea Adventures was propped open. "Let me know if there's too much wind from the doors. It's nice and cool over here."

"This is perfect," Erika said. She was going to paint from the sketch she'd made of Kal the night before. For the first time in months, she really felt as though she had something.

"Our routine on Tuesdays is that Grandpa takes Hiialo out for a fruit smoothie, and then in the afternoon she and I go to the library and for a swim at the beach. Is that all right with you?" Kal's mother asked.

It was—and with Hiialo, too.

Erika's project absorbed her completely, and while she transferred the sketch to watercolor paper, drawing faint lines for Kal's face, the folds in his T-shirt, the shadows on his guitar, it was comfortable to think about him. And, strangely, comforting.

Hiialo left with her grandfather for a smoothie, then returned, and at lunch Erika took a break to eat Chinese take-out on a picnic table outside with her and Mary Helen.

After lunch, she began actually painting, and a few customers, tourists from the mainland and also from Japan, stopped at her table to observe. While Mary Helen took care of several framing jobs, Erika visited with a couple from New York who debated on and then rejected one of her prints.

At last Mary Helen came over to see her work in progress. "That's Kal."

"Yes." Erika knew she had captured him. His intensity. His absorption with his music. The grief that was part of him.

The watercolor was neither happy nor sad, but it was real.

Mary Helen stood back for a time, watching her paint, and Hiialo, who had been practicing *hula kahiko* nearby—some ancient hula Danny had taught her—stopped and asked, "Will you paint a picture of my dad for me?"

No request had ever pleased Erika more. "Yes, I'll do that, Hiialo."

"Thank you."

Mary Helen touched Erika's shoulder, and when she looked up, Kal's mother was turning away with a smile. "Come on, Hiialo. Let's go for our swim."

When they returned, Erika had finished the watercolor, and as she cleaned up, Mary Helen came over to admire it.

"You did that so quickly. I'm amazed."

Erika was elated. For years she'd seen other artists convey depth of personality with their subjects. Others were able to show what lay beneath the surface. Emotions. In contrast, her people always seemed flat. But the watercolor of Kal and his guitar... This was what she wanted to be able to do—what she'd told Adele she hoped to do. Standing, stepping back to look at it some more, Erika said, "I'll take it home and press it tonight."

"I can cut the mats for you," Mary Helen volunteered. She frowned at the picture.

"What's wrong?"

Kal's mother laughed. "Nothing. I want to buy it."

Really? But she couldn't take money from Kal's mom. She would give her the painting.

Tired of looking at the picture, Hiialo stood in the French doors slurping the remains of a soft drink from a paper cup. Erika glanced at her and saw her blow through the straw, spraying red pop out the door and into the flowers just as Kal came up the porch steps. He gave her a tired smile.

Erika supposed blowing pop at plants was harmless.

"Kal," said Mary Helen, "look at Erika's painting."

He came inside. The watercolor was beautiful. He found a place to stand and stare, and Hiialo trailed after him, making bubbling noises with her straw and soda.

Then she blew through the straw into the cup. The drink sprayed out the top, and Erika saw red liquid spatter her paper, across Kal's face. Involuntarily she cried, "Oh!"

Kal turned. "Hiialo!" He snatched the cup and straw from Hiialo and crumpled them.

Hiialo began to cry.

"Hiialo," Mary Helen said, "that was very naughty. Oh, Erika, can you fix it?"

Hiialo cried louder. "I want my drink! I want my drink."

Kal told her, "Get your things together."

"Nooo!"

He picked her up and took her out of the gallery.

Her face etched with anguish, Mary Helen gazed after them before she turned back to Erika's watercolor.

The worst was in some shadows on Kal's face where the paint was still wet. The pop had made the colors run together, dark areas streaking across the untouched highlights. Erika carefully dabbed at the affected area with a sponge. The pop and the paint came up, but the result was blotchy, dirty-looking, and Erika doubted she could make

.it right again. Her only successful piece of art in months, and Hiialo had ruined it. Erika could still hear her shrieking outside. Anxiously recalling Kal's anger, she asked Mary Helen, "He won't spank her, will he?"

"Oh, no." Mary Helen's eyes softened on Erika's. "We don't hit children or dogs." She smiled sadly. "Though we might occasionally want to. Oh, Erika, I'm so sorry. You must let me reimburse you."

"It's not *your* fault. It's my fault. I was supposed to be watching her." Erika stifled a choked sound. She could attempt the watercolor again—or try to fix it—but it would never be as good.

Kal's mother said, "Well, let me write a check for having you in today."

"Oh, please, no." How embarrassing. Did Mary Helen guess that she had no money? She'd never mentioned paying her till now. "Really, I can't accept payment."

Kal came back in the door with Hiialo on his hip. Mary Helen looked as though she wanted to argue more, but at last she turned to her son and granddaughter. "Hiialo, what are we going to do with you?"

Hiialo sniffled. "I'm sorry, Erika. I didn't mean to wreck the picture."

Erika knew it was true. Just an accident. "That's all right, sweetie. We had a good day, didn't we?" She smiled at her, trying to cheer her up. "And tomorrow you can watch me try to fix it. Remember I said sometimes you can fix mistakes?"

Something made her turn her head, and she saw Kal's blue eyes on her, and they lingered the way they had Sunday morning on his parents' couch. He didn't shift his gaze as he said softly, "Ready to go home?"

And Erika felt, for one moment, that his home was hers, too.

IT WAS A TENSE EVENING, and Hiialo was slow going to sleep. She got up repeatedly for drinks of water and to go to the bathroom and to gaze at Erika and Kal with dark eyes, as though suspecting them of having a good time without her.

Erika sat on the couch, waiting to talk to Kal, to ask what he liked for lunch and offer to prepare it for him the next morning. Unfortunately he was standing at the sink eating antacid tablets, holding his guitar in one hand and growing angrier at Hiialo.

When Hiialo's face appeared between her curtains for the fourth time, he said, "Get back in bed *now*."

Hiialo started to cry, returned to her bed and wailed.

With an unemotional glance at Erika, Kal went outside. She heard the swing creak, but no sound from the guitar.

Hiallo sobbed behind her curtain door, and Erika couldn't help going in to see her. A tear-streaked face peered up from the bed.

Erika sat down on the edge of the bed and picked her up. "Honey, don't cry. Your daddy's just tired. That happens to grown-ups, and it doesn't have anything to do with you. But when he asks you to go to bed, your job is to get in bed and stay there."

Hiialo sniffled, wiped her nose on her nightshirt, one of Kal's T-shirts. She didn't answer. She looked very sleepy.

"Maybe we can go somewhere special tomorrow. Is there a place you like to go?"

Hiialo nodded. "The *heiau*."

Oh, yes. The old hula platform. She'd mentioned that on Sunday. "Okay," said Erika. "That'll be fun. And remember, tomorrow night's your dad's birthday, and we'll go to Grandma and Grandpa's and visit the puppies, and you can give him your present. Now go to sleep, so we can have fun in the morning, all right? That's a good girl."

Hiialo lay down and whispered, "Thank you, Erika. I like you."

"I like you, too." She'd try to fix the watercolor, and if it didn't work, she'd paint something else, something just as good. But the thought was like a prayer.

Erika covered Hiialo, tucked Pincushion and Fluff on each side of her and went out to the front room, just as the screen door opened again.

Kal came back in, bringing the wind. Apologetically he said, "I'm going to sleep."

He looked pale. Tired. He had to work again in the morning.

"Kal?"

He'd started toward the hallway but stopped.

Erika leaned against the paneling where the hall met the living room. He was just a foot or so away, still holding his guitar.

She asked, "Is there anything I can do?"

About what?

Her eyes answered the unspoken question. Kal saw himself reflected in their expression; he was strung too tight, worn too far. His gut twisted. The pain increased. "I'm fine." He smiled at Erika, then moved by her into the darkness of the hall and pushed through the beads in his doorway. Without turning on a light, he hung the Gibson on its hook and pulled his shirt over his head. *Is there anything I can do?*

There were things a wife could do, things Maka had done. Not all of them were taboo between him and Erika.

Shirtless, he went back through the beads and out into the front room.

Erika stood by the kitchen sink, staring at his day pack on the counter. Seeing him, she started, and he saw her cheeks flush. "What do you like for lunch?" she asked.

"Lunch?" He ran a hand over his hair absently. "Oh, tabouli. Tofu. Brown rice..." He couldn't think. "Why?"

"I thought I'd make it for you." Erika glanced at him, afraid she might actually be staring at his skin, his taut stomach muscles. René, her fiancé, had been five-nine, slightly built, and he'd put some effort into reducing a nascent beer belly.

Kal...

He was the kind of man who could make her think sex might be different with him. Might be good.

But men had never been the problem. *She* was the problem.

And Kal wasn't looking for a lover.

"Hey, that's really nice of you."

She remembered she'd offered to make his lunch.

He opened the refrigerator. "Okay, well, that leftover blackened tofu and stir-fry would be fine for tomorrow. Stuff with garlic is good for me. Easy on the dairy products—milk produces acid. There's Tupperware in the cabinet down there." He shut the fridge. His eyes raked over her.

Erika's legs felt like long rice.

His speculative expression made her wonder if he was going to ask if she did windows. But what he said was, "So, Erika. Do you give back rubs?"

CHAPTER EIGHT

SHE FOLLOWED Kal into his bedroom, where he flicked on the lamp and lay down on his stomach on the purple-and-lavender quilt.

Erika wondered if she should have excused herself to change. She was wearing a wraparound knee-length sage-colored skirt and a crocheted sleeveless cotton sweater. Well, she wasn't going to straddle his body in any case. Sitting carefully on the edge of his bed, she put her hands on his lower back, above the waistband of his indigo blue cotton shorts.

She'd never had trouble touching men. What she didn't like was their touching her.

But touching Kal was scary.

Smooth sun-browned skin.

He shifted on the bed under the motion of her hands, laid his cheek on the quilt.

Outside, leaves rustled.

She tried to think of something to say. Something impersonal. Nothing came to mind. Except that he was beautiful.

Making herself look away, she studied the quilt. There were letters stitched on it. MAK... Both their names. The quilt must have covered their bed.

Distracted, she massaged his back more deeply, feeling the muscles, imagining what Maka must have felt, losing herself.

To Kal, the change felt erotic. As his sudden erection tried to carve room for itself in the mattress, he moved slightly, trying to get comfortable, and closed his eyes. To blot her out.

Her hands felt so different from Maka's. And so good.

"Hiialo wants me to take her to the *heiau* tomorrow. Can you tell me how to get there?"

Her voice made him jump. The *heiau*.

"Um...you follow the main road to the very end, to Ke'e Beach. Hiialo can show you from there." This way he wouldn't have to go with them and remember Maka dancing on the hula platform.

Erika's hands slipped down the sides of his chest. He wanted to roll over. Wanted her to touch him. Wanted someone to touch him. *I'm lonely, Erika. I can't help what's happening. I know you don't like sex.*

After a long time her hands gave his back a last stroke and went away. "How's that?"

"Great. I don't want to get up." If he did, she'd see...

"Don't then." She turned off the lamp on his desk. "Good night, Kal. Sleep well."

He heard her go out, the beads clacking behind her. He needed to brush his teeth, but he lay in the darkness until he thought he heard her sit down on the couch. Then he got up and went through the beads.

They collided in the hall, Erika's arms full of art materials. Him still aroused.

Erika saw, and her heart gave one explosive beat.

"Excuse me," she gasped, and hurried past him. When she reached her room, she shut the door and leaned against it in the dark. *Oh, Kal...*

She knew how sex was supposed to be. When she'd begun recovering from her accident, she'd found herself in a relationship with an acupuncturist. Missing David and Chris, seeing their happiness with Jean, Erika had been determined to make things work. But sex was bad. So bad she'd given up, and in the ensuing months, when she'd met someone else she liked, a film director, she had read up on female sexuality. She'd studied the mystery of orgasm, considered taking up tantric yoga, and dosed herself with herbs to increase her sex drive.

No luck.

Like the first, her second attempt at a sexual relationship had repelled her. It disgusted her to have a man touch her body with its scars, her body that had been flaccid and useless in a wheelchair.

In her mind, she saw Kal as she'd seen him in the hall. Something stirred in her, something that felt right. But she couldn't believe in it.

Sex would be the same with Kal. She was sure of that now.

In fact, it would be worse.

Because it would matter much more than it ever had.

WHAT ERIKA HAD DONE to him wasn't going to let him sleep unless he dealt with it. The solitary orgasm was release, but afterward he was lonelier than he'd been before.

And he couldn't remember Maka's face.

With a sense of panic, he turned on the light, reached down and opened the desk drawer. Knocking off the top of the shoe box, pushing aside the tape case, he found a photo. Maka grinning from the edge of the crater on Diamond Head.

It was easy to remember then.

He touched the picture, his eyes filling, his throat swelling. Swiftly he switched off the light so that if Hiialo or Erika came out of their rooms neither would see him cry; and he lay in the dark with the photograph as though it was her.

The other pain came as well, uninvited, the pain of dreams unfulfilled, of ambition stifled by practical necessity. He would turn thirty-one tomorrow. Time slipping by. *Too late, Kal. Let it go.* Blind in the dark, he opened the drawer again and felt for the tape case, and then he got up and found his headphones, so he could listen to his voice and his songs.

THE NEXT MORNING, Erika took Hiialo to Ke'e Beach, and they walked up the path to the *heiau*. The trail, which led through a fantastic garden of wild foliage, was narrow and muddy, and stones formed stairs that led up to the grassy terraces. Pausing on the path shadowed by palm fronds and large oblong tropical almond leaves, Hiialo said, "Eduardo, you must be respectful at the *heiau*. If you're good, maybe Erika will buy us shave ice later, 'cause it's Daddy's birthday."

Though Kal wasn't with them. *Working.* It made Erika hot all over whenever she remembered the night before. Which happened often.

As a gray-and-red bird suddenly took flight up into the trees, Hiialo called, "Aloha, Mr. Cardinal."

It must be a Brazilian cardinal; Erika had read about them in her Kauai guidebook. Her skin was dewy with sweat, and she hiked cautiously. Rocks that looked like good footholds were as slippery as algae-covered stream boulders, treacherous because they made tempting stepping stones. But Hiialo was a nimble hiker.

So were the elderly man and woman coming down the path toward them. The couple smiled in recognition of the little girl, and the woman said, "Hello, Hiialo. Do you know me?"

They were of Japanese ancestry, and Erika recognized them. These were the Johnsons's neighbors, the picture bride and her husband.

Hiialo pursed her lips, looking thoughtful. The woman held out her hand. "We are Mr. and Mrs. Akana, and we live next to your grandparents."

"Hello." Hiialo shook hands with her and then with Mr. Akana.

Erika stepped forward. "I'm Erika Blade. I'm a friend of Kal's."

"Oh, yes, his mother told me." Mrs. Akana beamed. Her skin was thin and smooth, the wrinkles draping gracefully around her fine bones.

Had Mary Helen told her neighbor how she and Kal had met?

"We were just taking some flowers up to the *heiau*," said Mrs. Akana.

That morning, Kal had told her to be sure to look at the offerings at the *heiau*. People, especially dancers, left *leis*, lava stones wrapped in ti leaves and other gifts for the hula goddess, Laka. Erika asked Mrs. Akana, "Do you know hula?"

"Oh, yes." She smiled. "When I was young. But just *bon* dancing now."

"*Bon* dancing?"

Mr. Akana spoke for the first time. "You don't know *bon* dancing? Kal should bring you over to learn. All the Johnsons used to go to the *bon* dances. Family thing. Very Hawaiian."

"Can I go?" asked Hiialo.

"You maybe little," said Mrs. Akana. She told Erika, "*Bon* dances are part of *obon*. It's a Buddhist religious festival, the Feast of the Dead, when our departed loved ones come back to visit us and we celebrate that they have achieved a higher state. A joyful time. Goes July and August. But *bon* dancing is for everyone. All you need is a kimono. *Happi* coat for men. Required attire."

The Feast of the Dead. Departed loved ones coming back. Did Kal see *obon* that way? Erika was fascinated. "I'd love to learn a *bon* dance."

"Good." Mr. Akana smiled in satisfaction. "But be sure you come before *obon*. We belong to a *bon* dance troupe, and we travel all through the *bon-odori* season."

"It is very nice to meet you, Erika." Mrs. Akana took Erika's hand in both of hers to say farewell, and then she and her husband continued down the path.

Her thoughts on *obon* and Kal, who loved a dead woman, Erika asked Hiialo, "Shall we go?"

Soon they rounded a bend in the path, and the stone-rimmed terraces came into view.

Walls of black lava stones supported gradually rising narrow grass terraces. Erika paused at the foot of the first terrace and turned toward the sea. The sun, still low on the horizon, shone through a strip of filmy clouds in an otherwise immaculate sky. The ocean was turquoise, the palms dark silhouettes in front of it. To the south was Bali Ha'i, the cliffs filmed in the movie *South Pacific*. Kal had pointed them out from the outrigger.

Erika followed Hiialo up to the wide platform on the highest terrace. This had been the *halau hula*, hula school. Against the cliff wall stood a rectangular altar built of shoe-size lava stones. It was perhaps six feet long, five deep and two feet high, and all along the wall beside it were shelves made of lava stone. On top of the shelves lay sun-browned *leis* and stones wrapped in ti leaves. Offerings.

Hiialo walked over to look at them, then skipped back to Erika. "Want to see the hula Danny taught me?"

"I'd love that." Erika sat down at the edge of the grass, beside the lava-rock rim.

Hiialo stood in the middle of the grass with her hands on her hips. Carefully she said, "Hula tells stories. This hula dance tells visitors to enjoy Hawaii." She crouched, sweeping one hand slowly down in front of her, then raising both, then pressing them down to the earth. Standing again, she pointed the tips of her fingers toward her lips, then sent one hand out to the side. She moved with a natural grace haunting in one so small. Erika was enchanted.

Hiialo completed an entire dance, concluding with one foot pointed on the ground in front of her and both hands forming a point, reaching toward the mountains.

Erika clapped, and Hiialo ran over to her. Erika gave her a hug. "That was wonderful, Hiialo. You're very good."

"Thank you. I'm going to practice more."

Erika watched her, delighting in her grace but also envying the woman from whom Hiialo must have inherited that grace.

Envy...

I'm not supposed to feel this way. He warned me. He said explicitly that he did not want another lover.

She tried the old formula. Think of the reality of sex. Think, *Yuck.* But instead, she saw the reaction of Kal's body the night before. She thought of him and imagined him touching her. She'd envisioned it before, her first night in Haena, but only embraces. Growing friendship. Now she pictured something more sexual. His hand on her bare skin. On her breast.

It wasn't distasteful.

But the reality would be. Horrible.

Her skin felt as though it was starting to burn, and she opened her day pack to look for sunscreen and to take out a sketch pad. She sketched Hiialo and memorized colors—Payne's Gray for the lava rocks, Hooker's Green Dark for the grass—while Kal's daughter practiced hula. *She really loves it.* Erika hoped Kal would encourage Hiialo to continue hula, perhaps go to a *halau.* He should like that she took after her mother.

The envy came back.

Get over it, Erika.

After some time Hiialo collapsed on the grass beside Erika like a little rag doll. "That was fun," she said. "What are you drawing a picture of?"

"You." Erika showed her.

"Oh. I like you," said Hiialo. "I don't have to go to day-care anymore. There was a mean dog there." She squatted on the grass and began trying to catch a bug. In a singsong voice, almost as though she didn't care whether or not Erika heard, she said, "And maybe my daddy won't be so sad anymore. He cries sometimes." Musingly, practically to herself, she said matter-of-factly, "And once he threw up blood."

Erika choked on a breath. Kal really did have an ulcer, didn't he?

"Then he had to go the hospital, and I stayed with Grandma and Grandpa for a whole week. I watched *Cinderella*."

"When was that?" asked Erika.

"I don't know. I was three." Hiialo sat down again. "Can we get shave ice, Erika?"

"Yes, darling." Troubled, Erika closed her sketchbook and put it away in her day pack. Hiialo needed her. And Kal needed her.

She had to get rid of these disturbing feelings for him. They had to make this relationship work—and within the boundaries they'd set.

Because even if those limits broadened by mutual agreement, sex would fail, and she would leave in the end.

And Kal would want her to go.

THAT AFTERNOON, she tried to fix the watercolor, showing Hiialo what she was doing. When she'd finished applying new paint to the affected areas, Hiialo exclaimed, "You *did* fix it."

Erika didn't have the heart to tell her that it was no longer good enough to sell or even give away. At least she could use it as a guide to paint another.

She asked Hiialo to play on her own, and she transferred a sketch she'd made at the *heiau* to watercolor paper. But her thoughts distracted her. From worry about her future as an artist and about money, she began to wonder what she would do if Kal decided he didn't want her to stay. Tension held her body stiff, but when she'd finished sketching in the faint lines, the composition was right. She saw the promise of a good watercolor.

And she prayed there would be no accident this time.

A TURQUOISE-AND-WHITE Sunbeam was parked outside Kal's parents' house when he and Erika and Hiialo arrived for his birthday dinner. Kal said, "That's my sister's car. Niau."

Hiialo skipped ahead as they made their way to the front door. Kal carried a huge salad Erika had made, their contribution to the meal, and Erika carried a paper bag containing Hiialo's gift and her own birthday present for Kal, a good stainless-steel thermos.

When they entered the roomy kitchen with its pale green spackled walls and maple cupboards, Niau, a strict vegetarian, was advising her father to feed an aggressive dog brown rice.

Teasing, King said, "No. Raw meat. Red meat. Hi, folks." Erika was closest, and he embraced her like one of the family.

The warm gesture increased Erika's disquiet, her sense of urgency about her future on Kauai. "Hi, King. Hi, Mary Helen."

She was introduced to Niau, whose smile glowed with romantic speculation. *So this is the woman who answered my brother's ad...* But after "It's nice to meet you," Niau turned swiftly away, as though looking for something to break the awkwardness. She pounced on Hiialo. "There's my favorite *keiki.*"

Hiialo said, "Niau, Erika is an artist."

"I know. I can't wait to talk about art with her over dinner." Niau ran the Okika Gallery in Poipu, on the south side of the island. She winked at Erika with a saleswoman's smile. *Isn't this the cutest kid you ever saw? Isn't my brother wonderful?*

Erika liked her immediately.

"Erika, were you able to fix the painting?" asked Mary Helen.

"Yes," said Hiialo.

Erika gave Mary Helen a private look, an answer that differed.

Mary Helen said, "Well, King and I have decided you can't sit in the gallery again unless you let us pay you. We know how it is for artists."

Kal glanced at Erika. Was she having money problems?

"That's very nice of you." She smiled at his mother. "Okay." Her eyes flitted toward his, then away.

Then, she *did* need the money.

Kal didn't understand his own response. A need to set her at ease. *I'll take care of you.*

"Grandpa, can I see the puppies?"

"Well, I think we can manage that." King picked her up. "You want to see them again, Erika?"

"Sure."

They went out, the kitchen door swinging shut behind Erika, and Niau said, "I saw Jakka and Danny in Hanalei. They want Kai Nui to get together again. Is Erika into it?"

Kal's stomach churned. "We're not getting together again." Quickly he said, "I'll still play at your wedding, though."

"I don't think *I'll* be the next one getting married."

"Niau, would you please pour drinks?" asked Mary Helen.

His mother stood on tiptoe, searching the cupboard for birthday candles, but Kal saw the worry lining her face—for him. He moved close to the chair to spot her. "You shouldn't be climbing up there when you've got tall people around, Mom." He held the chair as she climbed down, and when her eyes silently assessed him, he smiled. "I'm going out to see the dogs. And Erika."

His mother said, "Good."

But Erika wasn't with his father and Hiialo and the Akitas. When he pushed open the kitchen door, she was right there, ten feet down the shadowed hallway, contemplating a photograph on the wall. The door closed behind him.

She made a guilty movement, shifting her focus to a different frame.

Kal joined her. He stared at him and Maka in Fern Grotto, Maka in her white dress.

Erika thought, *You look so young*. Both of them. He must have been nineteen or twenty. But they'd had a good marriage, a normal marriage. Two people perfect in body. "What happened in the accident, Kal?"

"The other guy was driving too fast, passing on a corner. He was in her lane."

The other driver's car had had air bags. Theirs hadn't. It was a thousand-dollar car that was all theirs. *Poor but happy*. That night had made him rich and sad. A year and a half later, when he'd gotten the insurance money from the hurricane damage, he'd used that and Maka's life insurance to buy the bungalow from his parents. Start over in a place that didn't remind him of her.

What hurt most of all now was realizing how many of his memories didn't have her in them.

Life just went on.

"Was the driver prosecuted?" asked Erika.

"Twenty hours of community service." He looked at her. "What about your brother's wife?"

"Oh..." It was a startled word. "Oh, we didn't do anything." Maybe if she'd pressed charges, as David had told her to do, things would have turned out differently. Maybe she wouldn't have said—

"Erika? Are you okay?"

She lifted her face, and his eyes were concerned.

"Yes." She turned her head away. "I'd like to go see the dogs."

They went out to the kennel and leaned on the half door of the whelping shed and watched the puppy who looked like Jin. Kal said light things, talked about the Akitas and about Jin, and the obedience titles she'd won, but all the time his arm was touching Erika's and neither moved.

All the time, he wondered how it must feel to Erika that her sister-in-law had made a selfish wild mistake—had hurt Erika in an automobile accident—then slept with her fiancé. And finally, as though the guilt had caught up with her, she'd killed herself.

While Erika watched Jin's puppies, especially the one that she liked the most, Kal let himself examine her. Her thick hair sweeping the side of her face. Her slender muscular arms and small breasts.

Eventually she glanced up, and he was staring, but he didn't look away. He just gazed into her eyes until someone rang the dinner bell. She was flushed, and he felt that way, too. Tingly.

He wanted to say something, but he didn't know what, so they moved away from each other in silence.

THE PRESENTS WERE both successful. Kal seemed genuinely delighted by Hiialo's picture and told her exactly where he was going to hang it in his room. Unwrapping Erika's thermos, he said, "Now, this is what I need."

When they got home that night, they put Hiialo to bed, and then Erika went into her own room and changed out of her dress and into a tank top and track shorts. She had time to paint before she went to bed.

But there was a knock at the door to the hallway, and she opened it.

Kal asked, "Want some more birthday cake?" Mary Helen had made a coconut layer cake.

"No, thanks." Erika had stringent personal rules about sugar and fat. When she'd realized how hard she was going to have to work to get her legs back, it had seemed sensible to go all the way. Good diet. As few cellulite dimples as possible. She still hated her body, but at least she wasn't fat.

She stepped back from the door, an invitation.

After a moment Kal came in, wandered over to her art table to examine her drawing of Hiialo at the *heiau*.

"We met your parents' neighbors today," said Erika. "The Akanas? They were coming down from the *heiau*."

"Oh, yeah? Mrs. Akana looked after us some when we were kids. Taught us *bon* dances. My folks used to take us to *bon* dance clubs on weekends in the summer."

"I'd like to do that," Erika said, sitting down on the edge of her bed, on his quilt.

"You'd like the Floating Lantern Festival, too. That's part of *obon*. People send paper lanterns out on the water to guide the souls of the dead back to the other world." With his toe Kal nudged one of Hiialo's crayons, which lay against the baseboard. "I wanted to take part in *obon* the summer after Maka died. My dad and I practiced the dances. But..." He shrugged. "I didn't go." It had been too hard.

To Erika, it sounded like something he should have done. "Couldn't you still go? Couldn't you do it this year?"

"Oh..." Why did he feel threatened? "Yeah. Sure."

"Mr. Akana said he'd teach us the dances. But you probably know them."

"A few." He didn't want to talk about *obon*. He wanted to talk about why Erika didn't like sex. What she'd said the night they discussed it hadn't satisfied him. *And what happened last night...*

He crossed the room and sat down near her. Drawing a knee up onto the mattress, he faced her. "You rubbed my back last night. It was nice."

"I'd...do it again." She swallowed, hoping he didn't know she'd seen that hard unmistakable bulge under his shorts. Hoping that if he did know, he would assume she'd taken it for what it was. Meaningless. Without significance.

"Thanks for making my lunch, Erika. And the thermos."

"You're welcome."

"So," Kal proposed carefully, watching her face, "what do you say I rub your back tonight?"

Erika stilled. *Him touching her...* "No, thanks."

He was silent.

She had to explain. "I really don't like getting massages."

"Had a lot of them?" She must have been in rehab a long time.

"Yes."

They sat stiffly beside each other, and he wondered if she'd noticed his hard-on the night before, if that had anything to do with her answer. Because she didn't like sex.

Ah, Erika... He turned to her. "We'll go to the Blue Room tomorrow night, yeah? The place I told you about in Waikapalae Cave?"

She nodded, making a wordless motion with her mouth.

Nervous. He said softly, afraid of his own voice and of what he was saying, "I'm pretty gentle." He'd meant the back rub, or intended to mean the back rub. But he knew he was saying something else.

Erika knew it, too. Almost sick with tension, but unable to turn away from the wonderful thing she knew others enjoyed, she whispered, "You can rub my back."

SHE WAS NERVOUS. When she lay down on her bed, her arms near her head, she turned her face to the mountains, away from him. But Kal knew she trusted him. He touched the middle of her back.

Erika swallowed, feeling the heat in her face, not bothering to try to talk.

Kal knew she needed him to talk. He grabbed the first topic that came to mind. As his hands slid over her, over her tank top, he said, "Do you know anything about *obon?*"

Her jumpiness eased. "Just what I learned today. Mrs. Akana said it's a Buddhist festival that celebrates the temporary return of the souls of the dead."

Kal massaged gently, as he'd promised. "Right. It has other names. *Bon, bon-odori, urabon.* Supposedly *bon* dancing started in India with a dance performed by one of Buddha's disciples. He was allowed to see his mother in another realm after death, and she'd been reborn among the Hungry Ghosts of Hell. She'd eaten meat and denied it, so she had to hang upside down as punishment. She couldn't eat because food and water would turn into fire. So the son earned merits to help her, and when he saw her freed from her suffering, he danced for joy, and people around him joined in."

Earning merits for the dead. Erika liked the idea. Some people died too soon. Maka. *Skye.* If anyone could use some extra merits, it was David's late wife. *If I could help Skye...*

Kal saw her eyes drop shut. Completely relaxed. It wasn't fair to take advantage of this moment.

But it was necessary.

"So, Erika. Have you had any lovers since your accident?"

Erika's muscles went tight. Upset, she rolled away and sat up. Her throat felt dry and full of ridges.

Kal's hand was still on one of her shoulders as they faced each other.

She shrugged it off. "You don't have a right to ask that." And then—knowing her reaction was beyond her control, because she heard her own voice and knew how she must sound to him—she started to cry.

"Erika..."

She dragged her arm across her eyes. "Yes, you do. Yes. Yes, I have. I don't know what you want."

Kal swallowed, his chest heaving at the sight of her tears. Distraught tears. He didn't know what he wanted, either. She'd spoken the truth. He had no right to ask.

He risked it. Put his arm around her, drew her against him. She allowed it. Stiffly. He said, "I'm sorry. I'm sorry. Ah, Erika..."

He hugged her for what seemed like a long time, and then he said again, as though it was a solution, "We'll go to the Blue Room tomorrow. You'll want to paint it."

Erika was soothed by the thought. And by his arms around her body and his head against hers.

And by his voice, rough and smooth and familiar, saying, "We're still friends, yeah?"

THE NEXT NIGHT, after dinner, Kal drove down the road toward Ke'e Beach and parked on the shoulder, not far from the yawning mouth of a wet cave. As he turned off the ignition, he told Erika, "They say these wet caves are where the goddess Pele tried to build her volcanos when she first came to the islands. But her sea sister, Namakaokahai, whom she'd come to Hawaii to escape, destroyed them with groundwater."

Erika gazed out the window at the cave. "Are we there?"

"No, this is a different cave. We've got a little hike to Waikapalae."

That made sense. He'd suggested she wear her hiking boots.

Hiialo unfastened her seat belt. She was out Erika's door almost before Erika and raced toward a wide gravel path that led up into the woods in the direction of the mountains.

"Hiialo, please wait for us," Erika called.

Hiialo slowed her steps to a creep, then skipped over to a nearby rock, her fancy caught by a plant or a creature.

Wearing a neoprene knee brace and hiking boots, her swimsuit and a sarong, and carrying her waterproof 35-mm camera and her mask, Erika limped to the place where Hiialo stood. Hiialo had brought her mask, too. But Kal carried only an underwater flashlight to guide them down a short underwater tunnel to the Blue Room.

Though the sky had grown cloudy, it was warm out, balmy low seventies, and it wouldn't be dark for hours. As they climbed the path, the gravel disappeared, and the trail became rocky, twisting back toward steep cliffs. "I don't see how you two can hike in just flip-flops," Erika said.

Behind her, Kal corrected, *"Slippahs."*

"What?"

"Slippers. In Hawaii, they're slippers. *Malihini,"* he added, turning the word to a caress.

The kind of caress his hands had lavished as he'd embraced her the night before. Erika remembered his fingers on the back of her neck, his palm skimming her spine, his arms squeezing tightly. *Friends, yeah?*

Yes, thought Erika.

The road below vanished, and the air became quiet, as though the three of them were the only people on earth.

Kal said, "Here we are."

About seventy-five feet down a rocky slope was the curved dark entrance of a wet cave. Hiialo started scurrying down the slope with the ease of a squirrel, but then her foot went out from under her.

Erika gasped.

Hiialo fell hard on her rear end and let out a howl.

Kal scrambled down to pick her up. "Bet you'll be more careful next time."

Seeing Hiialo's face, hearing her sobbing, Erika wished he'd warned her *this* time.

With Hiialo in his arms, he returned to her side. "You can hold on to me, Erika. It's steep."

She opened her mouth to say she was fine, she liked to do things alone. But then she assessed the slope. Hiialo wasn't the only one who could fall. Without meeting Kal's eyes, she grasped his arm. "Thanks."

She had to take small steps, compensating for the weakness of her left knee, but he never rushed her, and she remembered when she'd been learning to walk again and had held on to David. Kal was as strong and surefooted as her brother. Like a pillar that would never topple.

The walk down seemed long, and the whole way her throat swarmed with feelings. *Friends.* He was a good friend. And the slope was so rocky, so slippery, it was as though she and Kal and Hiialo were on a dangerous sojourn together. Going to the underworld to meet with their own ghosts.

At the bottom of the slope, the cave looked about that inviting.

They set down their towels, took off their shoes and went in. The water was colder than the breakers off the north shore, and Erika shivered as she waded through the mud, then lowered her whole body and dunked her head. "Brrr!"

Kal grabbed the back strap of Hiialo's swimsuit to keep her from swimming away into the shadows, and she turned and clung to him, shivering. Watching Erika clear her mask, he said, "I bet you've dived all kinds of places."

"Yes." Everywhere. In Australia with sea nettles. In Hawaii, in water teeming with sharks, where she'd watched

a *longimanus,* an oceanic whitetip, bite her brother. She
rarely dived anymore. Trying it again with David and Jean
six months before, she'd been unreasonably afraid. Since
the accident, she'd been afraid of a lot of things that had
never bothered her before.

But David had said she was just getting older. Naturally
more cautious.

Kal said, "Okay, we have to swim down a tunnel for
about ten feet. Are you up to that?"

"Sure."

Hiialo let go of him and dog-paddled back into the cave,
and Kal and Erika followed.

At the back wall the top few inches of a tunnel arched
above the surface of the water. Erika pushed her mask up
on her forehead. It was so dark that Kal's blue eyes looked
like charcoal smudges, and the cave seemed huge around
them, the pool bottomless. Hiialo hung on to Kal's right
shoulder. In contrast to her small hand, he seemed big and
sturdy. Erika knew the feel of his shoulders. Briefly she
imagined their silhouette above her body in the dark.

"I'll go first," said Kal. "Grab my ankle if you want as
you're going through. The tunnel's really short. Then you
come up in the Blue Room."

"I'm ready." She cleared her mask again.

"Okay. Count of three, Hiialo?"

Hiialo said earnestly, "One . . . two . . . three."

She took a breath, and they went under together. Erika
watched the black outlines of their bodies in the light Kal
had switched on. They swam quickly through the tunnel,
Hiialo in front, and Erika followed easily, carrying her
camera and watching Kal's muscular legs and the fabric of
his surfing trunks moving with the water. Without wanting to, she remembered again the night she'd seen the shape
of his erection under his shorts.

The natural light in the pool beyond was blue—a mix of
Cobalt Blue and Turquoise—not as dark as the water in

the tunnel. Realizing she'd emerged from the passage, Erika rose to the surface. As she gasped a breath and caught, through her mask, a water-streamed glimpse of blue, she felt a warm solid touch, Kal's hand at her waist.

"You okay?"

Until you touched me. His leg brushed hers underwater. Her body tingling, Erika shoved up her mask and peered about in wonder. Even their skin was washed an eerie ghostly blue. "Oh, Kal—your eyes."

He was looking at hers and at drops of water on her lips. He swam away from her, over to a ledge where Hiialo could stand. Hiialo began using her mask as a bucket to scoop up water.

Erika was sure she was going to drop the mask, but said nothing and swam to the far wall where she could brace her foot on a slimy narrow shelf and focus her camera. "Kal, let me take your picture. I can paint from it." Her voice echoed through the chamber. "Sit up on that ledge."

He climbed up on the ledge, and Hiialo handed her mask to him, then abandoned the rocks and swam toward Erika. "Can I take a picture?"

"Sure. Then will you be in the picture with your dad?"

As Hiialo came near, Erika reached out and two small hands grabbed her arm. She pulled Hiialo over to the shelf and helped her find a place to stand.

"I want you to be in the picture with my dad."

"Not this time," said Erika.

"Why not?"

Erika decided to be honest. "I don't think we should both be so far away from you in this dark pool."

Hiialo's forehead creased with worry. "What might happen?"

Kal wanted to know, too. More than once after Erika had cautioned her about something, he'd seen his daughter look worried and fearful. Then, fortunately, her adventurous spirit took over again.

"Well, if you were to get a cramp and go underwater, it would be hard for us to find you."

Kal thought, *I'd find her.* He could tell Hiialo thought so, too. No wonder Erika didn't like sex. A person had to relax to enjoy it.

Then he remembered her tears.

Not that easy.

Hiialo tried to focus the camera on Erika. "Which button do I push?"

"The yellow one, honey. Right there."

He was the one who'd advertised for a celibate marriage. It was something he forgot more and more often lately. In the blue space of the cavern, Kal admitted it was something he no longer desired.

Celibacy was a way of clinging to Maka after her death.

But he wasn't dead. And watching Erika and his daughter figuring out the camera together, happy, liking each other, Kal knew he wanted to live. It was going to be hard to convince Erika. Hard to get to the bottom of whatever she didn't like about sex. But he would try.

He'd found someone who needed him as much as he needed her. And he didn't want to let her go.

CHAPTER NINE

BACK RUBS SEEMED a safe approach. Again that night he asked her for one, then lay on his bed while she stroked the muscles in his back. It was just right. Her touch stirred him, but this slow friendship was what he needed.

What she must need, too.

"Hey, Erika."

"Yes." Her voice faltered on the word.

"Let's do this every night. We'll trade off, yeah?"

Heat tingled in Erika's chest. Every night? It would become a ritual, like her making lunch for him, like tucking in Hiialo at night.

He might ask her about sex again.

Friends, she thought. In the deepest place inside her, she knew she needed a friend like Kal. A back-rub friend. A close friend.

She couldn't say no.

THE NEXT DAY he didn't have to be at work until noon, and Erika took advantage of his being home to get some time alone to paint. At the art table in her room, she completed a watercolor of Hiialo at the *heiau*. It was good, and when it was dry she tacked it high on the wall, out of reach of disaster. Then she took another sheet of paper, her drawing board and the ruined painting of Kal playing guitar and went out her back door. Sitting on a warped damp bench among the mock orange bushes, she drew.

Somewhere a band began to play rock and roll, but she scarcely heard. The drawing was as good as the first one she'd made, and by the time she finished, the sun had risen high over the mountains. Erika noticed the live music. It wasn't just Kal. She heard a drum, too, and another guitar inside the bungalow. Danny and Jakka? She climbed the steps to her door.

Inside, Erika consulted the clock on her nightstand. Eleven-thirty. She'd been working since eight.

Her bedroom door was closed, but she heard the song end, heard male laughter. Danny's voice said, "You gotta go to work?"

"Yeah. Where's Hiialo?"

Erika took her art supplies to the drawing table and paused there. Something wasn't right.

Then she saw. Gray goop spilled on the table, running into the bristles of four of her brushes. Dried.

The lid was halfway on the bottle of masking fluid.

Erika set down her drawing board, stored the drawing in her portfolio, then opened the door of Hiialo's room.

Hiialo was sitting on her floor, her head down, playing with Fluff and Pincushion. Though she must have heard Erika, she didn't lift her eyes.

"Hey, Hiialo?" Kal stuck his head in. "There you are."

Erika wasn't sure who to kill first. "Hiialo, were you in my room?"

Hiialo jerked her small round face up, her eyes big. She didn't answer. The terror of the guilty.

Kal came into the room. "What did you do, Hiialo?"

Her chin trembled, and she gazed down at her stuffed animals.

"Hiialo?" He bent down, picked up Pincushion and Fluff and tossed both on her bed. "Look at me."

Hiialo raised her head, met his gaze. "What?"

She was impossibly brave—or impudent, depending on point of view. Erika didn't know which way she felt. She was torn between wanting justice and wanting to protect Hiialo from Kal's anger. She was tempted to ask him, *Well, where were you?* But Hiialo shouldn't have to be watched every minute. She was old enough not to get into someone else's belongings.

Her mischief had been very expensive.

Kal asked, "What have you been doing?"

Hiialo began to cry. She rubbed her eyes and wouldn't speak.

Feeling the anger mounting in Kal, Erika said, "Hiialo, that was wrong to get into my things. You know I would have let you use the masking fluid if we were together."

Hiialo sobbed.

Kal stepped over her and around Erika and into her room. In a minute he was back. The muscles in his neck were tight, but Erika understood the expression in his eyes. Helplessness. *Why can't I control you? Why do you do these things?*

Erika had a good idea why. Because Kal loved Hiialo to distraction, and he didn't know how to discipline her. Maybe he only understood dogs. Disapproval for undesirable behavior, praise for good. It wasn't a bad place to start.

But it wasn't enough.

"Hiialo," said Erika. "Please get up."

Hiialo looked at her.

Erika stared back.

Hiialo bowed her head, picked at a scab on her knee. Then she slowly rose to her feet.

As Kal slipped back toward the window, Erika held open the door to her room and gazed expectantly at Hiialo. Hiialo went in.

Trying to stay calm and not to think about her last three hundred dollars or the watercolors she hadn't painted, Erika stood over the art table. "I would like you to clean this up. You'll need to peel all the masking fluid off the table." That would be fun; the rest was not. "And then you'll have to get it out of the bristles of these brushes. Now, you must be very gentle. This brush cost eighty dollars, and once a few bristles start coming out, the rest will come out, too. The brush is probably ruined, but you're going to try to save it and the others. And if it can't be done, we'll have to figure out a way for you to work to help pay for them."

Hiialo's eyes filled.

In the doorway, Kal thought, *That's unfair. She's too little.*

But he remembered the photos of Maka all over the floor of his room.

"Now please do what I asked," Erika said, and turned and crossed the room and opened the door to the hall. She went out.

Hearing her walk into something and swear, Kal remembered the amp was in the hallway and winced.

In her pink shorts and tank top, her face tear-streaked, Hiialo gave him a glance of appeal.

"Don't look at me." He went after Erika, took a minute to move his amp and found her on the lanai. She was sitting on the steps, her head in her hands.

Kal contemplated her slender athletic body, her back, her defeated posture, before he came and sat down beside her. "I'm sorry." He had to say that first thing. "It was my fault. Danny and Jakka came by. They'd stopped at Na Pali and knew I wasn't working."

"She's old enough to know better," Erika said. Kal couldn't be expected to spend every free minute with his daughter. It was just that he had so few. She moved her hair to see him. "Maybe you should take an antacid."

He smiled a little. His stomach was bothering him less today. The last few days. "I think you're my antacid, Erika. That sounds trivial. But it's not."

She knew.

"I'll pay for the brushes," he said. "I mean, she should do some work, but that's not really going to help you now."

There was no point, Erika decided, in assuring him that his four-year-old daughter *was* going to do one hundred and sixty dollars' worth of manual labor. She could fold laundry. She could sweep. They'd make a chart. And when those jobs were done, Hiialo would never ever again touch anything that belonged to someone else without asking.

"Hey, Erika, I know this set you back, so let me do it, yeah?"

It didn't seem right. She wasn't just a houseguest. She didn't want to be. If she was Hiialo's stepmother... "No, Kal." She had signed up for this. *At least Mary Helen said she'd pay me for going into the gallery.*

"You're not leaving, are you?"

"No." Did that mean— He didn't want her to go. She saw it in his face. He wanted her there. "I'm not leaving. Now," she added.

"I have to get to work, but there's an art store at the mall in Lihue. I'll take you there tonight, eh? I'll get a baby-sitter. We can have dinner."

Heat stole over her, and her emotions pulled on each other. Butterflies in her stomach. "Let me see what I can do with the brushes I have." Panicked, she met his eyes. "I don't want to... I'd rather stay home."

The moment was interminable, even the air immobile.

"I see," Kal answered finally. "Sure." And then he got up, as though he couldn't stand to be near her anymore, and hurried inside.

THE BRUSHES WERE RUINED.

That afternoon, Erika made a work chart for Hiialo, assigning dollar amounts to certain tasks. Sweeping the front room and the lanai was worth three dollars, folding two loads of laundry, five. If the jobs weren't done well, they wouldn't count.

Hiialo asked if she could start by sweeping, and she went to work, and soon Erika heard her singing a song from the Disney version of *Cinderella*.

With her remaining brushes, Erika tried to paint the watercolor of Kal, using a sponge for the wash because her good wash brush had been destroyed. But the effort was frustrating and eventually she stopped.

Why hadn't she agreed to have dinner with him? It had sounded so lovely. Perfect.

He likes you, Erika. He's held you when you cried. He said you could hold onto him when you walked down that slope to the wet cave. He said you're his antacid.

"How romantic," Erika murmured to herself.

But here she was, trying to paint with four small brushes, the wrong brushes, and she'd hurt Kal and he'd hardly said another word to her before he left for work, just tried to act very casual, like it didn't matter.

She abandoned her painting on the table and went to the bed and lay on it. What would it've been like if she had said she'd go? He would've bought her new brushes, bought her dinner.

And I would have been sponging. Because I can't be his lover.

Kal would be horrified if he thought she perceived the invitation that way—gifts in exchange for sex. But Erika knew that was what it always came down to in the end. Even her staying in this house . . .

Friends, yeah?

"Oh, Kal," she whispered into his quilt. "Let's just be friends."

She couldn't be more. With anyone.

HE CALLED HER at four and he sounded distant. "I need to do some stuff after work. Don't fix dinner for me, okay? I'll see you by ten at the latest."

"Okay." She wanted to apologize. She wanted things to be as they had before she'd refused his invitation to go to Lihue. "Kal, I feel bad about today. I—I don't know where we stand." It sounded so trite. What if he hadn't meant anything? What if he was just asking her to go with him as an extension of their friendship?

Then why get a sitter?

On his end of the phone, a car passed. He must be in the gallery with the doors open, or maybe at the pay phone in the park across the street.

His voice said, "Let's talk about this when we can see each other."

Her heart thumped.

"Is everything okay there?" he asked.

"Yes. Hiialo's been working. She's earned off ten dollars so far."

The sound he made might have been a laugh. Then, silence. After a time he said, "I'm not very good at that kind of stuff. That's why I asked you to come."

Erika felt bad for him. "She's perfect, Kal. You're a good dad. I love her." Who couldn't love a girl who sang Cinderella's work song while she was being punished by her wicked stepmother? Well...maybe *future* stepmother.

This silence lasted longer than the first, but eventually Kal spoke again. "Ten o'clock, yeah? Kiss Hiialo for me."

Erika agreed, and then they hung up, neither saying goodbye, as though if they did they might not see each other again.

Hiialo was out on the porch with her stuffed animals. "We're having a *luau*, Erika." One of her animals, who had the misfortune to be a pig, was covered with a layer of dirt. Erika was sure he'd been buried—cooked underground.

Laughter bubbled inside her. The last of her anger drained away. She didn't have room to be angry at Hiialo. She was too upset about Kal.

Trying to take her mind off it, she sketched and photographed Hiialo playing, and then she made dinner for the two of them. Hiialo asked for pancakes and supervised Erika's making them, pointing out when each began to bubble and the edges to pucker, and when Erika tucked her in bed that night, Hiialo said, "I'm sorry I was bad."

"I know you won't do it again. Now, here's a kiss from your daddy." Erika kissed her forehead.

Hiialo asked, "Are you going to live with us always?"

Always. She couldn't answer that alone. "I don't know, Hiialo."

Hiialo pulled her covers up to her chin.

"Good night, sweetheart."

"Good night, Erika."

SHE WAS STRUGGLING with her small brushes when she saw headlights in the driveway and heard the car. Leaving the painting of Hiialo's *luau* on the art table, Erika got up and gathered her brushes to take out to the kitchen to wash.

Kal was just coming in the front door with a paper bag in his arms, but he stopped when he saw her.

Neither moved.

The screen door swung shut behind him.

Erika said, "Hi."

"Hi." She'd changed clothes, and his eyes saw more than her tank top and shorts. Long legs and scars and brown eyes . . . It felt too long since he'd seen her. *Do this right, Kal.* He moved toward the counter, toward her, and set down the bag. "I got you these. I think they're like what you had."

Brushes. They were wrapped in tissue, and Erika watched his rough hands unfold the paper to show her. She studied the golden hairs on his wrists and forearms. She smelled his sweat.

She touched the fine camel hair of the brushes. She never used sable; the Siberian mink were endangered. Kal must have noticed her preference.

"They're just like what I had. Thank you." No need to look at him. She could feel him there beside her.

"I also got you this."

She couldn't see his hands anymore—or what he held. Had to turn.

It was a *lei,* made of pale green moss.

Erika's gaze crept up his chest and throat, stopping at his mouth. Looking in his eyes would make her head swim.

"In Hawaiian culture," he said, "the head and the shoulders are considered sacred. To give a *lei* is a sign of respect. And affection."

Erika had to meet his eyes then. His peered into her heart as he said, "And that's where we stand."

Placing his hands on her shoulders, he gently kneaded her muscles. "I think it's my turn to do this to you tonight."

She quavered. But she could smell the sweet earthy scent of the *lei*—and she'd never forget his words.

They went into her room, and she removed the *lei* so she could lie down without crushing it.

This time he didn't mention past lovers. He just caressed the tightness from her back and sang to her.

IT WENT ON LIKE THAT for almost two weeks.

Each day Erika awoke before dawn, practiced twenty minutes of yoga, did her isometric exercises and slipped out of the house and down to the beach in the dark. There, she walked the shore alone, two miles west along the sea and back, and she was lulled to peace by the inside-a-conch-shell churning of the waves, a roar louder than her thoughts, clearing her mind of everything but Kal.

Because each night they touched.

In between those mornings and nights came the long days without him, while he was at work. Hiialo had almost finished working off the paintbrushes she'd ruined, and Erika had completed several watercolors, which Kal's sister, Niau, had driven to Poipu to be photographed and made into transparencies for Adele. Now the originals hung in the Hanalei Okika Gallery.

On Thursday, two weeks after Kal's birthday, as Erika was returning from her morning walk, she spotted a shirtless man in loose indigo blue cotton shorts walking toward her. The papaya-colored ball of the rising sun was just a sliver creeping over the horizon, but she recognized Kal.

Instantly she was afraid something was wrong. Why wasn't he home with his daughter? When he reached her, she asked, "Where's Hiialo?"

The waves crashed.

"My mom took her to Lihue for the day. Relax." He was holding four mangoes. "Breakfast."

Relax, Erika. He said it often. When Hiialo ran ahead of them into the ocean. When she was quiet in the bathtub for too long. When she wandered away in the grocery store. When she went outside to play without telling anyone. When she practiced hula alone in the courtyard outside the Okika Gallery, just out of sight of where Erika was painting.

Kal stretched, his skin the finest color of the morning, a dilute wash of Yellow Ochre and Burnt Sienna. The pink-filtered dawn glowed over the ocean-facing side of his body, lightening his eyes, turning the irises the aquamarine shade of the sea. The line of dark hair dipping from his naval to beneath the loose waistband of his baggy shorts was an invitation to stare.

He tilted his head toward the high-tide line, gesturing her to sit down with him. "Want some mangoes?"

There was a mango tree behind the house, outside Kal's window. They ate a lot of mangoes. Mango ice cream. Mango bread. As they sat down together, Erika asked, "How long does mango season last?"

"July?" He lay back in the sand near her, and Erika could smell the juice of the fruit he was eating and the scent of the ocean and his body. The last brought familiar confusion. Earthy feelings she recognized as desire.

He wanted her, too. She'd seen him aroused more than once after she'd rubbed his back or Kal had rubbed hers. He knew when she noticed, too, and he smiled a little tensely and said something light. Once it had been, *Yeah, that happens.* Another time he'd said, *I guess you can tell I like you.*

She'd said nothing. She didn't want to tease him. She was afraid.

He knew that, too.

A black-and-white dog bounded up the beach barking, then splashed into the water and began swimming in the gentle surf. Erika saw his owner a few hundred yards away, throwing a stick for another dog, a golden retriever.

"We ought to get a dog to walk with you in the mornings," said Kal.

He said it as though she was going to stay. As though he took it for granted. Relief rushed through her, but she was still afraid to feel secure. His house already felt too much like home. And yet she always half expected to discover that her own ship would soon be weighing anchor, that she'd have to leave him and Hiialo.

But a man didn't talk about getting a dog with a woman he wanted to send away. "I'd like to have a dog, Kal."

His eyes explored her face. "Yeah?"

"Yes."

The surf broke, and the froth crept up the shore toward their feet.

Kal bit into his second mango, eyeing her. "You want to drive around the island with me today? I thought we'd go to the Menehune Ditch and Barking Sands. You said you don't surf?"

She used to surf well, by Santa Barbara standards. But her knee wasn't what it used to be, and Hawaii drew the best surfers in the world. "I can still do it. But I can't handle anything too hairy."

"During summer, it's tame here. We could put the rack on the car, try Polihale." He smiled. "I'll take care of you."

A lump formed in her throat, and her eyelids opened and shut hard, trying to keep the tears in. He was only talking about surfing. "Okay."

His eyes were sober, lingering on her face as though he was searching for something. Suddenly he sat up, turning his back to her. Patches of sand covered his smooth skin and sifted with the rippling of his muscles as he took another bite of mango and watched the Pacific.

Facing forty-five degrees away from him, Erika kept a vigil of her own, staring at the horizon, telling herself, *It's going to be okay.*

She needed the reassurance.

She knew what staying with him would require from her. Her only comfort was that he had the patience of the sea. And more gentleness than anyone she'd ever known.

Her fear was that she would disappoint him.

And break all of their hearts.

CHAPTER TEN

"IT REALLY BARKS!"

Kal grinned at her as they carried the cooler between them and a surfboard each across the warm "barking sand." It was a good day at Políhale, few people, no nasty kona winds.

He picked an isolated spot near some sloping green cliffs with rocky bases. They set down cooler and surfboards and shed their day packs. Clouds had floated in, cooling the morning, but Erika immediately fished in her pack for a tube of sunscreen.

The frayed edges of her loose faded cutoffs hung white against her tan. She pulled her T-shirt over her head and tossed it onto her day pack. Jade green bikini underneath. She squirted sunscreen into her palm.

Without asking, Kal put his hand over hers, collecting the lotion, and rubbed it into her shoulders and her back. His hands slid up her sides, and she stood motionless, a warm statue with soft skin... Moving down to the waistband of her cutoffs, he imagined unbuttoning them for her. *"I Wanna Be Your Man..."*

"Do you like it when I touch you, Erika?"

"Yes. But..."

His hands left her. He was done, and he moved to see her face.

In his, Erika saw the person who had become her closest friend. Because Adele was far away. Kal and Adele were like two sides of the same coin. Each knew things about her the other did not. Kal could never understand what it had been like Before and During. Adele could not share this magical part of After. Kal cared about her as a man for a woman, and Erika couldn't remember knowing his kind of caring before.

He waited, gazing down at her face, his chest just a few inches from hers.

"We said we were going to be celibate, Kal. Has that changed?"

"What do you think?"

She felt his hand push back her hair, stroke her cheek.

She answered the question, not the touch. "I think I'm frigid."

The word stopped Kal. It was ugly. He dropped his hand. "That sounds like something someone else said."

Her head shot up. "No. It's not like that. The men I've dated have been kind people."

His throat tightened. "I don't want to hear about them."

Erika clasped her arms about herself. He'd asked once. And she'd cried in his arms. A lot had changed since then. What she saw in his eyes and felt radiating from him was primal. Desire. For her.

"Why are you so afraid?"

How could she explain? It was so complicated. She could remember when she couldn't feel parts of her body. And sex was... She looked up into his eyes and told him the truth she thought he deserved and that she knew would push him away. "I'm not afraid, Kal. I'm repulsed."

He didn't move. "By...?"

"Sex." Because he didn't, she stepped back and turned away. She stripped off her shorts and picked up her surfboard.

"Wait. Just one thing. Are you repulsed by *me?*"

She turned and stared at him. His eyes were sky-water, translucent blue. "Of course not."

"Then I have a suggestion. When you wake up in the morning and when you go to bed at night and about twenty-five times every day, say to yourself, 'Sex is beautiful. When you love each other.'"

"You don't know how bad it is."

Her sister-in-law had nearly killed her, then slept with Erika's fiancé and killed herself. And Erika had spent three years in a wheelchair, her mind paralyzing her body. Now she was "repulsed" by sex. "I think I can guess." He picked up his board. "Let's hit the breaks, yeah?"

"WE SHOULD KEEP an eye on each other and the shore. The bottom drops right off here, and it's easy to get sucked away by the currents. See that knife-edge point at the end of that valley? Let's not go past it."

Erika nodded.

They had paddled out beyond the breakers. In the noonday sun, they'd found a spot of their own with easy peaks and hollows, fun for novice or advanced surfers. But Erika had butterflies in the pit of her stomach, reaction to being far from shore, surfing an unfamiliar spot, in a swell that seemed too big for summer. She started thinking about sharks.

Kal eyed the scars on her knee. "Feel okay?"

"I'm nervous."

"Just go whenever you want. I'll wait."

Erika took comfort from his voice. He was like the ocean for her. Necessary. Sometimes healing, sometimes too scary.

Together they watched the incoming set. It looked all right to Erika, and when she glanced at him questioningly, he said, "Go ahead."

She began paddling, and Kal watched soberly. Had he pushed her too much? It was summer, but the waves were overhead.

She was paddling.

The surf rolled under him, and then he couldn't see her anymore.

This is good for her.

Fear on her behalf was not something he allowed himself to feel. Accidents, destiny, could not be stopped.

THREE SHAKY RIDES and one battering wipeout were enough. Two hours later, Erika lay on her back with her shirt over her face, her left shin wickedly bruised, her body enervated, trembling with exhaustion. Overhead, the sky was cloudy. It smelled like rain, but the heat was intense.

Kal, still dripping from the ocean, lifted up her shirt, offered her some *mochi,* cakes made from pounded rice, that they'd bought in Waimea with their Japanese box lunches.

"Thanks." Erika sat up and took the chewy delicacy. Her hand was shaking, which embarrassed her. She rested her arm against her knee to steady it. She shouldn't feel sheepish about being unable to keep pace with a man who'd been surfing Kauai's waves since he was a kid. But she did.

He didn't, she noticed, ask how she was feeling. She was glad. She felt a little like throwing up. And if she opened her mouth she would say the words in her head.

I'm too old for this.

She didn't want to be too old.

For him.

ON THE WAY HOME, they stopped at the Menehune Ditch, an ancient irrigation ditch supposedly built by a mischievous race of little people with supernatural powers. It was raining, and when Erika got out of the car at the overlook, her legs ached.

When they were enclosed in the Datsun again, Kal reached across her to find the latch to put the seat back.

"Oh, that's great." Erika shut her eyes. She'd changed out of her suit in the bathroom at the beach, and her T-shirt felt soft against her skin, like sleeping clothes. Kal started the car, and the windshield wipers squeaked in a soft steady rhythm. As the Datsun began to move, Erika stretched her arms over her head and yawned. "I feel so relaxed."

"Mmm." It was a speculative sound. "Hey, I think I'm going to Jakka's tonight to jam. Is that okay with you?"

"Sure." Sleepily she turned in her seat.

Kal switched on the radio, low. Reggae was playing. "You Can Get It If You Really Want." Slowing the car to turn onto the Kaumualii Highway, he manually flipped the broken turn indicator back and forth.

As he pulled onto the road, Jimmy Cliff faded out and the DJ said, "And now we've got an old one from Hawaii. And I'll take a call from anyone who can tell me what happened to these guys. Kai Nui. 'Pau Hana.' For all the *malihinis* out there, that means 'quitting time.'"

Erika sat up, straightened her seat back. Had he said *Kai Nui?*

Kal murmured, "This should be interesting." Hearing what someone thought had happened to him.

The car filled with music Erika recognized. The song he'd played on the guitar that first Sunday when they'd gotten home from breakfast with his parents. "You have a single."

"More than that. We recorded a whole tape. Ten cuts. We used to get a lot of airplay."

Staggered, she gazed at his profile. His voice played in the car, coarse and beautiful. A voice that should be on the radio. Had she been oblivious or what? "Why hasn't anyone told me? Why haven't *you* told me?"

"It's not my favorite subject. It's past." He shrugged it off.

Erika listened to the song. God, he was good. They were all good. Jakka's backup vocals were spooky owl calls. Danny's drum was rock and roll and hula rhythm beating as one. It was a song for people who couldn't wait for five o'clock. *Pau hana.* Quitting time.

As the last notes faded out, the DJ said, "And we've got a caller on the line. You're on the air. What's your name?"

"Danny Kekahuna, drummer for Kai Nui."

Kal made a sound of irritation. But a smile twisted the corner of his mouth as he watched the road, driving with his hands loose and relaxed on the wheel.

"*Shaka!* So what happened to you guys, Danny?"

"A hurricane and some personal tragedy, Jim. I think you know we were slated to play on Letterman . . ."

Erika choked.

Kal listened to his friend tell every listener that "the tide always comes back in." High tide. Kai Nui. Shaking his head in disgust, he switched off the radio.

"You were going to be on David Letterman?"

"Yeah. The date was three weeks after Maka's death. And like he said, we had a hurricane in the meantime."

"Was there any way to reschedule?"

"That's the last thing I was thinking about. My wife had just died. My family didn't have food or drinking water. I didn't have a house. I had a baby girl who'd never drunk out of a bottle."

Oh, Kal. She ached for him.

"Is Hiialo why you stopped playing?" As she saw it, his band had never really broken up.

"I guess. And . . . I don't know. You get bad luck like that, and you see the writing on the wall." He shrugged.

"Would you want to play again? Professionally?"

"Um . . . *Sure.*" Twist my arm.

And now that I'm here, thought Erika, *he can.*

But she kept silent, for the most selfish reason of all.

If he asked her to stay in Kauai with him, she wanted it to be for herself.

THAT NIGHT, after Hiialo was in bed, Kal loaded his guitars and amplifier into the Datsun to drive to Jakka's home in Kalihiwai, twenty minutes away. When he'd left, Erika sat on the couch to rough out some sketches of the Haena Store, playing with photos she'd taken. Boys hitchhiking, an aging surfer selling plumeria *leis,* and a sumo wrestler on a picnic bench across from the gallery wolfing a pizza. Erika wanted to incorporate one of the images into a painting of the store.

She worked at the coffee table because the breeze from the trade winds was so pleasant. Time passed quickly, and soon she began to finalize a drawing on watercolor paper. By ten-forty-five she was ready to paint.

"Hello, Erika."

She started at the familiar voice, peered through the screen, then leapt up and ran to the door. "David!" Banging open the screen, Erika hurled herself at her tall bearded brother. "What are you doing here?"

"Visiting you. Thawing out." His face was windburned. In his long-sleeved rugby shirt, chinos and running shoes, he was overdressed for Kauai. But he'd been in Greenland.

He came inside, and Erika couldn't get over it that he was really there. "Where are Chris and Jean?"

"At Haena Villas. I walked over. We just got in, rented a condo, wanted to surprise you. But it's past Chris's bedtime, so Jean said she'd stay with him. She's a little worn out herself."

Erika saw a quiet gleam of pleasure in his eyes. It made her suspicious. "Is she pregnant?"

David nodded.

Because of Hiialo sleeping in the next room, Erika mellowed her cry of excitement. "How far along is she? When's the baby coming?"

"Valentine Day."

"How wonderful." Erika's joy was genuine, only slightly tinged by envy of Jean, who was going to know the experience of pregnancy and childbirth.

But I have Hiialo.

For now.

What she and Kal had discussed on the beach echoed through her. *Sex is beautiful....*

She'd try out the new mantra later. "Sit down, David. Do you want something to drink?"

"No, thanks." He glanced at the brown chair with the threadbare armrests and sat down. Casually he surveyed the front room, checking out his sister's home. "So, where are your housemates?"

Erika's windpipe seemed to develop a crimp, cutting off her air. "Oh." She perched on the edge of the couch. "Hiialo's sleeping. She's just four. And Kal's out playing music with friends. He plays guitar."

David missed little. "You're living with a man?"

She folded her arms across her chest. "Well...not the way you mean."

He grinned. "Jean thought it was a man. She said, 'Look, there's not a personal pronoun in this whole letter. It's a guy.'"

Erika wished David's wife would stick to marine biology.

But her conscience needled her. Kal had leveled with his family. She should do the same. "I answered a personal ad."

"*What?*"

"I answered a personal ad. In *Island Voice* magazine. That's how I met Kal."

Her brother sat back, rested one ankle over the opposite knee. "I thought you said it wasn't like that."

It took her too long to answer. "We're friends. Hey, want to see what I've been doing?"

"Sure. "

They went to her room, where Erika switched on the track lights, illuminating her studio. Her best work was hanging in the Okika Gallery. *Hiialo's Luau* and *Haole Guitar Man,* the painting she'd done of Kal on the swing, a copy of the one Hiialo had ruined. She had painted it with gouache, and, as with the first, Mary Helen had wanted to buy it, but Erika had refused to take money for it. She was less panic-stricken about finances now. Mary Helen and King paid her fifty dollars every Tuesday, when she came in to paint at the gallery, and Erika had sold an original watercolor of the Hanalei Bridge for three hundred dollars. She wanted *Haole Guitar Man* to be her gift to the Johnsons. That was where the matter stood, but Mary Helen had insisted that Erika prepare a slide to send to Adele. The piece had potential for a print series.

Erika wished David could see it, but it would have to wait till morning. Nonetheless, on her wall she'd taped up several other watercolors. A mother and two children selling bouquets of flowers at a roadside stand. The mango tree in the yard heavy with fruit. Two paintings of Hiialo at the *heiau.*

David examined the watercolors. "Has Adele seen them?"

"Not these. I've sent her some other slides." But what if Adele didn't see anything she wanted to publish? *I'll be all right. I sold a painting. I'm getting by.* "Tell me what you think, David."

"I like them." He was scrutinizing her now. "You look great, Erika. Relaxed."

"I ought to. We went surfing today, and I could barely walk afterward."

As they returned to the front room, headlights lit the bamboo window blinds. Tires crunched on gravel. Erika glanced at the clock. Eleven. "That'll be Kal."

She heard the engine go off, the door of the Datsun shut, Kal's tread on the stairs. He was singing. Not a cover, someone else's music, but a song he played at home, a song he'd written, called "Kona." The melody always stayed with her when he was through.

Erika heard Kal pause on the porch. Perhaps he'd seen David's shadow, the shadow cast by the lamp beside the couch. After just a moment, he opened the door and came in, smelling faintly of cigarette smoke, carrying his amp and the electric guitar case. Setting them down, he looked from Erika to her companion with the kind of black stare locally called "stink eye." He did not say hello.

"Guess who stopped by," said Erika. "My favorite man in the whole world. This is my brother, David."

Looking fractionally less irritated, Kal held out his hand. "Kal Johnson."

David shook it. "Good to meet you. Sorry I didn't warn anyone before coming by. We just had a long plane flight—a few of them. We checked into our condo, but I wanted to surprise Erika. I'll get out of your hair now. It's late."

Kal regretted being surly. "Don't go. I just came in, and—"

"I know."

Kal saw that he did.

David said, "What's your phone number here, Erika?"

"Oh, I'll write it down for you. How did you find the house?"

"Asked the right person. The woman who works the desk at Haena Villas had seen you at some gallery. Knew who you were and where to find you."

She squinted at him warily. And he hadn't known she was living with a man?

Unnoticed, Kal picked up his amp and guitar and took them to his room. He was about to step through the beaded doorway when the thought hit him that David Blade might know he and Erika weren't sleeping together, had planned not to. Or he might not know it.

It shouldn't matter.

It was juvenile to feel mortified at the thought of Erika's "favorite man in the whole world" learning that he and Erika weren't lovers. Did David know sex made her sick?

He went into his room without turning on the light, knowing the light would illuminate the nest of a widower. David Blade would recognize it. Kal set the guitar and amp on the floor and returned to the living room.

David stood with his hands in his trouser pockets, smiling at something Erika had said. She turned and bent to close her sketch pad, and Kal saw the backs of her thighs, tanned brown, sleek with muscle. With a slight yawn, he wandered to the couch, only glancing at her brother.

As Erika straightened up, sketchbook in hand, he touched her spine, the center of the muscular back he'd watched as they'd paddled surfboards that day. The back he'd rubbed with sunscreen.

"Get some work done?"

Erika met his eyes, remembering that morning, everything they'd said.

Sex is beautiful. When you love each other.

Now he was touching her. *Oh, Kal, you do scare me.*

She almost forgot her brother was there. She wanted to talk to Kal, just to ask him how it had gone with the band, to exchange news of the hours they'd spent apart. He had asked about her art. After too long she said, "I did work. I want to show you."

"I want to see." His arm was still around her, and his gaze slipped from her eyes to her mouth. As though he wanted to kiss her.

David cleared his throat. "Well, I'll undoubtedly see you both later."

His smile was contented, showing quiet satisfaction at something.

Her and Kal. *He thinks we're in love,* thought Erika.

Kal's faded green T-shirt had a picture of an outrigger and a Hanalei moon on it. She could smell the laundry detergent. She had washed the T-shirt with some of his other clothes and with Hiialo's things three days before. Hiialo had folded them. The washer and dryer were in a shed alongside the bungalow, outdoors, hidden by a flowering plumeria tree. Erika liked doing the laundry, helping him. His ulcer was bothering him less; she hardly ever saw him popping antacids anymore.

Kal released her and turned to David. "Well, it's good to meet you. Come for dinner tomorrow, eh?"

"Sounds great. We'll give you a call in the morning."

Erika stepped around the coffee table, hugged her brother again. "I'm so glad you're here, David. I can't wait to see Chris and Jean."

"They'll be glad to see you."

They migrated out to the lanai. The trunk of the Datsun was open, and Kal went down the steps to get his other guitar.

David murmured, "Erika, I think someone else wants to be your favorite man."

Erika put her bare foot on his instep and dug an elbow into his ribs. But he'd made her think, and she wished she hadn't called him that.

It wasn't true anymore.

Kal came up onto the porch with his guitar case, and David said, "Well, good night. Good to meet you. And good to see *you.*"

He hugged Erika, meeting her eyes. In his she saw the memory of their shared past, shared pain. The three years she'd spent on his ship in her wheelchair. The years before he'd met Jean.

He was all right now. Happier, in fact, than she'd ever seen him. And Chris could talk again, and he loved Jean. It was only Skye who...

Kal said good-night to David and took his guitar into the house. When her brother had left and Erika came in a moment later, she heard the shower running.

She went to check on Hiialo.

Hiialo had kicked her covers off and looked ready to roll out of bed. She slept with her mouth partway open. She wore one of Kal's T-shirts as a nightgown, and it was twisted around her little legs.

Carefully Erika picked her up and moved her to the center of the mattress where her head could rest on the pillow. Hiialo stirred just a little, and Erika said, "It's all right. It's just Erika."

Just Erika.

Suddenly weary of the uncertainty in her life, Erika straightened Hiialo's sheet and quilt and covered her, then retrieved Pincushion from where he was wedged against the wall and put him in Hiialo's arms.

In her sleep Hiialo murmured, "Thank you, Erika."

Erika's heart went warm. This was worth more than anything she had. For this she could live with her future unsettled. She whispered, "You're welcome, sweetie. Good night."

WHEN KAL CAME OUT of the bathroom, he saw light under Erika's door. He slipped into his room and pulled on some shorts and a T-shirt, then rapped on the door that adjoined their rooms, the door that was seldom opened.

"Come in."

He did.

Seeing him, she laid aside a drawing she'd been studying. "Hi, Kal."

"Hi."

He sat on the bed beside her, as he had many times before giving her a massage. David's appearance had made her forget their nightly ritual. It was her turn to be touched by him tonight.

She tried to relax. "How did it go? Playing?"

"Great." The jam session at Jakka's had made him euphoric, like a condemned man suddenly paroled. But they'd gotten into another argument over whether to start up the band again. He needed to wait and see if Erika stayed.

"I want a copy of your tape," she said. "Where can I buy it?"

"I'll give you one. I have a few."

"Let me pay you."

"Erika." Shaking his head, he stood up and went into his room. He returned a minute later with a tape case still wrapped in cellophane and handed it to her. "It's a gift."

"Thank you." The cover illustration looked like an acrylic. Kal and Danny and Jakka swimming through water wearing seaweed *leis*. And nothing else. "You had long hair."

"For a while."

She unwrapped the cellophane and took out the tape and the folded song sheet with the illustration. Inside were pictures of Kal and Jakka and Danny, looking four years, one hurricane and a death younger. Erika touched the picture of Kal's face. *You're so beautiful.* Remembering he was beside her, she read some of the lyrics, instead. All the songs were by K. Johnson or K. Johnson/J. Bennee. It was like holding his soul. She carefully folded the paper and returned it and the tape to the case. "Thank you, Kal."

"You're welcome." Why had she touched his picture that way? *She likes you, Kal. You like each other.* He liked

Erika enough that it had bothered him to come home and find a strange man in the house with her. Coming inside, he'd wondered if he was about to meet a part of her past she'd kept hidden. But it was just her brother.

Still, if he was going to be out at night much... "So, you said this morning you'd like a dog, Erika?"

He couldn't know how much. "Yes. Like I told you, I've almost always lived on boats. I couldn't have one."

The same way he couldn't have one until she came here. It mattered to him that there was something she wanted she'd never been able to have—and that he could give her.

"Akitas are independent," he said. "You have to work with them a lot and be assertive. It brings out the best in them."

One of his parents' beautiful Akita puppies... Erika frowned. "Do you think it's safe to have a dog like that around a child?" Then she wished she hadn't spoken. He would just belittle her fear.

"Depends on the kid—and the dog. You start with a good puppy and do the right things, and you should have a good dog. But any dog needs respect, and Akitas need ongoing obedience training. They're protective, and you don't want an animal who keeps your friends from visiting. If we got a puppy, we'd need to make sure it learned to accept commands from all of us, including Hiialo. And—like I said—the obedience work never stops. If you're really interested, let's borrow some of my folks' training books, eh?"

"Okay."

He eyed her sketchbook. "Show me what you did while I was gone."

"Oh. This."

Erika shared her drawing—three adolescents hitchhiking outside the Haena Store.

"That's good. I can't wait to see it when you're finished."

Her cheeks, flushed from the day on the beach, ripened more from his praise. Kal wondered if he'd ever tire of looking at her—or being around her. She was fingering the Kai Nui cassette case.

"Hey, Erika..."

She turned her head, her smooth brown hair moving in one sheet.

"Have you been doing what I suggested this morning?"

His eyes explained what he meant—*Sex is beautiful....*

"I don't believe it, Kal. What you said. Sex doesn't have anything to do with love, whatever people say. I can be crazy about someone, and it doesn't make a difference."

"Yeah, but that's not the kind of love I'm talking about."

The wind rushed past outside, carrying leaves.

Erika looked at him, and his eyes were intense. Serious.

"I'm talking about giving," he said. "You care about someone and try to make that person feel good. Sometimes it's better than other times, yeah? But it's a gift every time. It's not like, you have an orgasm, I have an orgasm. It's... being involved. Being close."

Her heart twisted. What did he mean? It wasn't like anything she'd read about sex.

But it sounded wise.

His eyes searched her face, studying her. Erika knew that expression, the one she probably wore when studying a nearly complete watercolor. Thoughtful. Preparing to act.

Her insides folded and turned on themselves with heat, unraveling.

Kal studied her mouth as he had earlier that night, and then he brought his face near hers and kissed her, his nose brushing hers in a light Hawaiian kiss to match the distant sound of the waves and the scents wafting through the window.

His hands circled her wrists, holding them, and she felt the calluses on his fingers that had come from making music. She smelled the soap on his skin, shampoo in his damp hair.

Give?

Give to Kal... Erika let her lips move slightly, bare millimeters, against his. She tried to kiss him more, but he eased gently back from her, his hands sliding up her arms, caressing her.

The touch of those hands had become familiar. And Erika realized she'd known all along that he could touch her like this, too. That he'd always been touching her this way.

Giving.

"Kal..."

He watched her eyes, waiting to find out just how much she hated sex. Her soft scared breaths whispered against his face, but she didn't try to move away, and Kal realized that something had shifted inside him. His tired craving for the impossible, for the dead to rise, had vanished.

"Baby..." It wasn't the word that was supposed to come out.

Erika heard it. Nobody had ever called her that.

Kal wanted to brush her brown hair back from her eyes, to slide his hands into it and hold her head as he kissed her again. He throbbed with wanting.

But this was like the back rubs. She dispensed her trust in thimblefuls. She'd just given him another one, and he should collect it and put it with the rest and not count it for more than it was.

Kal put his feet on the ground and stood. He tried to slip back into the platonic mode, tried to conjure up the distance of friendship.

Too late.

And he was the one who'd sworn he would never love anyone else after Maka. Stupid thing to say. To write. To believe.

"I'll get some books from my folks about dog training so you'll know what you're getting into."

"Thank you." A dog. They might get a dog.

He had kissed her.

Kal wanted to touch her again. Kiss her more. He edged toward the door to his room. "Good night."

Their eyes met again, and then he went out, closing the door behind him.

Erika locked her arms around herself and whispered inaudibly, "Oh, God. Oh, God." She was praying and didn't know what for.

CHAPTER ELEVEN

WHEN HE GOT HOME from work the following night, a woman and a boy he didn't know were visiting with Erika and Hiialo, and music was playing. His.

He'd barely come through the door when the beautiful athletic-looking woman on the couch got up and said, "Hi, I'm Jean, David's wife. Boy, your music's really great."

Kal recognized the model from Erika's prints. "Thanks." It was good to hear the tape—in a way that it hadn't been for many years.

After Jean introduced Erika's nephew, Chris, Kal ate some antacid tablets he'd forgotten to take to work, then helped with dinner. Putting on the rice, he noticed Hiialo huddling close to Erika's legs, never more than a few inches away from her.

"Hiialo," he said, "why don't you go play with Chris? Erika's going to fall over you."

Erika turned from cutting mangoes into halves. She touched Hiialo's hair. "She's fine, Kal." Hiialo's face showed so much consternation and uncertainty that Erika put down the knife and picked her up.

"Erika." A sandy-haired boy with a deep resemblance to his father got up from where he'd been folding paper at the coffee table with his stepmother. "See what I made you."

A paper crane. Origami. "How beautiful!" said Erika. "Thank you. I'm going to put it right here on the windowsill."

Hiialo buried her face in Erika's neck, and Erika hugged her more tightly. She'd been surprised by Hiialo's sudden possessiveness of her, first evidenced when David's family stopped by that morning. But at the moment Hiialo's attachment to her was comforting.

The day had been emotional, her happiness slowly deflating like an old balloon. She hadn't expected it to be so hard to hear Chris call Jean "Mom." She hadn't expected to feel such envy of Jean's pregnancy. Seeing her at all was difficult.

Her sister-in-law's thick curly hair swirled down her back like ribbons of gold. Her complexion was flawless, her body supple and slim. Jean's youth and beauty made Erika feel old in comparison, and she had dreaded Kal's coming home and seeing them side by side. He was like the dreams of her childhood, dreams she'd forgotten until she saw caring for her in his eyes. She didn't want to wake up.

Footsteps tromped on the lanai.

Kal said, "Looks like your brother found my mom and dad." David had gone down to the Haena Store to pick up some *shoyu*.

Through the front window, Erika saw King telling Raiden to sit, to lie down and to stay. "Can't Raiden come in?"

She was still holding Hiialo. Kal thought, *Erika, I want you.* "I think Dad's putting him on a long down. It's an obedience thing." He hoped his parents had brought over one of their dog-training books. Kal had called them from work that day and asked if Erika could borrow some.

Chris, still standing near Erika, peered out the window. "Oh, cool! It's an Akita. We saw some in Japan."

At nine Chris was already well traveled.

Turned sideways, talking to Mary Helen, David came in the house. He was saying, "The ship we'd chartered had ice problems, so we decided to cut our losses. We'll go back, but we thought we'd spend a month here first."

"I'll bet Erika's glad to see you," said King, who was holding three books. He smiled at her, his granddaughter and his son, then looked back and forth across the room, ready to meet Chris and Jean. Kal introduced everybody.

Recognizing her son's music, Mary Helen said, "Is that the radio?"

"Tape," Kal answered.

"It sounds nice." Mary Helen gave Erika and Hiialo a quick shared embrace. "How is everyone? I came over to peek at your paintings, Erika. Kal said you've finished quite a few."

Erika was pleased. "I'd love to show you. Can you stay for dinner?"

"We'd be delighted."

King handed the books to Kal. "Here you go. Let me know if you want me to hang on to one of Jin's litter for you. Kumi's are all sold. Danny bought one."

Erika's knee was starting to hurt. "I have to put you down, Hiialo." Setting her on the floor, she asked, "Would you like to help me make drinks for everyone?"

Chris bobbed up from the seat he'd just taken in a chair two feet away from Erika. "Can I help?"

"No," said Hiialo. "This is my house."

Her rudeness embarrassed Erika. Kal just lifted his eyebrows, but Mary Helen gave Erika a sympathetic glance and said, "Hiialo, dear."

Hiialo's face showed her acute insecurity. Erika crouched beside her and whispered so that no one else could hear, "Don't you want to show Chris what a good hostess you are? We can let him take the ice out of the ice trays."

Her eyes brimmed with tears. "No."

Kal and King exchanged looks of resignation.

Chris, showing the maturity of the older child, said, "It's okay, Erika. I'll make more origami."

David set the bottle of *shoyu* on the counter and looked inquisitively at Erika and Hiialo. Even at four, Chris had never behaved that way. But at four, Chris had been trapped in silence.

As Erika straightened up, King said to Hiialo, "How about a hug for your grandpa?"

Kal saw that lines of concern had creased Erika's forehead. He came over to the window to be near her. That night after Hiialo was in bed, they should talk. It occurred to him to ask David a few things about his sister. But it was David's first wife Erika's fiancé had slept with before she killed herself.

They ate on the porch, spreading out on the glider and on a bench under the window. Kal and Erika sat on the top step, with Hiialo huddled at Erika's feet, subdued but well behaved.

After dinner Erika took Mary Helen back to her room to share her most recent work, including the newest watercolor of the hitchhikers at the Haena Store, which she had painted that morning. Kal's mother was enthusiastic about all the pieces, especially those of Hiialo.

"You've really caught her vibrancy."

The word made Erika smile, and Mary Helen smiled, too, as though conjuring a mental picture of her granddaughter's "vibrancy."

Would Kal's mother have insight into his parenting style? Erika decided it was a safe topic. "You know, Kal and I have some disagreement over how to treat Hiialo."

Mary Helen lifted her eyes.

"I'm a person who always tries to foresee what's going to happen in the next moment. With a child, I try to anticipate possible accidents so that they can be avoided. And

Kal..." Erika's sigh was the buildup of weeks of frustration and anxiety. She didn't finish.

Mary Helen turned back to the watercolors, focusing on the hitchhikers. Her lips curved into an expression both thoughtful and wise. "You know," she said, "I think I know just how you feel."

Erika started. *Did* Mary Helen know?

"Look at this painting." Kal's mother regarded the hitchhikers. "Now, my parents always taught me that hitchhiking was dangerous." She faced Erika. "King, on the other hand, grew up hitching rides from tourists. And so you can just imagine the confrontation the day Leo first thumbed a ride home from Hanalei." She echoed Erika's earlier sigh.

"Erika, this is very difficult to accept, but in Hawaii it helps to remember the original meaning of the word *haole*. It didn't mean Caucasian. It meant foreigner. The longer I've lived here, the more I've seen that there are many ways to do things. And they aren't necessarily better or worse. Just different." Thoughtfully she regarded the *hau* tree outside the window. "If you look at Hiialo, for instance. She's wildly spontaneous and sometimes very naughty. But I also find her refreshingly brave, in a way none of my children were with the caution I tried to instill in them."

Erika twisted her hands together. Brave was all right. But children needed protection.

"The other part of it, I'm afraid," said Kal's mother soberly, "is Maka." Suddenly she blinked quickly, dug a tissue from her pocket, and dabbed at her eyes.

Horror crept over Erika. She'd made Mary Helen cry. But no, it was Maka. She stepped forward, wanting to offer comfort.

"I'm sorry. It was just so sad, so hard for Kal." Mary Helen sniffed and put away the tissue. "That accident— and Iniki, too, and what happened with his music—made Kal just a little bit fatalistic, Erika. I don't know what else to say.'' She arranged her face in happy lines and concluded the discussion. "Except that I'm glad you're here. You're so good for both of them.''

Erika pondered Mary Helen's feet in their casual slippers. A woman from the Midwest who had made Hawaii her home.

Raising her eyes, she said, "Thank you. For saying all of that."

Mary Helen answered, "I just wish there'd been someone to say it to me." She gave Erika a quick hug, and together they left the room.

WHEN KING AND Mary Helen had departed with Raiden, the others put on swimsuits and went down to the beach. As usual Hiialo ran into the water without waiting for anyone else, and Erika saw her brother wearing a faint frown of disapproval.

"Can I go in, too, Dad?"

"Yes," said David.

Erika watched Chris approach the water and scan the reef for urchins and stingrays. His caution was in marked contrast to Hiialo's full-speed-ahead confidence, and after her talk with Mary Helen, Erika found herself appreciating the latter. Kal's way of doing things had merit, too.

Not wanting to invite comparison between her body and that of her sister-in-law, Erika wore her sarong as she sat on the beach talking to her brother. Kal went into the water with Hiialo and Chris and Jean.

David said, "I like him, Erika."

So do I.

The waves roared, broke on the shore.

"The kid's a live wire."

Hiialo had done her jet-rocket imitation several times since he'd been there, running through the house, leaping off the porch. Sprinting for the sea and plunging in splashing. "She has a lot of energy. It's the way she is."

David smiled. "I wasn't criticizing. I'm glad you like her. And she seems to like you." The sun turned his face Burnt Umber as he squinted at the others playing in the surf.

Kal dove for something under the water and come up holding a hermit crab. It bit his finger. He yelped, over-dramatizing, and Hiialo and Chris had hysterics. Erika glanced at her brother, but David's eyes were on his wife, full of adoration.

He said, "I think I'm going to get wet." Soon he was out in the water with Jean.

Erika saw them playing, splashing... kissing.

Kal was entertaining the two kids by letting them take turns diving from his shoulders. Standing up, Erika removed her sarong and walked down to the water.

Chris yelled, "Hey, Hiialo, want to build a sand castle?"

"Hooray!"

As the children ran in, leaping over the foam, Erika dove into a wave and swam away from shore. The sea was like paint water, a Hooker's Green and Cerulean Blue wash.

Spotting Erika, Kal swam toward her. Somewhere behind him, Jean was wrapped around David in the water, the two of them glittery sunset wet, kissing. He'd held Maka like that a few times in the ocean, her legs embracing him. They'd been young.

Water beaded on Erika's lashes. What would it be like to hold her that close, only swimsuits separating them?

He moved nearer her, and they both stood on the sandy bottom, the ocean trying to push their feet out from under them as the surface spread around their shoulders. "Your brother and sister-in-law seem pretty crazy about each other."

"Yes... Well. They have a lot in common. For instance, they're both marine biologists. And martial artists."

"Really?"

"Tae kwon do. My dad did it, too." Erika admitted, "I never took to it. I don't like getting hit."

"I wouldn't like your getting hit, either. We have some things in common, too."

She turned away in the water. "Some things."

Kal's hands touched her bare waist. Wet. Soft. It reminded him of Maka. But the memory hurt only a little.

Erika let him draw her closer, and he spun her slowly around to face him. She saw water clinging to the edge of his scar. She saw her own image in his eyes.

He kissed her.

Feeling swelled her throat. She glanced toward the beach and the children and slipped away from him, swam farther from shore.

Kal followed her. Treading water beside her, he said, "So, your brother thinks Hiialo's pretty naughty."

"No, he doesn't!" While Kal dove beneath the surface and came up, Erika reached a decision. She ought to tell him about Chris. Once it had seemed too personal. Now she wanted him to know. "Kal, from the time Chris was three until he was six, he didn't talk."

Floating on a wave with her, Kal stared.

"He saw his mother go over the bow rail. Afterward he forgot everything. And he was mute."

The boy on the shore was dumping a bucket of water into a moat he and Hiialo had dug. Watching him point to something and speak to Hiialo, Kal recalled Erika saying, long ago, that Chris had hung around her while she painted. He remembered her telling Hiialo that she couldn't have a conversation and paint at the same time.

Now her mouth was bent with unhappiness and pain. Chris had seen his mother kill herself. The thought made him sick. Whoever David's first wife had been, he didn't like her. He'd never known anyone like that. "This woman sounds evil."

"She wasn't. Just...selfish. And messed up. She wasn't strong." Erika frowned. "I think each of us is the product of our life experiences. My childhood was good. Hers... Well, none of us know what it was." Why had Skye killed herself? What was the final trigger? A hastily spoken accusation that had sent her back into painful feelings born in childhood?

Erika shivered. She couldn't even discuss it with David anymore. He'd moved on. He was happy now.

This was her own burden. It always would be.

Fooling around in the water, eyeing the fuzzy silhouette of a dogfish two yards below, Kal considered what she'd said. Selfishness. It was what he and Maka had accused each other of when they fought. His music. Her hula. They'd both wanted to work nights. They'd compromised often. He'd become better because of her and she because of him. That was love.

Erika... Could he learn different lessons from her? Sure. But her past upset him; he recoiled from anything sordid. And what she'd told him was the stuff of horror.

She'd drifted away, twenty feet or so, and he swam over to her. "So how did Chris communicate with you?"

"Some sign language, but mostly just in his own way." The conversation had brought back those days on the *Skye,* the wheelchair, her prison. As the surf washed over her shoulders, Erika watched the children in the sand, one who had never completely been hers, one who might never be. "I think I'm going to go play with them."

"Sure." He swam with her toward the shore, but lingered in the foamy shallows to watch her limp out of the water, a goddess in human disguise. Namakaokahai of the ocean. But in fact, Erika the woman was more noble. A human who had triumphed over ugliness. *The battle's still going on, Kal.*

Sex.

She wouldn't have to wage that one alone. If she could learn to trust him...

Chris called, "Are you going to help us with our castle, Erika?"

From the surf, Kal watched Hiialo scramble to her feet and position herself in front of Erika's legs like a miniature Akita defending her own.

In a voice for the world to hear, she told Chris, "This is my new mom."

ON THE BEACH Erika swallowed, her heart racing. Hiialo hadn't really said that.

Chris, a bright boy with a stepmother of his own, asked, "Erika, are you going to marry Kal?"

"Oh, Chris..." She faltered. Where were David and Jean? Where was Kal? Had anyone else heard?

Yes, Kal had. Spinning her head toward the low breakers, she saw his face. Dumbfounded. Then, catching her eye, he shrugged and grinned before ducking under the water and swimming farther from shore.

Hiialo tugged on Erika's hand. "Pick me up."

Absently Erika said, "Magic word."

"Please."

Lifting her, in her wet and sandy swimsuit, Erika saw that Hiialo's eyes were fastened defiantly on Chris. She didn't really believe what she'd said; she couldn't. It was just a challenge, a way of marking her territory.

But Chris was watching Erika, waiting for an answer.

"I don't know." She eyed the round face of the little girl in her arms, and there was nothing to do but sigh.

And secretly wish that what Hiialo had said would come true.

"DO YOU THINK I should straighten her out tomorrow?" asked Erika as Kal rubbed her back that night.

He slid his fingers under the straps of her tank top, noting her slight shiver at the touch. Massaging her shoulders gently, he wished he could say the words in his mind. Soothing love words. Gentling sex words. His fingers slipped down her sides.

More quivering.

"Do you?" she repeated.

Think she should tell Hiialo that she wasn't her new mom? Kal said carefully, "That might be premature."

Premature? Did that mean he wanted to marry her?

She felt him move, the mattress sinking beside her, and rolled onto her side. "Kal?"

He lay facing her. They stared at each other, bodies inches apart.

Kal waited until he was sure she wouldn't move away. Then he reached up and smoothed back her hair. "I want to kiss you."

The words were soft, but she knew what he'd said. She shifted closer on the mattress, and so did he, and he kissed her.

Erika shook. *Give,* she reminded herself. It wasn't hard.

Sensing trust in her lips, Kal wrapped his arm around her, pulling her close. But he hadn't lain in bed with his body against a woman's since Maka, and it was Maka who came to him, a soul-vision filling up his mind, making his eyes burn.

The emotion shocked him. He'd thought it was over. Upset, he pulled away.

Erika saw his face, his confusion, as he rolled onto his back. His hand groped for hers on the mattress, and their fingers wove together.

"Kal?"

Think about her, he thought. *Think about Erika.*

He sat up, searching for something appropriate to say. Some excuse. But when he saw her brown eyes watching him, he didn't want to lie. And the truth was unspeakable. You couldn't tell a woman that kissing her had made you miss your dead wife.

He stroked her hair and bent to kiss her forehead. "I'll see you in the morning."

"Is anything wrong?"

"Not with you." He hugged her. "Everything's fine."

He got up, and Erika stared at his back and saw the door close behind him as he went out.

What's wrong, Kal?

Had she done something wrong? That had to be it: he didn't like the way she'd kissed him. It was too awful to ponder, that after all this *she* repulsed *him*.

To get rid of the thoughts, she crawled across the bed and took one of the Johnsons's dog-training books from her nightstand. *The Art of Raising a Puppy* by the Monks of New Skete. It took her a long time to focus, to shake off what had just happened with Kal, but soon she was absorbed, and she read the introduction and three chapters.

By then it was past eleven and her eyes were drifting shut. Kal was probably already asleep. She should go to sleep, too.

Erika got up and opened her door to go down the hall to the bathroom.

A bed creaked. It was in Kal's room, and she heard his feet hit the floor. Starting down the hall, she schooled herself not to glance through the beads into his room.

But as she reached the bathroom, she heard a drawer open, and her head jerked toward his door by its own volition.

Through the beads she saw him.

There was a photograph in his hand. He was putting it into a shoe box in his desk drawer, a box full of other photos.

He must have known she was there, because he turned his back as he shut the drawer. Erika quickly did the same,

to pretend she hadn't seen. She pushed open the bathroom door and slipped inside.

When the closed door hid them from each other, she
drew a breath. But her heart was pounding and she felt
sick. The knowledge was so crushing that she clung to one
of the towel racks, drawing deep breaths.

He wasn't over Maka.

THROUGH THE DANGLING bead curtain, Kal looked at the
closed bathroom door. She hadn't seen. Wouldn't think
anything if she had. It was his guilt doing this.

The ancient Hawaiians had believed you shouldn't keep
a dead person's possessions close to you, that it caused
their souls to stay near in an unhealthy way. Was that what
was happening to him?

But these were only photos. Iniki had taken everything
else. Everything but the quilt in which he'd wrapped himself and his daughter those nights at the shelter.

Casting another glance toward the bathroom, Kal
opened the drawer again and removed the shoe box. He
slid the closet door open and put the box on the highest
shelf, on top of some photograph albums and videos of
Maka dancing—the remains of their past.

He shut the door, and when Erika came out of the
bathroom, he stepped out into the hall and said, "Hey,
good night." He put his arm around her and hugged her,
and she smiled before she hurried down the hall to her
room.

He watched the light disappear as she closed herself inside, and he stood in the hallway and told himself again
that she hadn't seen him with Maka's picture.

ERIKA COULD SEE no change in his treatment of her, and
she tried to forget what had happened Friday night. Saturday, after Hiialo was asleep, she massaged his back, and

when she was done they embraced, cheek to cheek, and he kissed her briefly and warmly, looking long into her eyes.

He's still getting over Maka. It's not going to happen all at once. She told herself that whenever she remembered the shoe box in his drawer.

Sunday night David took the three of them—Kal, Hiialo and Erika—out to dinner in Hanalei with his family. They were going to the Hunakai, a seafood restaurant and bar. As they waited for the hostess to return from seating some people, Hiialo exclaimed, "Look! Hula! Can we go watch?"

She was gazing out the front window at a park across the street where two men in short sarongs were running along the walkways lighting torches.

Kal picked her up. "Sorry, Ti-leaf, we've got a dinner reservation."

Jean leaned around them to peer out the window.

"Please," begged Hiialo.

The hostess arrived to seat them.

"Blade, party of six," David said.

Kal shook his head at his daughter.

"I wouldn't mind seeing some hula myself." Jean shrugged at Erika. "I guess they'll be gone when we're done eating."

"Yeah." Kal kept his back to the window, though even from across the street they could all hear the long eerie blast of a conch shell.

Hiialo's face began to quiver, to melt into unhappiness.

The hostess led the way into the shadows of the restaurant, and David waited for the women to follow. Erika went ahead. Outside, behind her, the hula drum beat. *It must make him think of Maka.* There was no way it couldn't. Did it bother Kal to see hula now? How did he feel about Hiialo's interest?

When they reached the table, David pulled out a chair for her and another for Jean. As she sat down, Erika heard a familiar sound—sniffling—and saw that Hiialo, in Kal's arms, had begun to cry because she couldn't see the dancers.

Kal said to David, "Excuse me. We're going outside for a minute."

Erika hoped he wasn't taking her to the park; she'd been told no.

But he was carrying her in the opposite direction, toward the back door. When Hiialo realized this, she began to scream. Patrons all over the restaurant gaped. Her wail rose and fell like a siren as Kal slipped out the back door. Sitting quietly in his seat, Chris stared after them with an expression of amazement that anyone could behave so badly.

Jean and David opened their menus, and so did Erika, but her heart and her thoughts were outside, and she barely heard the conversation around her for the next fifteen minutes, until Kal and Hiialo returned.

THE FEELING AT THE TABLE wavered from relaxed to tense while Kal and Erika tried to keep Hiialo happy, giving her anything she asked for to preserve the peace. But whenever the adults began talking, she grew bored and misbehaved, blowing the paper on her straw across the room— much to Chris's amusement—playing with her silverware, kicking the legs of the table.

She had eaten half her dessert and was looking cranky again when Kal felt hands on his shoulders and looked up.

The owner of the Hunakai, a guy who'd gone to school with his brother Keale, said, "Howzit, Kal?" He smiled at the other guests. *"Ono?"*

Tasty.

"Very," said David.

Seeming satisfied, the owner turned to Kal and spoke quietly. "Hey, I saw Jakka Bennee the other day. He said you guys are getting Kai Nui together again. How 'bout a Fourth of July gig?''

Erika's eyes were riveted to Kal's face. She saw his surprise, but he hid it fast.

"Love to. Let's talk about it.''

"Good.'' The owner clapped him on the shoulder, nodded to the rest of them and left the table.

Kal stared at his plate, wondering why Jakka had said they were a band again. They'd talked about it Thursday night, but nothing had been decided. Now he'd accepted a gig—without even discussing it with Erika.

Erika...

He looked across the table, trying to catch her eye.

Erika smiled. "Good,'' she said, and then turned to the fish on her plate. But her appetite was gone.

Because of her, Kal could play music again. He would be grateful. But how would he ever separate that from his feelings for her? Would he even try? Or had he simply accepted what he'd said in his letter, that he would never love another woman the way he'd loved Maka?

"Hey, Erika.''

His low voice summoned her from her thoughts.

Across the table he smiled, and his eyes were a kiss.

But the timing was all wrong—too soon after he'd gotten the gig—and it intensified rather than extinguished the doubts in her heart.

As HE RUBBED her shoulders that night, he said, "Sorry about the Fourth. Saying yes without asking you.''

"It's fine.''

It wasn't fine, thought Kal. It was complicated. She'd been with him three weeks. He'd promised her three more to make up her mind about Hiialo. And since then everything had changed. One gig was no big deal, but he knew Jakka and Danny wanted more. It was a commitment he couldn't make. Not till he knew Erika would be there for Hiialo.

He stopped rubbing her shoulders and lay down beside her as he had two nights before. She rolled onto her side to look at him.

Kal wasn't afraid of the Maka feeling coming back. He'd figured out the problem. Firsts. Most of them had happened in the year after she died. First Christmas without her. First birthday without her.

But he'd forgotten about first kiss.

First sex would be something else.

Just part of going on.

As he hugged her, Erika let her body slide alongside his. It felt good. Only her doubts bothered her. When she felt his lips touch hers, she wondered if he wished she was Maka. It wasn't something she could ask.

His mouth formed a word on hers. "Erika..."

"What?"

He shifted, and she felt the shape of his erection through their clothes. His hand touched her jaw, and she saw his eyes and spun in them.

She'd never felt this way before, when all she wanted was to gaze into a man's eyes and never stop. Helpless, she knew the truth.

I love you.

He was talking. "I know how I asked you to come here. We both know everything's changed." He moved his face against her cheek, getting closer to her, and his nose stroked her skin. "I don't want you to leave."

Heat saturated her body, pouring into her legs, one of which was somehow between his, skin to skin. What was he saying?

"But I can't have a celibate marriage to you." He pressed his lips to her jaw, let them creep up her face. Her mouth was looking for his, too, and they kissed again, drawing closer. When he looked at her, those brown, almost black eyes were open, wholly present.

He said, "I love you."

Her breath stretched. *He loves me.* The arms around her, the face so near to hers. The friend who'd seemed too faraway ever since that night she'd seen him with a photograph. But this was Kal, who had told her that love was giving. And he loved her.

He kissed her again.

"Kal..." It felt like the beginning of sex, but she didn't care. There was no man she trusted so much.

Kal turned his head, coaxed her mouth open with his. *It's all right, Erika. This is how we go farther.*

His tongue slid inside.

She kissed him back, and he knew she didn't know she was rubbing against him, trying to get closer. It lasted quite a while, and he wanted much more. As he pulled his mouth away, he watched her. She didn't move her hands from his shoulders. Her lips were flushed, her face bright, too. Her eyes were misty.

"You," he said softly, "are not frigid."

"I don't want to get hurt." She didn't mean to say it, but it came out.

"There you go again," he said softly. "Worrying. Why don't you think, instead, that here's this guy who loves me and maybe it'll work out?"

Her heart heaved, and she placed one of her hands in one of his.

Kal kissed her again and did not say what *he* was thinking. That if anyone got hurt, it would probably be him.

CHAPTER TWELVE

AFTER HE'D SAID good-night to her, he went out on the porch to play guitar, but he ended up laying aside the instrument and staring out at the hot humid night. She'd said, *I don't want to get hurt.*

She'd been hurt before, by her fiancé. Maybe by other guys.

Kal had married Maka when he was barely twenty, after she'd been his girlfriend for more than a year. He'd had sex once before that, on the beach after a party, with a girl who liked his voice and the way he played the guitar. In a half-drunken state, he'd realized what he was doing. He still remembered feeling, *This is intense. This is real life.* Then he'd looked into the blurred face of a stranger and pulled out and said, "I don't want to do this."

Maka hadn't changed him that way; she'd proved him right. Sex was like...getting a puppy. You were inviting someone to fall in love with you, and if you turned your back...

He wasn't going to turn his back on Erika. He knew that already. But unless they made some real promises, he wasn't sure she wouldn't do that to him.

She wasn't Maka.

And her feelings about sex differed from his in more ways than one.

THE NEXT DAY Adele called to say that she wanted to publish three of Erika's paintings as prints. Erika met Kal after work with an ecstatic hug, and his parents, hearing the news, decided to host a spur-of-the-moment potluck to celebrate her success and Kal's new gig. It was the start of a busy two weeks.

On evenings when he and Erika and Hiialo weren't busy with David's family, Kal played music with Danny and Jakka at Jakka's house in Kalihiwai, on the other side of Hanalei Bay. When he was home, he practiced with the band tape they'd made. He wanted the Fourth of July show to be great—the start of a comeback.

If all went well, it would be the start of something else, too.

Something more important.

Erika.

On the Fourth of July, she would have been in Haena more than five weeks.

ON THE FOURTH, he and Erika and Hiialo gathered on the beach to light fireworks with David's family. The kids would be going to his parents' house for the evening, Hiialo to spend the night because he'd be out so late. Chris would stay only till midnight; David and Jean wanted to see Kai Nui play, but because she was pregnant, they wouldn't stay till the end.

When the last sparklers had been lit, David and Jean corralled the children into their rental, and Erika and Kal got into the Datsun to drive to Hanalei to the Hunakai.

Kal was wearing white cotton twill pants and a beige aloha shirt with navy blue guitar players on it. Erika wore a thigh-length emerald green silk dress with no sleeves. It was Kal's favorite of her dresses—and the color seemed like a good omen. The same shade as something he wanted to give her. The small square box weighed down his shirt pocket. He'd lock it in the trunk before the show. And afterward . . .

As he turned the car down the street beside the Huna-kai, planning to pull into the back lot, Erika spotted a sign in front of the community center. Bon Dance Club. "Kal, what's that?"

Obon. It was that time again. It hit him as it did every year, perhaps because his parents used to take them all *bon* dancing in the summers. The festival marked the years. Since Maka had died, it had marked the years without her. He didn't know why.

"What did you say?" He couldn't remember what Erika had asked.

"What's a *bon* dance club? They have clubs? I thought it was a Buddhist thing."

"Well, the dancing has become pretty secular. People still go to temples to dance but also to these clubs. *Bon* dance clubs have musicians or taped music for the dances. Sometimes they have dancers who perform alone. Sometimes the dancers travel, like the Akanas. You can join a *bon* dance club and go every weekend."

"Do you think we could go visit the Akanas?" asked Erika. "I'd really like to do that."

"I'm sure they're traveling with their troupe now."

Erika was disappointed. *Obon* appealed to her. Her life had been altered by death. Her parents'. But even more, Skye's. Maybe honoring it somehow would help. Help to shed the guilt.

And maybe if Kal went, he would stop missing Maka.

He loves you.

He'd only said it once, and sometimes Erika wasn't sure she believed it. For the past two weeks, he'd been wrapped up in the band, sometimes coming home too late for their back-rub ritual.

But she treasured the memory of a night she'd awakened in the dark to find him covering her up. He'd kissed her good-night, with soft words and a brief embrace that left her able to drift easily back into sleep, his voice and touch imprinted on her mind and heart.

As he turned into the narrow lot behind the Hunakai, Kal noticed her silence. *Bon dances.* She wanted to go. He should take her. His parents knew several dances. They could teach her, and he could take her to a *bon* dance club some weekend. It didn't have to mean anything; it never had when he was a child or a teenager. It was just a thing his family had done.

He parked behind the restaurant, and Erika gathered her purse and pulled on her door handle. Kal almost reached out to stop her, just to say, *I'll take you bon dancing, Erika.*

But the grief, the hurt of the past, stopped him.

He knew what the *bon* dances meant. And he couldn't dance with joy that Maka had moved on. He wasn't that generous.

He'd never wanted her to go.

He opened his door, and the trade winds gusted in and brought her voice into his mind, answering him.

That's why I've never gone.

Erika was already out of the car. Kal paused, gazing at a hole in the interior of the driver door.

Bon-odori.

Maybe this was the way the souls of the dead came back. By speaking through the subconscious of the living. But it felt like Maka in his heart. Real Maka, loving him.

In that moment Kal knew that she *was* there, had been there since the day she died. Maybe she slunk through his house in a *mo'o's* guise as Eduardo, playing with his little girl. Maybe she hovered around his head and shoulders, keeping close to him in his pain. But Kal knew now the power of his own love for her, of the love they'd shared.

She'd never turned away.

And she never would—until he let her go.

"Is EVERYBODY HAVING a good time?"

The screams and shouts from the dance floor were deafening, muted only slightly by the earplugs Kal had given her. It was after midnight, and Erika stood against the wall, some distance from the stage. David and Jean had already left, and now she was alone, a spectator because she didn't dance.

From the shadows, she watched Kal at the microphone. He was sweating, his hair wet with perspiration, as he grinned at the responsive crowd.

"One more song, and then we're gonna take a break. This is a dedication."

Erika hadn't thought he knew where she was standing, but his wink hit her with the accuracy of a laser, and when he strummed that first chord, she recognized the song. "I Wanna Be Your Man."

Her heart swelled, the way it did when he kissed her. The way it had when he said he loved her. But as he played, his joy seemed more intense than love, than anything Erika had known that could happen between a man and a woman. She wondered again if it was *her* that he loved.

Or simply the freedom to be where he now stood.

She watched his body, his touch with the guitar, the grin he rained on the crowd, the way he moved. He seemed like some god, unattainable, whose attention to a mortal woman could only end in tragedy.

She wasn't like him. She wasn't beautiful enough. Her body was ravaged. And the way she'd lived in that wheelchair. The indignity. She didn't ever want him to know how she'd been. He would be disgusted. Even if he *didn't* feel that, she did.

Watching him on the stage, she faced what she'd known the first time she'd seen his picture.

That the highest love was for the beautiful.

And that she was not among them, while Kal was.

If he loved her, as he'd said, it was for his daughter and for his life, his music. He could not be *in love* with Erika Blade.

AFTER THE SHOW Erika helped Kal get his equipment together in the back room and waited while he loaded the car. Although Jakka and Danny were friendly, she felt out of place. What did she know about music, about this late-night scene? It was obviously something they'd all done many times before, and she pictured Maka with them, knowing which electrical cords belonged to Kal, helping coil them.

Or maybe just knowing how to speak pidgin with Jakka and Danny.

Erika only knew better than to try.

But when she climbed into the Datsun with Kal, when the doors were shut, the tension rolled off her body and evaporated. This was Kal, her friend, who rubbed her shoulders at night, who hugged and kissed her before he left for work, who had, just two days before, left a note on her pillow that said, *Sex is beautiful.*

Her doubts faded into the night.

"You're so good, Kal."

"Thanks." He grinned at her as he started the car, and then he leaned over and kissed her mouth. "Gonna be my number-one fan?"

I want to be.

I Wanna Be Your Man.

She had to believe. She'd been reading to Hiialo. When the fairy godmother came and provided a dress, you put it on. You could worry about the pumpkin coach and the midnight curfew later.

"Yes," she said. "I think I already am."

He didn't put the car in gear. He maneuvered over the stick shift to hug her. "I love you."

Wear the dress, stupid. "I love you, Kal."

Their eyes locked and the stars swirled and the waltz began. Erika felt the warm skin of his neck against her cheek and knew that she'd never known anything so divine. *He does love me. He's not a man who would lie about love. This is Kal. Kal...*

He sang as he drove toward Haena, stopping in the middle of songs to ask her questions. "Did you hear that weird bass thing in the middle of 'Kona'?" And, "Were the lights too bright?"

She pushed back the seat and felt as relaxed as she had after surfing Polihale. It was so easy.

Before they reached Haena, Kal pulled off the road and parked the car.

Erika sat up. "What are we doing?"

"Introducing you to a new beach." He grabbed an old wool blanket from the back seat. Erika waited, accepting his quick kiss before she opened her door. Close by, waves crashed.

As she stood hugging herself in the breezy night, Kal rustled around in the trunk, undoubtedly checking his equipment. "Ready?"

"Yes."

He came around the car to collect her, to take her hand. She clung to it tightly, and sometimes to his arm, as they hiked down a rocky trail to the water. Kal spread the blanket in the sand on a vine of *hunakai*, white beach morning glories, and they both sat down.

Erika drew a breath, inhaling the night. Overhead a sprawling ironwood tree leaned toward the sea, dividing the view of sky, but between its limbs she could see the stars. "This is beautiful."

"Thanks. I told the Visitors' Bureau to make it just for you."

He was teasing. Affectionate. When Erika turned to give him a look, she saw the box in his hands.

"Except I hope you're not just a visitor."

Her heart thudded too hard. She forgot to breathe and couldn't help glancing at the box again.

"It's what you think."

She lifted her eyes.

His tilted up a little at the corners. "Want it?"

Erika edged back slightly. *Just ask, Kal. Don't do this to me.* But he *was* just asking. She should just answer. "Yes."

Kal moved to surround her with his legs. Erika's own stretched out under his bent right knee. She studied the shadows in the folds of white fabric. He was silent, and at last she looked at him.

"Will you marry me, Erika?"

Her eyes got hot. Dammit, couldn't she ever keep from crying? "Yes."

Kal held her, tears and silky strands of her hair under his cheek. His hands found her spine through her dress, found all the muscles and hollows he knew. "I'm asking you to make love with me, Erika. To be my real wife."

Real wife. She quaked, made herself small to be closer to him. "Yes. I want to be your real wife."

His legs pressed around her, all of him holding her, and it was safe, the safest place she'd ever been. She tried to wipe her eyes and he pulled back. "You can use my sleeve. I empty my pockets before shows. I don't have a handkerchief."

"I have a tissue." She found it, and she laughed as she blew her nose. "I'm sorry I always do this."

"I'm not." Smiling, Kal opened the lid of the box and sang some words from a David Lindley song, asking for her hand.

Her left hand. Erika couldn't remember giving it to René. She recalled how she'd received that ring at a jewelry store. It had been a conscience gift. She'd gone months with no symbol of their betrothal, only his words, which were worth little.

Giving her hand to Kal was different. He held it and kissed it before he slipped something cool and metallic over her finger. Erika looked down. In the moonlight, she saw an emerald. The ring was thick, textured, gold.

"It's a *haku lei.* I had a guy in Kapaa make it."

"It's beautiful, Kal." Not wanting to take her hand from his, she leaned closer to examine it.

His musician's fingers stroked her cheek. Then he gently twisted the band against her skin. "How does it feel? Too snug?"

"I think it's right. It won't come off." *Ever,* she vowed silently. Kal was not René. And she would fulfill the promise she'd made.

Fear stole over her.

What *had* she promised?

All of love.

Panic-stricken, she repeated the words he'd taught her. *Sex is beautiful. When you love each other. Sex is beautiful. When you love*...

How soon? When would it have to happen?

Kal read the fear on her down-turned face, like Hiialo when she was nervous or uncertain. But Hiialo had the sense to lift her brown eyes to him, to say the name she called him.

Erika had forgotten how to love or trust like a child.

I can teach you, he thought. But all he said was, "So you still owe me a back rub."

Her eyes did look at him then, just like Hiialo's. *You won't make me do it tonight?*

He treated her as he would have Hiialo when his daughter was avoiding a scary inevitability. Never releasing her left hand, he used his other hand to smooth her hair away from her eyes and gently told her again that it would really happen. "We'll have a nice long honeymoon."

She nodded, frozen-faced, and Kal had to quiet more than a ripple of misgiving in his own heart.

What if she never learned to love sex?

"DADDY, YOU WOKE ME UP," Hiialo said, rubbing her eyes the next morning.

"I know. I want to talk to you before I go to work. Erika made some mango bread last night." At three in the morning. She'd told him she couldn't sleep. He'd played the guitar while the bread baked. "She said we could have it for breakfast. So get up, sleepyhead."

"Okay, Daddy." Hiialo gathered Pincushion, Fluff and her favorite blanket and got out of bed. She followed him into the front room.

Kal heard Erika stirring in the back of the house, and a song rose in his mind, one that had tried to write itself while he lay sleepless on his bed. Rejecting some lyrics, trying to make others wait till after his conversation with his daughter, he collected the pieces of bread he'd cut for himself and Hiialo. "Can you carry that cup of juice? Let's go out on the swing."

The sun wasn't yet poking through the branches of the trees. About now it was probably starting to show above the ocean's horizon. Too bad the bungalow wasn't on the beach. When he'd bought it from them, his parents had asked if he wouldn't rather have the oriental beach house. That house had seemed big for him and Hiialo. But now there were three of them. Something to think about.

Beside him on the porch swing, Hiialo helped herself to a piece of mango bread.

"So, Hiialo. How would you feel if Erika lived with us always?"

Hiialo squinted at him thoughtfully. After a moment she said, "Okay. Would she be my nanny, like Mary Poppins?"

"Ah . . . no. Remember that day on the beach when you told Chris Erika was your new mom?"

She didn't look at him. Caught making things up. She hadn't known *he'd* heard.

Kal let it sink in. It never hurt to let her think he had the powers of Santa Claus. "Hiialo?"

"Yes. I remember."

"It turns out you're right. I'm going to marry Erika. She'll be your stepmother."

Hiialo peered up at him anxiously, and then her eyes filled with tears.

Kal's heart gave one hard thump. "What is it?" She was the one who'd said Erika was her new mom. He gathered her up, mango bread and all. "What's wrong?"

"She'll make me do all the housework. I don't want a stepmother!"

"Do all the housework?" He thought. "Didn't you finish paying for the paintbrushes?"

"Yes." Hiialo still looked troubled. She closed her mouth and wouldn't talk.

"Tell me what you mean. Does she make you do housework now?"

Hiialo simply shook her head, her lips drawn tightly together.

"Well, I am going to marry her. We love each other. And we both love you. I wouldn't marry someone who didn't love you."

Hiialo began to cry, not a screaming tantrum, but quiet deep sobs as though she was afraid she'd be overheard. "No, Daddy. Please don't make her be my stepmother. I don't want a stepmother."

Kal heard Erika in the kitchen putting on water for tea. "Why don't you want a stepmother? I thought you wanted—"

"She'll be mean. And you might . . ." Her voice trailed off on another incoherent sob.

Erika came out onto the lanai to see if Kal wanted something to drink. She was sleepy but happy—until she saw Hiialo's tear-streaked face. "Hiialo, what's wrong?"

Hiialo took one look at her and buried her face in her father's shoulder. She sobbed softly and continuously.

Erika searched Kal's face in the dim light, and he tilted his head toward the seat, inviting her to join them on the swing. Erika sat down. She put a hand on Hiialo's back. "Can I hold you, Hiialo?"

Hiialo shook her head hard and hugged her father convulsively.

Kal said, "Hiialo, let's finish our breakfast, yeah?"

"I don't like it."

Erika knew Hiialo was trying to hurt her. And there could be only one explanation. Kal must have told her they were getting married.

But she told Chris I was her new mom. She loves me.

"Hiialo, do you need to go back to bed?" suggested Erika. She usually wasn't up so early.

Hiialo shook her head.

"I think that's a good idea." Kal stood up with her in his arms.

"Nooo!"

The tantrum began, and Erika tensely rocked the porch swing, hugging herself, heartsore.

The last thing she'd expected was that Hiialo wouldn't want her.

DAVID STOPPED by the bungalow that afternoon while Hiialo was sleeping. She'd had another tantrum at noon, throwing her plate lunch on the floor.

When Erika saw David at the door, she wasn't sure if she was sorry or relieved. They sat out on the steps of the lanai in humid sunshine filtered through clouds, and she told him she was going to marry Kal.

His eyes shone. "That's great. That's really great, Erika."

"Hiialo's not happy about it."

He quirked his eyebrows. "No?"

"She cried."

David rubbed his chin, ran his tongue along his teeth thoughtfully. "Chris wasn't too happy when I told him I was marrying Jean."

"He loved Jean."

"Sure. But getting a new parent is threatening. Hiialo will come around."

A skink raced over a boulder beside the step. Erika tried to believe her brother's words.

"I'm really happy about you and Kal, Erika. I've worried. For a long time."

Erika knew since when. She had no secrets from David. He'd been privy to everything. Not just her private struggles on his ship, things no one else knew. But what had happened with Skye that day in the hospital.

He had said, *Don't even think about it. Her decision, if she ever consciously made one, had nothing to do with you.*

Erika still couldn't quite believe that. Her chivalrous brother would say nothing else. But if she owed him anything now, it was to set him at ease, the way he'd always tried to do for her.

"Everything's fine." She smiled like a newly engaged woman.

And tried not to wonder what would happen when she and Kal tried to make love.

THEY DECIDED to be married in the Awa'awapuhi Valley on the Na Pali Coast. They would get there by Zodiac and be married by Kroner, Kal's boss, who was a mail-order minister; he'd sent away for a license from an ad in the back of *Rolling Stone*. Kal had said he'd like to write the vows—did she want to help? No. Erika felt incapable of planning. Trying to help plan made it too real.

After the ceremony Kal's parents would host a party at their house. In Hawaii, Kal explained, hardly anyone attended the wedding; but everyone came to the reception.

And that night...

Kal had ten days off, two before the wedding, a week after. Mary Helen and King would be looking after Hiialo. And they'd offered the beach house for a honeymoon getaway. Erika hadn't objected when Kal asked her. There was nowhere more beautiful than Haena, and it didn't matter where the honeymoon took place, anyway.

She couldn't hide from him.

On Monday, the week after the Fourth, Erika was washing dishes at the sink and wishing she could break through Hiialo's moodiness, her strange anxiety about the wedding, when a white rental car came down the driveway and pulled into the Datsun's empty space. *David or Jean,* thought Erika.

But when the driver door of the automobile opened, the person who stepped out was a heavyset woman with spiky burgundy hair and enormous yellow-and-black art deco earrings. Chrome Yellow blazer over a Lamp Black dress. Erika squinted at the visitor for three seconds before recognizing her.

She limped quickly to the door, banged open the screen and made fast time down the steps. "Adele!"

"Hello, Erika!" Adele burst out. "You look like an engaged woman. All aglow."

The two friends embraced, both talking at once.

"I didn't expect to see you yet."

"As the matron of honor, I had to come and make sure everything's set for this wedding. Do you have a fabulous dress yet?"

Erika rolled her eyes. "I've heard enough about fabulous dresses from Jean. She keeps taking me shopping. Try this on for size. We're going to land on the Na Pali Coast and hike up into a place called the Awa'awapuhi Valley. There is no fabulous dress involved. I'm going to wear ti leaves."

Adele broke into laughter. "If I had your body and was marrying the Haole Guitar Man..."

My body. No, you don't want that.

Pausing in the middle of the sun-splashed little lawn, Adele regarded the bungalow. "It's so cute, Erika. Now, I just have to know this. Didn't you and I read some personal ad from an SWM in Haena?"

Erika couldn't help smiling. "Yes."

"I see." Adele threw back her head and laughed again. "Well, you didn't do too bad for yourself, and neither did he. Where's the *keiki?* And is your intended home?"

"At work." Erika opened the screen door.

Hiialo was coloring at the coffee table. Just fifteen minutes before Adele arrived, Erika had tried to talk to her about the wedding, to ask what was bothering her. Hiialo had clammed up and shaken her head, refusing to talk.

All Erika could do was love her. Try to make her happy.

"Hiialo, I want you to meet my special friend, Adele."

Hiialo got up, her face still puckered with worry.

"How nice to meet you, Hiialo," said Adele. "You just call me Auntie Adele. I love to spoil little girls. Are you going to help me find a wedding dress for Erika?"

Hiialo swallowed, looking frightened. "Okay," she whispered.

Adele lifted her eyebrows at Erika like, *What gives?*

Erika shrugged. To divert attention from Hiialo, she said, "Adele, I've been out with Jean three times this week looking."

"Jean schmean. You don't shop for a dress with Cindy Crawford, you know what I mean? I can't even sit at the same dinner table with your sister-in-law. Too beautiful. Adele is in charge now."

Erika brushed Hiialo's hair, and the three of them went out to the rental car. Hiialo brought her blanket and Pincushion and Fluff and sat in the back seat sucking her thumb, looking troubled.

"Now, tell me where you've been already," said Adele. "Rest assured, if we don't find it on this island, I'm taking you to Honolulu."

"I am not going to Oahu for a dress." As they passed the Haena Store, Erika said, "Okay, we've looked in Kapaa, Lihue and Poipu."

"Have you tried Hanalei?"

They visited a Hanalei boutique that sold cotton and silk imports. Exploring the racks, Erika tried to imagine getting out of a Zodiac in a dress.

Adele corralled a petite salesgirl with a long dark braid, who asked Erika, "You're from the mainland?"

"But she's marrying a local guy," said Adele to Erika's dismay.

"Who?"

No hiding it. "Kal Johnson."

The girl's eyes widened. "Kalahiki! He some *ono.*"

Adele laughed richly. Even Erika had picked up enough Hawaiian to know the word for "tasty."

In the corner of the store, Hiialo sat placidly on a chair, sucking her thumb, holding her blanket and stuffed animals. Erika sighed without sound. What on earth was wrong? She told Adele, "Let me browse."

When Adele and the salesgirl began searching together, she joined Hiialo in the corner and crouched beside her chair. "Darling, please tell me what's wrong. Why are you so worried?"

Hiialo took her thumb from her mouth. Her face tightened painfully. She swung her legs under the chair, as though contemplating whether she should speak.

"Please tell me. I thought you wanted me to be your new mom."

"Mom," said Hiialo. "Not stepmother."

Erika blinked, startled by her confusion. "Honey... I can't be your mom. You grew inside Maka before you were born. She'll always be your mom. But if I marry your dad, I'll be your stepmother. And I'll take care of you like a mom."

Hiialo's eyes grew tearful, and her mouth and face crumpled. She turned her face toward the wall, trying not to cry.

"Honey, look at me."

She did. And whispered anxiously, "Will you make me do the housework?"

"What?" Was this about the paintbrushes? Had she been too harsh? Erika didn't know what to say. She couldn't promise Hiialo that she wouldn't have to do any chores. "Well, we all do some of the housework. You're such a help to me when we fold laundry together."

Hiialo bit her lip. "What if my daddy dies?"

Erika opened her mouth. "Why would that happen?"

"I don't know." She clamped her lips shut, hugged Pincushion and resumed swinging her legs.

The salesgirl said, "You like this?"

Erika glanced up in distraction. She had an impression of a pale yellow dress. She couldn't wear that color.

Adele made a polite indecisive sound. "Don't worry, Erika. Your fairy godmother will take care of all."

Fairy godmother...

Erika felt like slapping her head. "Just a minute. I'll try something on in a second."

Adele slipped away to confer with the salesgirl, and Erika turned back to Hiialo.

"Honey, are you thinking about Cinderella?"

Hiialo nodded gravely.

"Oh, no no no." Erika took her in her arms and embraced the little body. "I love you, Hiialo. Nothing like that will happen to you. Stepmothers don't have to be mean. Why, Jean's a stepmother.'' She pulled away to see Hiialo's worried face.

"Really?"

"Yes. Yes."

Hiialo seemed to think it over. At last she picked up Pincushion and her blanket again and leaned closer to Erika, asking to be held.

Erika picked her up and sat down in the chair, hugging Hiialo on her lap. *My little girl now.* She'd answered a personal ad, and now this small person was part of her life. She felt thankful. "You talk to your daddy about it when he comes home tonight, okay?"

"Okay," whispered Hiialo.

"Will you help me pick out my dress?" Softly Erika confessed, "I want to look special for your dad."

Hiialo handed Erika her blanket and stuffed animals, then slid off her lap. "Okay, Erika. I will help. But my daddy already thinks you are very pretty, and that's why he kisses you."

Leaving Erika, she began to wander through the store, touching dresses. After a moment she found Adele, plucked at the edge of her jacket and said, "Auntie Adele, I'm ready to help find a pretty dress for Erika."

CHAPTER THIRTEEN

HIS LIPS WOKE Erika Sunday morning.

She smelled coffee and saw his blue eyes and his naked shoulders and remembered what day it was. "What are you doing in here? It's unlucky. I shouldn't see you till the wedding."

He shook his head, smiling, and climbed over her on the big bed. "Paid attention to all that stuff the first time. This is the lucky way."

Her eyes began to focus. Sunlight flooded through the screen door to the outside. She'd begun to sleep with the door open because the evening breeze was so pleasant. With Kal so close by, she felt safe.

He was very close now.

She'd seen those worn-out cutoff pajama bottoms before. They always seemed on the verge of falling off his slim hips. They were all he wore as he lay on his stomach and propped himself on his elbows to face her. "Your coffee's on the nightstand."

She looked. Two cups. "How's your ulcer?"

"I forgot I had one till you said something. Must be getting good medicine."

She touched his arms, his biceps. She couldn't help it.

Bending his head to kiss one of her hands, Kal thought, *It's going to be fine.* Whatever the problem, at least she was able to get aroused. Phrases like "repulsed by sex" he barred from his mind. There were better things to consider. Day-to-day happiness. He and Hiialo had a secret from Erika. A good one.

Her hair was messy, a sexy halo on the pillow.

"Like having me in your bed in the morning?"

"Yes," said Erika. "When I came here, I wondered why you'd made it so big."

"You had good legs. I could tell from your picture."

Erika searched his eyes. Good legs. He didn't mind her scars. "Really?"

He shrugged. "Well, I don't know why I made your bed big. But I do like your legs. All of you." He didn't want to talk about how he'd felt before she came. He didn't want to think about it. He had hurt so much without Maka every day. Thinking about that time brought it back. He slid his hand to Erika's side, against her breast, and laid his head on the pillow beside hers.

Her brown eyes wouldn't meet his. They seemed to be trained on his throat as she asked, "Are you going to sleep in here, then?"

"That's the idea."

What about the quilt on his bed? she wondered. What about the photos of Maka in his bottom drawer? She didn't want to look at those things in his room day after day.

She didn't want *him* to look at them.

As he kissed her again, a shadow cut out the sunlight from the door.

"Ahhh!" screamed a voice as the screen creaked. "What's *he* doing in here?"

It was Adele. Erika giggled as her friend came inside, clutching a paper grocery bag. The older woman waved her free hand at Kal. "Scat! Get out. You're bad luck."

"I'm the groom." He gazed into Erika's eyes. "Go away, Adele. We'll be done in a minute."

"Oh, good grief. It's your funeral. I mean, your wedding." Adele opened the door to the hall and went through to the kitchen. "Hurry up!" she called over her shoulder. "Erika has to get dressed."

From the bedroom, as Kal kissed her again, as she allowed the now familiar touch of his tongue against hers, Erika heard Adele's voice soften. "Why, good morning, Hiialo. Are you ready for the wedding?"

"Kal . . ." whispered Erika.

"I love you," he said. "It's going to be a good day."

KAL SHOWERED and left in a car with his brothers to go Erika knew not where. She and Hiialo and Adele sat on the lanai and ate the croissants and fresh pineapple Adele had brought in the paper bag. Hiialo seemed ready to burst and finally said, "Auntie Adele, I have to tell you a secret about Erika. Two secrets."

Erika rocked dreamily on the swing while they went inside. The fairy tale hadn't stopped. This was how a wedding day should be.

It didn't matter that she'd seen Kal before the ceremony. He was right. It was a good omen.

Hiialo took a bath and put on the tie-dyed cotton-jersey dress she'd picked out in Hanalei to wear to the wedding. It matched Erika's tank dress, which was tie-dyed as well— her wedding clothes. *Why not?* Adele had said. *You're young, you're skinny. And it's cute that you match.*

More to the point, Erika loved it that Hiialo wanted to dress like her. Looked up to her. Maka would always be important to Hiialo, but each day Erika recognized the influence *she* was going to be in Hiialo's life.

If only it was the same with Kal.

But where Kal was concerned, it would take her seven years to catch up with Maka.

Adele was blow-drying Erika's hair when Jean showed up. David and Chris had gone down to the beach, she said. Erika slipped into the bathroom to take off her robe and put on her dress, and when she came out, Jean was in the hallway, staring into Kal's room.

Strange that for Jean—who must have worried once that David still loved Skye—Erika found herself making things up. "We'll probably use that as a spare room. Or a music studio for Kal. Maybe Chris could sleep in here if he comes to visit alone."

Jean's slanted blue-green eyes regarded her curiously. But she betrayed no suspicion that all was not right when she said, "Maybe you'll have another kid."

"Oh." Since Kal had asked her to marry him, she'd forgotten to want a baby of her own. She had Hiialo. "I'm thirty-six."

"Thirty-six works," said Jean. "Hey, your dress is beautiful."

They all walked down to the beach. Erika expected to see a Zodiac; instead, she found Kal's outrigger, draped in blossoms. Danny held the paddle, and David waited at the water with a maile *lei* for her hair and another *lei* for her to give Kal. The *leis* made of the fragrant leaves of the maile plant were highly prized for all special occasions. Erika carried Kal's *lei* over her arm. *Leis* for other people were not supposed to be worn by the giver.

Only she and Hiialo were to ride in the canoe with Danny, and as they left the shore, Erika noticed that, though hot and humid, the morning was also tranquil and clear. That would change; north shore rain came daily. Erika sat with Hiialo nestled against her, the matching fabric of their dresses blending together like flowers in the same bed.

Hiialo held on to both of Erika's hands. "My daddy planned this. He wanted you to ride in an outrigger like a princess."

"I love you, Hiialo," Erika whispered.

Near Hanakapiai Beach, a Zodiac passed them, familiar faces on board. Kal's parents, Adele and Kurt and their son, Jean and Chris and David. The outrigger had almost reached the steep lantana-green walls of the Awa'awapuhi Valley before Erika spotted a canoe coming from the other direction. As it drew nearer, she recognized Kal's body, the way he moved. He and another man were paddling the canoe, and two others were with them. The Zodiac was already beached with a little group of people gathered around.

As Danny landed the outrigger, jumping out to hold the gunwale, King and David waded through the water. "Hi, beautiful," Kal's father greeted Erika, then picked up his granddaughter to carry her to shore.

Accepting the support of her brother's arm, Erika stepped barefoot into the low breakers, holding up the shin-length skirt of her dress.

Soon she was on the beach, beside green cliffs like skyscrapers. The other outrigger was landing. Kal had rolled up the legs of his long white pants to pull it onto the beach. He unrolled them before he took some *leis* his brother Keale had been holding and walked down the beach toward Erika.

It felt like a lifetime since Erika had seen his face. But as she moved toward him on the hard wet sand, the crash of the surf echoed the pounding of her heart. *I'm crazy to be doing this. What if I never learn to like sex?*

Of course you will. Look at him, Erika.

They met midway between the canoes.

"You look beautiful." He touched her dress, then put *leis* of maile and of pikake, jasmine, over her head, around her neck. Drawing her near, he touched her hair, her head, with both hands and kissed her cheek. "How do you feel?"

Her stomach yawned, turned on itself.

If worse came to worst, she could fake it.

No, not with him. Not with Kal . . .

"I'm fine."

A PATH EDGED WITH LAVA rocks led up into the green valley. The steep slopes rising around it were covered with vegetation; it wasn't the dark green of the north shore but more vibrant, Hooker's Green Light, new grass in spring. From a distance the valley seemed to be lined with emerald velvet. Up close, Erika discovered that all that grew there were air plants and thorny lantana. The ginger for which the valley had been named was gone, eaten by goats.

Kroner, in cutoffs and a Na Pali Sea Adventures T-shirt, led them to a place under a dry falls where a lush hanging garden of watercress and maidenhair grew. In the muggy air Kal and Erika held hands, the others gathered in a semicircle around them. Adele was beside Erika, Kal's oldest brother, Leo, beside him.

Kroner said, ''We're here today to witness the wedding of Kal and Erika and to let them know that we, representing the larger community of their *ohana,* will be with them throughout their marriage, ready to offer support.''

Erika felt the salt spray that had dried on her skin. The sun beat on her bare shoulders through intermittent clouds. The air had grown oppressive with the threat of rain, and each time clouds passed over the narrow valley, the walls of the landscape, the mossy cliffs too steep to be scaled, seemed to press in a little more.

Kroner read from a piece of paper in his hands the words Kal had written. ''Do you, Erika, take Kal as your husband and mate, to love by giving and receiving, by growing with him and respecting him, in married faith and devotion, till death divides you?''

Erika's eyes blinked against the sun. Kal's hands wrapped around hers, and the clouds shifted impatiently in the sky as though waiting for her promise.

''I do.''

His face was near hers, his eyes holding a soft smile full of love as Kroner repeated the question, substituting Kal's name for Erika's and hers for his.

"I do," he said.

All was silent, the valley still.

Kroner pronounced them husband and wife. "Kal, you may kiss the bride."

Erika saw the light sheen of sweat on her husband's upper lip as he met her eyes. He put one of his hands over the back of her hair, over her neck, and he murmured, "We're really good at this."

Trying to stop the nervous sickness in her stomach, Erika gave herself to the sensation of his lips on hers. Lips she had tried to recreate with her paintbrush. Lips she had watched as he sang. Lips she had seen kiss away Hiialo's screams, her tantrums. Lips that had made her believe in the love of a good man. They were kissing her mouth, saying, *Trust me now. Give yourself to me.*

She did. He was strong, and she felt all the muscle and power in him as he held her. All was relaxed, but his strength felt like security, like permanence.

She believed in their love.

IN HIS PARENTS' YARD, long tables covered with floral sheets held sushi, chow mein, *lumpia, kim chee,* long rice, squid *luau* and *kalua* pig, which Danny and Jakka had roasted in an underground oven. Foreboding of the night ahead made it almost impossible for Erika to even look at the food, particularly the glazed pig. But after the hula chant and blessing by Danny's dance troupe, she helped herself to everything on the tables, saying, "Oh, how wonderful." The start of a headache thrummed in her temples. Maybe she'd feel better after she ate.

Maybe Kal would be tired after the reception. Maybe he'd drink a lot and pass out, and...

Remember what it feels like to lie against him and kiss him. Sex won't be so different.

But it always was. It was hideous.

She and Kal had barely sat down at the head table when the guests began banging silverware on glasses.

For Kal, the sound echoed the past. His first wedding. Heeding the custom, he leaned toward Erika and kissed her. His bride's pallor cut through the memories of Maka, the sense of her all around.

"You okay?"

She nodded, sick with apprehension. "There are a lot of people here," she said, as though that was the problem.

Time crawled. She was introduced to dozens of people and spoke to others she'd met only briefly. The Akanas had made a point of getting back to Kauai for the weekend, and they came up to congratulate Kal. Danny introduced her to the men and women in his hula troupe.

They cut the cake and fed it to each other, then sat down with mango ice cream. Trying to take her mind off her nausea, Erika told Kal, "I really didn't know there were so many ways to eat mangoes."

He lifted his eyebrows, touched his tongue to his lips. "I know another way to eat them. I'll show you when we're alone." His eyes reached into hers. "Now that we're married."

It was a gentle flirtation. She knew he intended something sweet . . . sweet as mangoes.

But her nerves, her fears and too much unfamiliar food, triumphed. Remembering the sight of the *kalua* pig, she stood up abruptly, trying not to fall over the chairs, and limped toward the house.

"Erika?"

She heard his chair bang behind her.

Her mouth filling with bile, Erika headed blindly in the direction of the kennels.

"Erika."

Kal's shadow was beside her. She pushed her hand at him, wanting to tell him to go back to the table, but if she opened her mouth she'd throw up. Which she did, in the first flower bed she saw. And on her beautiful *leis*.

One of the Akitas began barking at her.

Kal said, "*Toshi.* Enough." He touched Erika's back and she waved him away.

"Please . . . go."

He didn't, but he discouraged his mother and sister and a few other people from approaching. And tried to tell himself it wasn't the thought of sex with him that had made his bride vomit.

He *had* been talking about sex, hadn't he? Mangoes . . .

There was a hurt inside him.

Too much excitement, that was all. He stuffed his hands in his trouser pockets and waited for Erika to turn to look at him. She didn't. She was taking off her *leis,* dropping them into the flowers as though she didn't know what else to do.

Kal remembered that Leo had handed him a handkerchief that morning. It was still in his pocket, and he gave it to Erika. "Here, baby."

Erika couldn't face him. She needed to go in the bathroom and cry. "Thank you." Weak, she turned from the heliconia and from the party.

Sliding an arm across her shoulders, Kal guided her toward the kennels. They'd go in the house the back way.

"Kal, don't..." The tears began streaming. To throw up on her wedding day, at his parents' party.

"Shh. It's all right. You're a trooper to eat everything at your first *luau.*" *Not sex. Don't let it be the thought of sex that did that to her.*

Erika wiped her eyes on his handkerchief. They'd reached the kennel runs, and the puppies in Jin's litter were barking at her. She searched for the one that looked like Jin, the one she'd liked. But the puppy was gone.

She started crying again. Dumb to hope Kal would really get that dog for her. He would pick a dog for other reasons. He'd pick the one that was right for them.

Oh, God, she needed to think about how *he* was feeling.

Kal watched her pull herself together, dry her eyes. Face him.

She was bedraggled, but still beautiful to him.

"I need to wash up."

"Sure. I'll ask my mom to find you some clothes. She's worried about you." He pulled her against him, hugged her tight. He was worried, too. "I love you, Erika."

Each of her breaths fell hard against him, gradually evening as he stroked her hair. "Kal..." she whispered. "I love you. Don't ever leave me."

"No...I won't. I won't." He subdued his own fears, told them to go away. Hers mattered more.

THERE WAS A LOT of traffic upstairs. Mary Helen brought Erika bath towels, a new toothbrush, one of Kal's T-shirts and a pair of his gym shorts with a drawstring waist. Grateful, Erika took a shower in the bathroom that had been Kal's. When she emerged, comfortably dressed in his clothes, Niau and Mrs. Akana and Jean and Adele and Mary Helen were all in the upstairs bedroom waiting for her.

Jean, looking a little green herself in early pregnancy, said, "Don't feel bad, Erika. My sister, Cecily, threw up on a runway in Paris."

"Before takeoff or after landing?" asked Niau.

"Cecily's a *model*," explained Adele. "She means she threw up at, like, a Ralph Lauren show."

Mary Helen put her arm around Erika's waist. "Enough about throwing up. Erika, what can I do for you?"

"Nothing." She met her mother-in-law's eyes. "You've been so good to me, and I'm so sorry about this, Mary Helen."

Kal's mother looked at her sweetly and corrected, "Mom."

Erika tried not to cry again. In no hurry to leave the comfort of the room full of women, she moved toward the window to gaze out at the party. People were playing volleyball. She couldn't see Kal.

Mrs. Akana smiled up at her from a striped wing chair beside the window. Noticing her, Erika said, "I'm so glad you could come today. I was disappointed I didn't learn *bon* dancing from you before you went away on tour."

Rising gracefully to her feet, the elderly woman touched Erika's arm comfortingly. "Mary Helen and King know *bon* dancing good. And I will brush up with you in the fall, yeah?"

"Okay. Thank you." A peace settled over Erika. These were nice people. Kal was a good man. She was going to be all right.

On the other side of the room near the door, Adele was laughing at something Niau had said.

Mrs. Akana smiled and told Erika, "I threw up at my wedding, too. Maybe something picture brides do."

Erika took the older woman's hands in hers and met her eyes and knew she'd found a friend.

She began to leave the room, and she saw the tall figure in the threshold, his blue eyes waiting for her, and when she went into his arms again, she knew he was her dearest friend of all.

She hoped that she could be the same for him.

That she could be the lover he needed.

THE AFTERNOON was a celebration of *ohana,* of family. Within a few hours, Erika was almost able to laugh at the recollection of what had happened earlier. She enjoyed last moments with Adele and Kurt and sixteen-year-old Jason, who would all be returning to the mainland the following day, and with David and Jean and Chris, who were ready to head back to Greenland.

Talking to David near the volleyball net, Erika said, "You know, I'm sure Kal and I can arrange to see you guys next week before you go."

Her brother's lips twisted upward, amused. "Erika, I want your husband to like me. I'm not going to pull you away on your honeymoon."

She started to object, to say it didn't matter. But she knew it was right that she and Kal have that time alone. And she was going to do her best to make it right—for him.

She told David, "I'm going to miss you."

"We'll be back. At least you live by the ocean. Besides—" he glanced about the garden, his eyes softening "—you've got quite a family here."

As the sun began sinking in the sky, the band—which was Kal's band, playing without him but with his brother Keale—began tuning up.

Kal found Erika. "I think we're wanted." He steered her toward the area in front of the band.

She said, "Oh, I don't dance."

"Mmm. You're not good for much, are you?" The misty *pali,* the cliffs, loomed above them as Kal took her left hand in his right and put his other arm around her.

They danced slowly to two songs. On the second, others began dancing, too. Then Kal led her up toward the band and sat her down on a folding chair and took the guitar Jakka handed him. His Stratocaster.

He spoke into the microphone, to Erika but also to the crowd, as he had in the bar on the Fourth of July. His ragged, distinctive voice, that sweet low voice, came through the mike. "Okay, no more jokes about my beloved eating that *kalua* pig. She does good, yeah?"

Everyone laughed and cheered and whistled, and Danny gave a drumroll. Erika would have buried her face in her hands, but Kal's eyes were holding hers. Their expression cherished her.

She couldn't look away.

When the guests were finally quiet, Kal said, "I guess it's no secret how Erika and I met. Through a want ad in *Island Voice*. We sent our pictures and our stories to each other, and I asked her to come here. This is a practice that has a history in Hawaii, a history some of our guests have experienced firsthand, the old way. Erika and I did things a little differently. But I wrote this song about our way of finding each other. And about her."

The blue of his eyes went through her eyes, into her heart and soul. *You really love me*, she thought.

He and his band spent a couple of seconds tuning, then broke into the song.

Mainland girl
I thought you'd turn your back
on me and my life,
but you'd sold your Karmann Ghia for a plane ticket
here
You were running like me,
running to me . . .

He knew things he'd never revealed, but he was telling them all now, telling everyone. Erika had believed that her feelings were secret from him, that he hadn't known when she'd fallen in love with him. But he knew. He sang about lying in the dark thinking about her and seeing her in the kitchen in the mornings and knowing she was afraid to look at him, afraid to let him see she loved him. He watched her as he sang, and the song got sexier and more personal, and his voice was doing that thing to her, playing her. Erika sat on the stage, flushed, knowing she was going to have to go home that night and make love with this man who was telling their secrets.

Knowing she wanted to.

As she gazed out over the dancers, her eyes stopped on two figures near the edge of the crowd. Mr. and Mrs. Akana were dancing slowly in each other's arms, gazing into each other's eyes, smiling the shared contentment of lifelong friends.

The sight gave Erika courage as nothing else could.

Except Kal's voice singing "Picture Bride."

CHAPTER FOURTEEN

"SHOULDN'T WE GET groceries first?" asked Erika as Kal turned down their driveway. The headlights illuminated the foliage and the familiar dirt road, but they passed the bungalow and continued to the blue house on the shore. In the moonless night the drive seemed long and dark.

"My brothers stocked the house for us." Telling himself she wasn't really stalling, that she'd lost all her lunch and was just hungry, Kal took his hand from the steering wheel and squeezed hers.

Erika clung to him. She had cast off from a safe port and headed for open sea. She'd said goodbye to Jean and Chris and David. In this new land she had one friend. Kal. Her husband.

Who wanted to have sex with her.

He parked, they got out of the car, and the breeze rushed at them from the sea the night had swallowed. The waves roared invisibly. "Want to go down there?" Kal asked. To the beach.

"Okay." The blackness and the ocean beyond seemed safer than the house, a bed with expectations. Sex could be easy without expectations.

Kal was swinging the key to the rental, which was on a ring with a plastic pineapple on it. "Let me check some things in the house. I'll meet you out here."

Erika nodded. In the blackness he crossed the patio and unlocked the glass doors of the beach house. Barefoot, still wearing his old clothes, Erika wandered through the deep sand and scooped out a seat for herself near the dark shape of Kal's outrigger. The wedding gift from Maka had brought them back home together from their wedding ceremony.

After several minutes Erika heard a dog breathing and the faint sound of a leash and collar, and she looked about the beach to see who was walking a dog. Fur brushed her arm, and she started as something bounded around her, kicking sand. The tall shape standing over her, sitting down beside her, was Kal.

"What is this?" But then she knew. The puppy explored her hands, licked her. Feeling its thick fur, Erika made out the markings. It was the one she'd wanted, the dog who looked like Jin. "Kal! Does Hiialo know?"

"She and Chris were playing with him in my parents' den all day."

The excited puppy squirmed, then settled down under her hands.

Erika turned her head to say something, and Kal's mouth was there, kissing hers.

"I want to make you happy, Erika."

His voice wasn't quite steady. Was he nervous about making love, too?

He has to be. I told him I find sex revolting.

And Kal wasn't arrogant enough to assume he would be different for her than other men. He had told her only that love would make the difference.

I need to love him. To give to him.

The puppy contentedly licked Erika's hands, shifting only occasionally in her lap, showing no signs of going anywhere. The sea made its long slow beats in breaking waves.

His arm behind her, his hand resting in the sand, Kal said, "He's got a Japanese name a yard long. What are you going to call him?"

"I don't know." Kal hadn't yet turned on any lights in the house to shine to the shore outside, but her eyes had adjusted to the dark, and she could see his legs on the beach beside her. She could make out the pattern of his aloha shirt. "His mom is Jin." She thought it over. "Kin?"

"Like family. That's nice." His foot held down the end of Kin's leash. He'd asked his brother to bring the dog out to the house a half hour before, so that it would be there for Erika. A distraction to calm her. *Baby, I won't hurt you....*

What was that aching in his heart?

He put both his arms around her and eased her back till her head was cradled on the sand. The puppy climbed over his body and moved away to explore.

"He won't run away..." said Erika.

"I've got him."

His leg settled between hers. The beach felt soft under her, the sand a cushion that molded to her body, and there was relief in the intense blackness of the night. Kal's hand touched her cheek, and he eased against her so that she felt his erection. A dark confusion swirled inside her. It felt good. They'd come this far before.

She let her left hand reach up and touch the front of his shirt, then grasp his arm.

Kal moved closer to her. "I love you, Erika."

Magic words to peel away the last tension in her limbs. Then there was only his mouth, gently kissing her, starting something that might go on for hours, unrelieved for seven days. His voice, rough and quieter than the ocean, whispered soft things to her, the gentle murmurings of a lover. Things about sex, about her getting wet and pressing up against him. Erika felt as though she'd become the earth beneath her body, become the rocking tide before the waves hit the beach in that slow steady rhythm.

She loved how he smelled and tasted. His mouth didn't seem to be driving things toward an inevitable end. His mouth seemed unconscious of time. His body had melted into hers, so that they were both part of the sand, except she wanted to be closer to the top layer of sand that was him, heavy and warm and hard above her.

"Kal..."

His hands were in her hair, cradling her head. He didn't want to let go, didn't want to stop being so close to her. He brushed his face against hers, feeling her smooth skin. Her head went back, and he touched her face, touched her lips with his tongue.

"Oh, Kal..."

No protest, just saying his name. She was ardent. Her breasts pushed up against him. She held the sides of his chest, his arms, his shoulders, in turn, trying things. His lips kissed hers again, and then he felt the puppy walk over his back.

He moved carefully, not wanting to roll on Kin.

Erika felt his weight shift, leave her. He caught the puppy, letting Kin kiss his face. Erika sat up, knowing there was sand all over her, that she was wearing a man's clothes sizes too large, not caring because Kal had transfigured her, made her beautiful.

She was chilled without his body.

He asked, "Want to stay out here for a while or go inside?"

Inside... She wished they could stay on the beach forever. He wouldn't make love to her on the beach. And on the beach they couldn't quite see each other. Erika couldn't see the lines on her own hands when she touched him.

He gave her the puppy, set Kin in her lap, and then he hugged her tight from one side, held her as though she was something he had wanted for a long time. "Let's go in."

Kal opened the patio doors of the oriental beach house, and he and Erika went in, Erika still holding the end of

Kin's leash, not tugging at all because the puppy wanted to
go in, too.

Ahead of her in the darkness, Kal turned on a light
above the kitchen stove. The front room was filled with
gifts. Leo and Keale had brought over the gifts and one of
Kal's guitars, too. Even the crate for the puppy and its
leash and brush and food were there.

The gifts made it all terribly real to Erika. *Married...*

Returning from the kitchen, Kal glanced at the presents
without interest. "Want a tour?"

"All right."

"Pick up Kin. We'll put him in his crate soon."

Erika collected the fluffy puppy and unclipped his leash,
which she dropped onto the couch.

The floors were ceramic tile, as in his parents' house. Off
to one side, a bar separated the kitchen from the rest of the
room. A window room divider cut off the sleeping area,
with its king size bed, from the living room. Folding koa
blinds could be drawn across the opening in the partition
for privacy. Matching doors closed it off, as well.

"The bedroom," said Kal. The clothes they'd packed
for the week were in suitcases at the end of the bed. Kal led
her down the hall. "There's another bedroom here." With
two full-size beds. "Bathroom across the hall."

As they made their way back to the glass-fronted room
opening onto the patio, Kal said, "Let's get Kin used to his
crate."

"I can't believe your parents let us bring him here.
Aren't they worried about accidents in their rental?"

Kal was taking the crate into the bedroom. He emerged
and picked up an old bedspread his brothers had dropped
off. "For one thing, the only rugs in here are area rugs. For
another, my parents feel that if a puppy has more than a
couple of accidents, you're housebreaking wrong." He
folded the bedspread. "They also consider dogs first-class
citizens."

Erika followed him into the bedroom, stroking Kin. Kal took the puppy from her and coaxed him into the crate. It was a large crate, the size for a full-grown Akita.

Kin sat nervously at one end and looked out at them.

Kal didn't shut the door. He said, "Good boy, Kin. You're a good dog. Kin, stay." The puppy started to come out.

Kal put him back in. "Stay."

The puppy sat down.

"I love him, Kal. I really wanted a dog. Thank you. And thank you for the song. I don't have anything like that for you."

He sat back on his heels, eyed her. "You have something for me."

Erika was glad for the darkness. The only light on in the house was the kitchen light. "Kal, I . . . I'm still uncomfortable about sex."

"I know." He changed the subject. "I'd like a shower. If you want to sit in the tub for a while first, I'll watch Kin."

Relaxing in the bathtub sounded good. On the nightstand, the glowing numbers on the clock read nine-thirty-three. She picked up her tote bag and set it on the bed.

She had packed it the night before, but when she opened it, the first thing she saw was an unfamiliar garment. Who had put it there? Adele? No. Though he wasn't looking at her, though he was on the floor reassuring the puppy in the crate, she knew Kal was paying attention to everything she did.

She pulled out the fabric, which was coffee-colored silk, sheer enough to show every shadow. A thigh-length chemise. Simple, with slits six inches up the sides. "Kal, do you . . ."

He told the dog, "I like lingerie."

He had packed it, on top of her other clothes, like a word. *Please.* She took it out and started to leave the room, but Kal, at her feet, playfully nipped at her calves. His eyes were loving, and Erika swallowed.

I want to please him.

She went down the hall. The bathroom had been stocked with soaps and bath salts from the Island Soap Co. On the edge of the tub was a bottle of papaya-scented shampoo. She drew a bath, using some salts, and as she soaked in the fragrant water, she tried to relax her mind. *It will be okay. Just try to enjoy it.*

When she got out, she dried off in front of the mirror and saw the hard-won muscles in her arms and legs, saw her tan lines. She put moisturizer on her face and looked closely at her eyes and her face and did not find the wrinkles many. She removed the towel from her hair and drew the coffee-colored chemise over her body. It fit, and the private shadows showed as she had known they would. *How do I really look?* It was hard to step outside herself and tell. But the chemise was clothing; it masked her.

Nudity... *I'm going to hate it.*

She emerged from the bathroom with wet hair and smelled popcorn. She followed the scent and the sounds of popping to the kitchen. Kal's back was to her. "Kin's in his crate. I shut the door. He seemed happy. We should check on him in about ten minutes."

Erika said, "It's like having a baby."

When he turned around, her face was red, as though she'd made a blunder. Kal switched off the burner. She was the woman he wanted, and it made his blood rush just to see her muscular legs and arms, her firm body, her proud features, faintly lined with age but sexy to him. Beautiful.

"Come here." He took her hand, led her down the shadowed hall to the living room, which still lay mostly in darkness.

She sat on the couch while he wandered through the presents, too many presents, too many good wishes for them. He found a large package with no corners. Heavy.

Sitting on the couch, he laid the bundle across both their laps. Erika knew it was a quilt.

She opened the inexpensive floral card. "A wish that all the gifts of love will shower you from heaven above." Beneath the printed message was scrawled, "With love to Kal and Erika from Mary and Jessie Kekahuna and the Makanalua Quilters."

"Maka's mom and her aunt," said Kal. "They wanted to come to the wedding party, but Aunt Jessie is sick."

Erika pictured the old quilt on Kal's bed, the quilt he had shared with Maka. Would the quilt in this package ever look so old and tattered? Together she and Kal unwrapped it. It was green, yellow and white; the flowers were anthurium, lilies.

Kal unfolded it and laid it over her. He pulled her legs up onto the couch and rubbed her feet before tucking them under the quilt. As he kissed her lips, there was a whine from the bedroom.

Kin.

Erika's glance followed the sound.

"He doesn't have to go out. It's too soon. This is when we let him cry for a little bit. Like a baby," he said just as she thought it.

For a moment their eyes held.

He broke the connection between them. "Want to watch old surfing movies?"

It sounded good.

"Let me have a shower first." He stood up, opened the doors on an entertainment center, then went into the bedroom. Erika heard him talking to the puppy. "You want to come in the bathroom with me? Or you want to go see Erika?"

He brought Kin out to her, and she cuddled the puppy, stroking his fluffy body, while the shower ran. She couldn't see the ocean through the plate glass, but the surf was au-

dible, and the trade winds periodically gusted through the
screen doors.

The dog licked her hands.

She heard Kal come out of the bathroom, then go into
the kitchen. When he joined her, he was carrying the bowl
of popcorn and wearing a pair of baggy cotton shorts that
looked new. They hung low on his lean hips, and when he
sat down beside her it was hard not to stare at his skin.

Kin sniffed at the popcorn.

''No,'' said Kal. ''Time to say good-night.''

Erika hugged her dog, gave him a kiss, wanted to take
him to the crate herself. But Kal said, ''I'll do it,'' and then
he was gone, and she heard him putting Kin in his crate.

Erika fished a large flat package from the stack of presents. Obvious. Not half as sweet as a puppy. When Kal sat
down with her again, she handed it to him. ''Here's your
present.''

''Thanks.'' He tore off the white envelope containing
her card. The card itself was a small original watercolor,
an outrigger on a beach. Kal opened it and read the message.

Dear Kal,
I love you, in the giving way. I want to make you
happy.

                                                    Erika

He closed the card and gazed at the front. He said,
''Receiving, too. Did I mention that?''

''No.'' The look on his face—strong and vulnerable at
once—caught her heart. ''But you gave me Kin. I received him.''

Yes, thought Kal, *but what about my fingers between
your legs, my tongue licking you?*

Repulsed by sex.

He hadn't expected those words to come back now.

And scare him.

Concentrating on her gift, he removed the paper and found an oil painting similar to a watercolor that was hanging in his parents' gallery. His favorite, *Hiialo's Luau.* The oil was better. He knew it was worth more money, but it was the other that she'd decided to publish. This one was just his. "Thank you."

He set the picture at the end of the couch and gazed at it for a while. "There's a skink in it that wasn't in the other one. The pig looks better in this one, too."

The pig reminded them both of the pig at the wedding party. Of Erika's throwing up. Of what Kal had suggested just before.

"Erika." The quilt shifted as he drew her closer, met her eyes. "Were you just nervous today? I know what I said was... I didn't mean to scare you." Or make you sick. *Tell me it wasn't me.*

"I was just nervous. I still am."

It was easy to kiss her then. It made him excited, and he thought of just taking what he wanted. A reasonable pace. If she wouldn't be seduced, she would at least let him . . .

Cool it, Kal.

He got up to go to the VCR.

Watching, Erika saw the front of his shorts distended, hiding nothing.

She shut her eyes, surrendering to the dizziness, the yearning that mingled with uncomfortable things, that went into the world of nakedness, a teetering place between the beautiful and the grotesque.

Since neither of them would be watching it, Kal didn't ask her opinion about the movie. It was a distraction for her. If it didn't work, he'd bring out Kin, another distraction. A ball of fur she could touch—so she could forget that a man was touching *her.*

Carrying the remote control, Kal went to the kitchen and switched out the light, then returned to the couch. He turned the volume very low before he sat down on her left near the end of the couch. In the faint glow from the television, everything was blue. Kal put one leg against the back of the couch and reached for her.

She accepted the warmth of his bare chest, his legs surrounding her. Rolling on her side, she stared at the TV, the waves, the start of the film. Kal covered her with the quilt, held her beneath it. She felt every muscle, every hair, every line of his body. She felt his penis.

All of it seemed safe. He made her safe. She pressed her face to the smooth skin of his chest.

Kal wasn't hungry, but he grabbed a handful of popcorn and passed her the bowl. "No butter," he promised.

Erika took some popcorn and feigned interest in the movie, as though he wasn't holding her waist, stroking beneath her breasts. He was doing everything right. But it would make no difference.

She said, "I can't have an orgasm. I've never had one with a man."

He dragged her closer, his arms and legs speaking the language of affection and security. "I'll have to send you back to the mainland."

Erika buried herself deeper in the den of his body and the quilt and touched his leg, moving upward.

"Erika, don't." He caught her hand, the hand moved by practice rather than passion. By what she thought he wanted. They had to talk, and it should happen in the bedroom.

With luck, something else would happen there, too.

He picked her up, her and the quilt, and stood. Erika closed her eyes and let him carry her to the bedroom. He left open the shutters that separated the king-size bed from the next room, from the soft sound of the television. Setting her at the foot of the bed, he drew back the spread and the sheets and blankets.

Erika crawled up to the pillows, where he joined her and pulled the covers over them. They turned toward each other.

"Tell me what you like," he said. "What you don't."

I've already told you! Why did you marry me? "Maybe we should just . . . do it."

Well, it wasn't the worst idea. But he shook his head.

He kissed her mouth, and Erika's breath went away. She kissed him back, slowly. His ribs were against her hand. His skin was warm. She wanted to touch him. He was beautiful like no man she'd ever known. But her own body felt tight as a spring.

When he drew her near, she tensed.

Kal took a silent breath, eased his hold on her.

"It's okay," she said.

He didn't answer.

In the next room the television talked low. Through the partition, the trade winds, carrying a breath of plumeria, blew over their skin.

"Really," said Erika. "I can just do this. Let's not try to talk about it."

"Okay."

But all he did was make a place for her in the crook of his arm, intimate with the scent of his skin. It would be so comforting to roll over and put her face against him in the night. She could get used to his lips resting half-parted against her forehead, as though he drank her like a sleeping draft.

She must be making him crazy. He was tense now, too. Pained, she crunched up her eyes, her forehead. This was her wedding night. Where was the magic?

The clock had struck midnight. The pumpkin was smashed.

Kal felt her small tense breaths. Under his hands, her back knotted. *Relax,* he thought. *Relax, Erika.*

"Hey, Erika. Just remember the stuff about love, yeah? I want to try to give to you. Just...let it happen. It's okay if you don't get excited. But just know that I'm doing it because I'm in love with you. Humor me."

She nodded, strangely glad. No decisions to make, except to love him.

"I'm so in love with you." His mouth kissing her jaw, her throat, her closed eyes, he rolled her onto her stomach, and she resisted only slightly, then lay tensely with her face to the pillow. Kal rubbed her shoulders and arms, territory they'd covered before. Then places they hadn't. The backs of her legs. Her naked bottom.

She moved beneath his hand with the restless stirrings of pleasure. *Good.* "That's right. Just relax." He drew her chemise up her body, and she sat up and let him take it off.

There was a horrible gulping feeling in her throat, alien qualities at war. She huddled back under the sheets, hiding. *You don't have to have an orgasm. He doesn't care.*

Kal took off his shorts and reached for her again, sliding down the sheet.

"Kal..."

"You're so pretty. You make me so hard, Erika."

She'd heard words like that before. They were different coming from him. Kal she believed. Not that she was pretty. But that he found her so.

And his hand felt so good against the skin of her back. His body settling against her, pressing close, cradling her.

It didn't feel as she'd imagined. It was earthy. Body hair. Muscle. Heavy male body. The smell of sex. It was in the air already, and it brought a choked feeling to her throat.

Suddenly she wanted to escape. *I hate this. I hate this.*

"I love you."

Give, she thought. *Let him.* But, oh, the feeling inside her. It would be easier to touch him, and she tried to roll over. He wouldn't let her. He kissed her shoulder and rubbed her spine, gentle-hard. "Don't move."

"No," she said, trying to move again.

He slid away from her and she from him.

Her eyes were big, desperate. Like Hiialo waking up from a nightmare. "Let me give to you," she said.

Kal knew she was choking on her feelings. She hated it. Had hated having him close to her. He shook his head. "No." Like her, he couldn't talk. Except the most familiar words, the only safe words for this moment. Gently he leaned over and kissed her cheek. "I love you."

And he got up and left their bed.

THE PUPPY WOKE THEM in the middle of the night. At the sound of his whining, Erika remembered where she was, what had happened. Kal was beside her, and though it was dark, though the light from outside was the blue shade of night, she didn't want to get up because she was naked. Bleary-eyed, holding the sheet, Erika searched for her chemise on the bed.

Kal sat up, crawled to the foot of the bed and opened the door of the crate, catching Kin's little collar as he came out.

"Let me get him, Kal." She hunted for her chemise and couldn't find it.

Observing her panicky movements and figuring it out, Kal said softly, "Come on. It's all right. I think you're beautiful."

Naked in front of a man. Oh, well, it was hardly less than her bikini. She let the sheet fall, and without meeting Kal's eyes, she stood up and walked around the end of the bed to take the puppy.

Cool air all over her skin, she carried him out the screen door to the garden area in the starlight. Kal followed, drinking a glass of water, and when she turned from the puppy, she found a big beach towel waiting for her.

He slipped it behind her, but didn't close it. Erika saw him stare at her breasts in the dark, saw his eyes drift down. This was part of what she didn't understand about sex, why it should excite her to see him look at her, to see it give him an erection.

She swallowed.

He closed the towel and met her eyes, and they both remembered how she'd gone to sleep alone.

She said, "Please . . . I want to try again. I won't be that way."

"Oh, we'll try again," he assured her, not quite lightly.

But they didn't just then.

They sat on the patio and played with Kin, throwing him a rubber ball. Finally they took him back to his crate and got back into bed together, and Kal tried to forget that he had an ego. He knew it would get in the way in a hurry if he couldn't make her respond.

Just kiss her. You've kissed a lot. She likes it.

Erika sensed his tension, a kind of tension she'd seen before. The inevitable. Frustration. She closed her eyes and begged of forces she didn't trust that she could make love with her husband.

And then, desperate, she thought rationally again. *I love him. This is loving.* But now there was a double enemy against them. Experience. What had happened earlier that night. And fear of its repetition.

Kal touched her face and kissed her. A voice spoke inside him. *Open your heart, Kal. Stop thinking about you and fantasies of making her come. Just tell her how much you love her.*

"Erika . . ." He kissed her with his tongue, keeping his body a little apart from hers. "Just let me touch you. I love you. That day we went to Polihale, I just wanted to take off your shorts, take off . . ."

He told her more, and he kissed her, and she drew nearer. The weather was gathering inside her, the sticky hot of hurricane season. Her mind tried to find a thought to hang on to. She deliberately stopped it and felt his tongue against hers and his hand on her breast.

"It's all right," he said. More kisses.

She lay back, but when his hand slid down her front, she was nervous and rolled onto her stomach. "Don't stop touching me," she said.

"I won't." Her back, her sides curving to her breasts. Lower. The backs of her thighs.

She responded.

He touched the insides of her thighs, slid his hand up, pressing his lips to her shoulder. Wet...

Erika felt his fingers stroking her, and the room became a cloud.

"Kal...Kal."

"You're all right. Shh. We'll just do this for a while." A long while.

She forgot about him, about anything. It felt good. So good. It was a long time before she wanted to turn, and then they were kissing again and she reached out to touch him.

"That's right," he said. Her hand on him, stroking. Shaky hand. Like his touching her. Petting like teenagers afraid to go all the way.

"I want to make you come," she said. "Show me what to do."

He kissed her, held her tight, until he found the power of speech, and sometime later they knew their first shared climax, which was his.

And as she lay in his arms afterward, Erika felt like his wife.

WHEN SHE AWOKE in the morning, it was with an awareness of Hawaii, of the warm air, of the smells and the humidity, of the hue of the light—the faintest dilute wash of Payne's Gray and Alizarin Crimson. The windows in the beach house had invited the outside in.

Smelling something frying—plantains, she thought—she started to get up, but Kal came in, naked, and said, "Don't move." He brought her Kin, who had been in the kitchen with him, and said, "Watch over this guy, all right? I've already taken him out, so he should be okay."

Erika propped the pillows up behind her, and the puppy crawled over the blankets, exploring. After a moment she caught him and stroked him while he looked into her eyes.

Kal carried in two plates, handed her one, set the other on the bed and picked up the dog. "Back to your crate, Kin." He got in bed beside her, and they ate plantains and eggs and drank guava juice.

After breakfast she washed the dishes and they put on their suits and went out and swam together, a quarter mile along the shore.

The sun was coming out, and Kal said, "This is really nice. I never have time off like this, without Hiialo."

The sea was the color of his eyes.

Erika said, "I've never had a time like this, ever."

They stopped swimming and stood in the sand, a wave riding over Erika's shoulders, washing his chest. He held her tightly, a bear hug.

When they returned to the beach house, they fed Kin and took him outside and trained him, working on teaching him to come, to answer to his name. Then Kal sat under the gathering clouds and let Erika sketch him for a painting of the Blue Room.

After lunch he put Kin in his crate and said, "Want to lie down for a while?"

The wonderful nightmare that would never go away. Erika had pushed it out of her mind all morning, but now it was back.

They were salty from the ocean, still wearing their swimsuits, but they went into the bedroom. He unmade the bed she'd made that morning and they lay down. Soon he was hard, stiff, wanting sex. The way they were kissing made it more intense, and he reached for the zipper at the back of her high-necked aqua maillot. He pulled it down.

Erika swallowed the sound she wanted to make. She didn't want him to stop.

It's going to be okay, he thought.

He nudged her swimsuit off her shoulders, tugged it down her front, revealing her breasts. His yearning mounted.

Sitting up, Erika slipped the maillot off her arms. But she could see herself in the light, and—

Kal pulled her against him, kissing her, his hands sliding under her arms, rubbing her shoulders. But she was rigid, tense.

Their eyes met.

Instinctively Kal raised the sheet to cover her.

Erika closed her eyes, closed him out. *I hate my body.* "I think it's because I was in a wheelchair." *I don't want to say this. I don't want him to know.*

"I think so, too. Tell me what it was like. You can tell me anything, Erika." Her eyes opened, and he moved his head closer to hers. "We live together. I'm going to know more about you than anyone, and you're going to know more about me. That's the beautiful thing about being married. You know each other's weaknesses, and you love and are loved, anyhow."

"Character weakness is one thing . . ." Erika began.

"It's uglier than anything on your body. Just like goodness is more beautiful. You know that."

She knew it. But only because he'd said it.

"I love you," he said. "And nothing you say is going to disgust me."

And so he held her and she told him. She told him what it had been like every day, the horrible ways her body had not worked right, things she'd never discussed with a lover. About falling on the ship, between her wheelchair and her bunk. About feeling half-human yet knowing she was fully human.

Kal never let her go, and her words moved from matters of the body to the spirit.

"I didn't know what to do. I was a diver. I was an artist, but I was an athlete, too. I was so ugly suddenly, and René couldn't even stay in the hospital room with me. When Skye came, I wished she was there, instead of me. I told her she was a self-centered bitch and the world would be a better place without her. I said why didn't she do us a favor and get out of our lives? I said my brother would be happier without her. I told her she was ugly inside. . . ."

Whispers. No tears. Erika, who cried so easily over flowers, did not cry about this, he saw.

"Then she slept with René. And then— Oh, Kal, it wasn't better without her. It was horrible, for David and for Chris. I never stop wondering if what I said was the last straw. What if she killed herself because of me? I can't stand it. I think about it every day. I always will. I want to believe she's moved on to a higher place, but I *don't* believe it. She was a weak woman, and she chose a weak way out. I think she's in hell, and I put her there. She could have stayed on earth and become a better person—"

"Erika." Kal sat up. "Wait. Stop. This woman tried to ram your brother with a car. She was trying to hurt him, and she hurt you. You got mad. That's all that—"

"I shouldn't have. It doesn't matter what she did. I have to think about what *I* did. I want to participate in *bon-odori*, Kal. I want to do things for her. I want to try to be good for her. If anyone might be with the Hungry Ghosts of Hell, it's her. I need to close this somehow. I need peace."

Obon.

Kal wanted to groan. Of all the ways she could deal with her guilt, she had to ask that.

Gone was any hope of experiencing the *bon* dances in a secular context. Erika understood the symbolism of the festival, and it held meaning in her life.

Unfortunately, the same was true for him.

If it wasn't, he would have encouraged her to rejoice for Mr. and Mrs. Akana and learn some *bon* dances. He would have taken her to the temples, where the slow enchanting rhythms floated on the summer night.

But he didn't want to rejoice for the souls of the dead.

He didn't want to feel Maka leave on the last night, to see her as a candle afloat on the water, a flame that could no longer be held.

Angry, knowing there was no chance in *hell* that he was going with her, knowing Erika was going to have to do this one alone and without his blessing, he said, "Yeah, I hear you." And he scrambled to the end of the bed and opened Kin's crate. "Come on, boy. Come on out."

CHAPTER FIFTEEN

THE AFTERNOON WAS HUMID and sultry, billowing clouds choking the sunlight without cooling the day. At six Erika and Kal pushed the outrigger down to the shallows and out into the surf and paddled toward Keʻe Beach. It was crowded, full of tourists and, sweating, they went on to Hanakapiai. They paddled until their arms were sore, and when they reached the beach it was nearly deserted.

"We're going to be alone soon," said Kal. "Maybe we can have a romantic time." *Instead of talking about the bon festival.*

They dragged the outrigger far up into the sand, then went into the water, swimming down to the wet caves at the southwest end of the beach. A lava boulder protruded above the surface near the caves, and Kal paused behind it. The placid water was still translucent under the dark sky. But he and Erika were alone, as he'd wanted. He watched her rinse the sweat off her body and dive down to touch the sand, and he dove after her, grabbing her beneath the surface as they came up.

Erika relaxed in his wet embrace. When the water cleared from her lashes, she saw how dark the sea and sky had made his eyes.

He kissed her, touching her face, the way he always did. "Put your legs around me, Erika."

Shaky from the emotion of the afternoon, in which she'd learned to depend on him, she put her hands on his shoulders and did as he asked. Her legs around his waist.

Kal's hands on her bottom drew her all the way against his penis, which was trying to penetrate barriers of cloth.

They kissed again.

"Kal...this feels good. I like it in the water." The ocean was hers, the blue wash in which they floated a part of her. She had been born in it and raised in it like a thing of the sea.

"Does this feel good, too?" A taste of how it would feel...

"Yes."

Kissing her salty wet mouth, he whispered, "I love you even more than I did at noon. You're brave. It's okay, Erika. All that stuff is okay."

Skye... That would never be okay.

"Feel what you do to me, Erika. You've got me so turned on."

He said more. The tension left her body. All that remained was natural response to him, to his excitement. She let him take off her bikini and set both pieces on the lava rock, out of the way of the tide. His shorts, too. He reached for her again, wrapped her around him. All the barriers between them had vanished. She felt only his skin. And she trembled.

He kissed her lips again, teasing her with his erection, feeling like he was going to come from the sensation. "This could make a baby."

"Not now." She liked the smoothness pressed close to her. She wanted him inside her and couldn't remember ever feeling that way about anyone.

"That's not a very reliable method."

Erika just looked at him. She knew her own cycles.

He pushed into her and she opened to him, letting him guide her, grateful for the buoyant salt water to support her. It felt good. It felt life-giving, like his tongue in her mouth. Making love.

Her awfulness—the ugliness she perceived in herself—passed over her and through her. She shuddered, shaking it off. "Kal..."

"Don't think." He couldn't think, either, or he'd think about Maka. Hard to have another woman. Hard to be inside her, feeling her wetness. Beautiful, too.

But this wasn't *a first time without*. It was all Erika. It was exactly what he wanted.

Bride, he thought, and he held her tighter, wanting to protect her and give her everything. Her mouth was against his shoulder, kissing him, pressing hard with her lips as she made love to him. He held her tighter, went deeper, his own urgency making him half-crazy. "Oh, God, Erika. Just..." The next sound was a quiet moan.

It was hers.

"There, baby..."

She was lost, different from how he'd seen her before, and he was different, too. They were in the same place. Adrift.

Erika buried her face in his shoulder, and he held her down on him, moved gently against her, his blue eyes half-closed. She cried, and a small wave, a tingling baby breaker, swept through her. What happened to Kal was stronger, more intense. His lips bit down on her wet hair, arms crushing her. Shaking. "Erika..."

They held each other afterward in the water, and Kal wished they were back at the house in bed and never had to get up. Because he wanted to tell her things, as she had told him.

"Let's go sit on the beach," he said.

They put on their wet swimsuits and swam around the lava boulder and back to the beach. Their towels were in the outrigger. Wrapped up in them, they sat on the still-warm sand, and Kal told her about the night the police cars came and when he had to go and identify her and crying at night with Hiialo. He told her about the hurricane that came eight days later and tore apart the rest of his life and ravaged the island that was his home.

In the end, as the sun became just a dome on the horizon, as he felt the urgency that they must leave, he told her the truth. As close to the truth as he could speak.

"Erika, I can't go to the *bon* dances with you. They mean something to me, and I don't want to go. That time was too painful. If I participated in *obon*, I'd live it again."

Maka's death. Erika understood more than he'd said. He didn't want to face Maka's death again because he had never let her go.

Silencing the cry inside her—that he was saving parts of himself for Maka, that he was putting a dead woman before his wife—she said the only thing she could. "That's fine, Kal. The last thing I want is to cause you pain."

Unfortunately the price of saving him pain was accepting it herself, by living with the ghost of Maka, not a beloved memory, but too strong a presence in his heart.

THEY MADE A PIZZA for dinner, with a thick whole-wheat crust loaded with vegetables. Afterward they walked Kin on the beach in the dark of the new-moon night, beginning leash work.

"You've got to understand," Kal said, "that this dog is going to grow. He'll be big and powerful, and it's his nature to want to be in charge. But *you* have to be in charge. Never give a command unless you have the time to make sure he obeys it. If you let him disobey, he's one up on you."

He didn't apply the same rules to Hiialo. Erika remembered Hiialo's heedless behavior. And she remembered Kal's face above her the morning of their wedding, the bad luck of her seeing him before the ceremony. Even though he said it wasn't bad luck at all. For no reason a shiver ran over her.

They played with Kin in the sand in front of the beach house, working on getting him to come when his name was called. Erika loved his three-colored coat. He was a good dog, a baby who looked up at her with concerned brown eyes.

When the sky grew dark, they took the puppy inside and put him in his crate where he lay down to sleep. Erika and Kal opened wedding presents, and Erika wrote down who they had come from. Many people had given them money, and Kal counted it with satisfaction. There was almost six hundred dollars. "What do you want to do?" he asked. "We could go to Honolulu and stay at the Royal Hawaiian. Eat and dance and order from room service and go to the aquarium and Pearl Harbor. Or we could be practical and trade in the Datsun. Buy another car. I have a thousand dollars in savings."

Erika had almost that much herself. "Where do we get a new car?"

"Lihue, if we want to trade in the old one. Or we can check the papers, see if there's something we want to buy."

They decided to go to Lihue the next day. Erika asked, "Are you going to practice with your band this week?"

Kal shook his head. "It's our honeymoon."

"Kal."

He lifted his eyebrows, waiting.

"It's okay with me. The music. I just want you to know. It'll be hard—with you gone at night. But I'll stay with Hiialo." Erika stopped speaking. She realized the truth, and it was ugly. She was doing what she'd never done before they were married. Bribing him—to love her.

Love me like you loved Maka. Love me more.

She got up from the couch where they were sitting and went into the kitchen to get a drink and regain her dignity.

Kal's voice called to her cheerfully from the couch. "Thanks."

And she knew suddenly that while she had been bestowing a gift, it was actually something he had been planning to take all along.

LATER, WITH THE PATIO doors open and a light burning in the front room like a night-light, they went into the bedroom. The bed was unmade and a little sandy from that afternoon.

Erika began hesitantly to remove her tropical-print rayon dress.

"Not yet. Come here." Kal wrapped his hand around hers, coaxed her toward the bed. When they lay facing each other, heads on the pillows, he said, "It's just like the ocean."

She moved into his arms and it was.

"I didn't let you take this off because I wanted to." He unbuttoned her dress. Beneath, her bra was of some fine navy blue fabric, sheer enough to see through. Like her dress, it opened in front. He pressed his face to her. "I loved that today."

Erika's eyes were closed. *Don't wake up from the dream. Don't think about During.*

Kal kissed one breast, one nipple. She put her hands on his head, in his hair, and imagined the ocean around them. As he touched between her legs, she stayed in that sea of blue, a sea that had become his eyes. She didn't know when she'd opened hers again. He made her sit up and helped her out of her dress.

Then he was touching her, talking to her, sliding off her underwear. *I'm going to die of this,* thought Erika. She heard him taking off his clothes.

"Look at me, Erika."

She did and saw in the half-light what she had not seen in the water. She swallowed. "Kal."

He was moving against her body, embracing her, rolling her onto her stomach. He rubbed her spine as he had so many nights, then lay tenderly against her, cradling her, protecting her with his body. Erika could feel his heart, his mouth on her neck and her jaw, his weight on her.

She wanted to be one with him. He put on a condom— "I don't trust your method"—and touched her as he pushed inside.

Erika gasped softly, and her eyes watered. He cradled her with his arms and went in deeper.

"I love you," she said. "I'm so in love with you."

"Two of us are in love." Deeper. "God, Erika." He held one of her breasts, and he pressed his mouth against her shoulder, then the side of her face. "I love you."

He kissed her jaw for a long time while he tried to get as close to her as he could. He felt that place inside him that remembered Maka, too, and he knew that loving her—and losing her—had allowed him to love this woman more. But he expelled Maka from his thoughts.

His cheek to Erika's, he asked, "Are you all right? Comfortable?"

"Yes." The sheet swallowed the word. She'd never before known what it was like to be in love with someone and to have him inside her this way.

Kal covered one of her hands, which had twisted into a fist. He talked to her quietly, exciting her. He was going to make it happen, just like before. Erika felt the loss of control approaching, and she didn't fight it, just felt the closeness of their mating, of their movements against each other.

"Kal..." Her voice was odd, too high. Sounds came from her and she couldn't think. There was just a feeling like waves crashing in her head. She tried to hear the surf, and when she listened she did, but then she just felt Kal and the hot liquid sensations he was making inside her.

"I love you," he said again, moving inside her.

He heard her gasping lightly, and that made it hard not to come. He had to focus on holding on, on not letting it end. But when he heard her deep cry and felt her clench around him, he surrendered. They were both shaking hard, coming, and the tears were released from his eyes because he remembered what it was like with Maka and this time it was so completely different.

They separated, and Kal pulled off the condom. The end was broken.

"And you don't trust my method," said Erika. "Where'd you buy that thing?"

He dropped it in the trash, grabbed her, tickled her till she screamed and begged him to stop. In the dark he said, "Do you want to have a baby, Erika?"

She was practicing never lying to him. "Yes."

The next second was long. She had no clue what he was thinking, but finally he hugged her tighter. "Let's get busy, then. *Hana hou.*"

THEY WENT TO LIHUE the next day, traded in the Datsun and spent two thousand dollars on a rusty twenty-year-old aquamarine Thunderbird, then messed around a nearby shopping mall. They bought a T-shirt and a new Barbie doll for Hiialo, a new paintbrush for Erika and three CDs for Kal. On the way home Erika spotted a red-and-white-striped bandstand in the middle of a courtyard outside a Buddhist community center. Around the tall square bandstand was printed BON DANCE CLUB.

Kal saw it, too.

Neither of them said a word.

WHEN THEY GOT HOME, they made dinner, took a hike to Waikapalae Cave and swam in the Blue Room, naked, until they were both cold. Back at the bungalow after-ward, Kal played his guitar and Erika tried more sketches, using a photograph she'd taken the first time they'd gone to the Blue Room. In the picture Kal was sitting forward on the ledge talking to Hiialo, who was out of camera range. As she was working, a gecko crawled over the arm of the couch. Erika stopped sketching and stared at it, trying to make out its features. Without daring to turn the page, she roughed out a sketch of the lizard.

In her mind something clicked. She remembered weeks before, at the gallery. Hiialo had asked for a picture of her father. Suddenly Erika knew what she was going to do. When the gecko moved away, she got up to try to see where it had gone, but it had disappeared. She went to the bedroom and collected watercolor paper, palette, paints and brushes.

Kal had been sitting across from her, figuring out a song, repeating the chords he'd learned, experimenting with finger-picking, but when Erika returned to the room and started working, when she actually began painting, he stilled his hands and watched her face.

She didn't notice that the music had stopped.

She was gone far away.

He absorbed her presence. How long would it take him to shake the little whispers of disloyalty and guilt, the pining for Maka? After a bit, he put the Gibson in its case and went to the bedroom to let Kin out of his crate. He took the dog outside and played with him in the dark in the sand, and when he came back in, Erika was still working. She painted as the hours crept on, and he didn't disturb her, though sometimes he came near enough to see what she was doing.

It was him. He must have been talking to Hiialo when she took that photo. He hadn't known he seemed so earnest when he spoke to her.

In Erika's watercolor he wasn't talking to Hiialo.

He was speaking with Eduardo.

He wanted to put his hands in Erika's hair, to touch her. Instead, he let her be. He went back to his guitar, taking breaks to stare at her, to watch her eyes, so deeply focused on the paper. Taking a long break to walk back to the bungalow and collect some of the last mangoes of the season from the tree.

She finished at two-thirty in the morning. She set the watercolor on the coffee table, and they both stood over it, studying it.

Kal said, "It's great."

"It's for Hiialo. She wanted a picture of you."

"She'll love it."

Erika was amazed he was still awake, still there, waiting for her. When she was painting at night, René had always gone downtown to the bar. Where there were other women ...

She cleaned her brushes and they went to bed. She knew that was what Kal had been waiting for, to make love again.

He tried to take things further. He'd tried in the Blue Room, but she had known what he wanted and had dodged him, trying to say every way but with words that she didn't want it. She'd just gotten used to making love with him, to feeling desire.

In bed with him she couldn't swim away.

"Shh ..."

"No," she said. "I really don't like it, Kal. Please don't."

His mouth was on her flat stomach, on the slender area that, though she was thirty-six, had never grown full with a child. He kissed the hollow beside one hipbone. He nudged her thighs apart.

"Please don't, Kal."

He sat up, touching her.

She wouldn't look at him.

He couldn't say to her, *Why doesn't it excite you?* He couldn't say that Maka had liked it. He couldn't even remind her that love was giving.

"Erika?"

She opened her eyes, stared in the dark.

"You know Sam-I-am, the guy selling green eggs and ham?"

"Yes." She looked wary.

"Try it, you might like it?" He lifted his eyebrows. "Two minutes?"

I know what it's like, Kal. Been there, done that. She didn't want to remind him.

Give. As he was trying to give to her. It was, she knew, a sweet act of love. But she hated the exposure, the intimacy. It was almost more than she could bear. As soon as one level of closeness was reached, Kal went deeper.

"Okay." It was a whisper.

Kal pressed his cheek against hers, kissed her mouth. Then he bowed over her, and she saw his shoulders in the dark. She wanted to shut her eyes, but he was too beautiful. Unable to look away, she saw his head go down and his mouth kissing her, and there was so much love in him that something changed inside her. She dared herself to look at the body he kissed, her hips, the juncture of her thighs. Herself. Seeing herself as the object of the love he bestowed, she thought with stunned pleasure, *I'm beautiful.* It was the first time in five years, perhaps in her life, that she had loved her body. Seeing what he was doing. His hands opened her. His tongue probed her, caressed her.

Erika's breath grew ragged, and the dark world came, the sex world that was as out of control as she had been during those three years on the *Skye*. She hadn't been able to control the feeling in her body, to get it back.

She couldn't control this, either.

The only control was to choose not to do it, to tell him to leave her alone.

Or to give the control to him. To let him play her like one of his guitars.

She gave. Love. Trust.

"Kal..." His name became a cry, and she tossed, enjoying a body she had forgotten how to do anything but hate, feeling suddenly proud and beautiful, as beautiful as he said she was. The sounds she made didn't matter to her, but he soothed her and held her, controlling her, not letting her escape, as though she could have escaped.

Kal felt her reborn in his hands, from the love he gave with his mouth.

And the night was so good and so long that in the morning, after he'd taken the puppy outside and brought him back in, he wasn't afraid to go into the kitchen and retrieve the mangoes he'd picked the night before. When he returned to the bedroom, Erika's dark eyes were watching him as though she wanted him.

Crawling onto the bed with her, he said, "At our wedding, it just for a minute crossed my mind that the thought of oral sex with me made you throw up."

"Well, it did."

He kissed her smile. "Guess what we're having for breakfast in bed, *ipo*." Sweetheart. Lover.

Erika welcomed him into the sheets, and together they learned more about love and joy.

CHAPTER SIXTEEN

"YOU TWO LOOK WONDERFUL," said Mary Helen, when they came to pick up Hiialo on Sunday night, one week after the day they were married. She kissed both of them, and Erika wondered if Mary Helen, too, had feared that Kal would never really get over Maka.

An inarticulate unhappiness tugged at the edge of her mind, and she pushed it away. *Don't think about his room, about the quilt on his bed. Think about the room and the bed you're going to share.*

Hiialo was eager to see Kin again, and though it was past her bedtime when they got home, they let her play with the puppy for fifteen minutes before bed. During that time, Erika walked down the hall to her room, the room she would share with Kal.

On the way she paused beside the beads in his doorway. He was unpacking. The purple quilt lay smooth on his bed.

It probably didn't mean anything. She should just suggest he pack it away somewhere, for Hiialo.

Oh, right. And how are you going to word that request?

But Erika slipped between the beads.

Shutting the closet, Kal saw her. "Hi." He grinned and came nearer to hold her. "We can try out your bed together when Hiialo's asleep."

Their lips touched. It gave her courage. "Do you want to move your things in there? We could use this room for...I don't know." She shrugged, wishing she hadn't gone so far, hadn't actually suggested taking apart his room.

Kal glanced around. "I've got a lot of stuff. It's probably better for me to keep using this closet. We'll see."

It's not important, she thought. *Let it drop.*

But the feeling, the twinge of jealousy, had become an entity inside her and it would not rest. After Hiialo was in bed, Erika went into the room that had been hers to find Kal spreading their new wedding quilt on the bed. The older one, his birth quilt, he'd folded and set on a chair.

A better chance would never come. "I love that quilt," said Erika, nodding to the one his grandmother had made. "Maybe we could use it on your bed."

Intuition pricked Kal. There was something in her voice that told him she wasn't just talking about redecorating. Or maybe his own guilt made it sound that way. The purple quilt on his bed . . .

He turned. "You're right. Good idea."

Surprised by his agreement, Erika watched him take the yellow-and-red quilt through the door that adjoined their rooms. She looked in to see him folding the purple quilt and opening his closet.

A gravity fell over her, and she moved from the door.

He knows. He knows how I feel, so he put it away.

But the action of changing the quilts on the bed hadn't accomplished what she'd hoped. It had only, for some reason she didn't understand, confirmed the belief that bled inside her.

He could strip all signs of Maka from his room and his house, in courtesy to her, his new wife.

But Maka would still be there, first in his heart.

DAVID AND JEAN and Chris had gone, returned to Greenland. Adele was back on the mainland. Erika resumed her schedule of painting at the gallery on Tuesdays, with Hiialo, and sold two more watercolors, after which she asked Kal if he wanted to shorten his work hours some. Gladly he arranged with Kroner to have both Wednesdays and Thursdays off, yet Erika saw no more of him than she had before.

He had become a professional musician again, with a dedication that showed her how much it meant to him— and that increased her niggling suspicion that he'd married her so she would be there for Hiialo and he could play with his band. It had to be at least partly true.

But he did love her. Erika believed that, because there was no room for that kind of lie in the double bed they shared. She slept well in his arms. But when the sun shone outside or when the lights still burned in the house, he played music. And Erika kept waiting for the joy to end, for the tragedy that would explode her happiness.

Kai Nui had a gig in Honolulu, at a popular club in Waikiki, on the third weekend in August.

Tragedy came two weeks before, on August first.

It wasn't the tragedy Erika feared or anticipated, that Kal would cease to love her.

It was something she'd forgotten to fear.

The first was a Thursday, Kal's day off. Erika took Kin with her on a painting trip to Wailua Falls, halfway around the island. She would've liked to take Hiialo, too, but Danny had promised to come over and teach her some hula that day.

Kin seemed fifty percent bigger than when Erika had first received him as a wedding gift from Kal. A family dog, the Akita possessed deep affection for Kal and especially for Hiialo, but most of all he responded to Erika and she to him. She loved him as she'd never known a person could love an animal, and driving home from the falls, she worked on his automobile manners. Sit. Stay. He sat patiently on the seat, and Erika was feeling happy when she turned down the driveway in the rain and steered the huge Thunderbird into the spot beside the garden shed.

As she was getting out of the car, Kal walked out onto the lanai. Erika told Kin, ''Go see Kal.'' Tail wagging, the puppy trotted to the porch. Gathering the tote bag that held her art supplies, Erika checked to see that the water-color she'd completed was protected from the rain.

Barefoot, Kal came down the steps and across the lawn. He held the car door open for her.

''That was fun, Kal. Thanks for letting me get away for the day.'' When she kissed him, she saw in his eyes that something was wrong.

''Kal?''

The rain beaded on his hair and his eyebrows and nose. ''Come inside.''

She was scared. ''What is it?''

The car door was still open.

Kal held her arm, looking into her eyes. ''Kurt just called. Adele had a heart attack yesterday. She's dead.''

''Oo-ooh.'' The wavering sound had nothing to do with words, just with pain. Kal couldn't take it away. He wasn't Adele, who could laugh at the antics of men and children, who could tell Erika that René had never been worth a single tear, that Skye had charted her own course to self-destruction, who had said all the right things Before, During and After. Who could always make her laugh. Who had saved her with art.

''No. No...''

She didn't remember going inside. ''Where's Hiialo?''

''My folks' house. It's just you and me.'' He took her to what at first had been only her room, to the bed they now shared, to lie down and feel numb.

''Kal...''

He could hold her against him as though she was Hiialo. Sobbing woman.

''She's my best friend. I need her... Oh, God, what about Kurt? And Jason?'' Their son.

Kal's hand held her hair, her head.

After a while Erika lay back, staring vacantly at the ceiling. Where was Adele? "I have to see her. I have to go to California."

He was holding her hand. He knew all those things.

He hated death.

"Kal . . ."

They both wanted to make love, to make death go away. They joined their bodies while the rain poured off the eaves and the sky darkened with the end of the day. Then they drank *mai-tais,* Erika to try to blunt the pain, and they made love again. After that, Erika called Kurt and talked to him for an hour and a half.

When she got off the phone, her eyes were hollow, and Kal saw her walking around trying to function, an imitation of how he had been four years before.

Hiialo was going to sleep at his parents' house, but once it was dark they went over, anyhow, walking Kin through the rain. When they went in the door, Raiden approached to sniff the puppy and Mary Helen emerged from the kitchen and embraced Erika.

"Oh, darling," she said.

Erika began crying again. "Mom."

She went into the kitchen with Mary Helen and Kal, and she told them about Adele and how when she couldn't walk, Adele had been there, always ready with a wisecrack and never with pity. *Why should I feel sorry for someone who can paint like you? Get outta here.*

King came in and leaned against the counter with Kal.

Mary Helen told of when her friend Lou had died of breast cancer. Talking story.

Talking story.

Kal thought about when Maka died, but none of them mentioned it, because it was too hard to think about how she had looked. They'd all seen her in the casket, fixed the best the funeral director could do. After a while Kal left the kitchen and went down the hall and looked at the photo of them in the Fern Grotto, and the hurt caught him and made him cry.

Death was a fishing net, and it gathered up all the old deaths, too.

He went outside and lay on the wet lawn with Raiden and cried, holding his stomach, trying to forget.

He would never forget. He had a new wife, and he loved her, but Maka would never go away.

"Kal."

It was his father.

Kal sat up, found. He shook off the tears and stood.

"Erika's looking for you." There was a quiet warning in his voice.

Kal didn't hear it. He straightened his face, dried the tears, glad it was dark. "I love Erika," he said, in case his father got the wrong idea, that he didn't. "I really love Erika."

King pressed a hand on his shoulder and said nothing.

A man who'd been happily married thirty-five years might doubt that you could love a new wife as much as an old one.

But in some ways, I love her more. Instinct pulled his eyes toward the house.

Sickness crept over him, and he knew why his father had not responded.

Erika stood on the patio, watching him through the twilight.

His stomach felt like lead.

It's nothing. You were just crying.

No, he'd been sobbing. And Erika would know it hadn't been for Adele. He felt like throwing up. Like she'd caught him in bed with another woman.

His father slipped away into the night, walking toward the kennels as though fleeing the scene of a disaster.

On the patio Erika was motionless.

Raindrops hit his face.

He walked toward her.

Erika saw his dark form, the tall broad-shouldered body. The sound of his sobs was still with her, would never leave her, nor those words of denial he had cried to his father. *I love Erika. I really love Erika.*

As though he needed to convince them both.

This was not the stroke of twelve. This was not Cinderella locked in the tower while her stepsisters tried on the glass slipper downstairs.

This was real. Water spilled on the painting of her life, flooding the colors to gray.

Her husband faced her, and she saw his features wet with rain. She saw the pulse at his throat, evidence of the heart that had pounded against hers when they made love.

She had never seen infidelity till now.

He spoke her name on a breath. "Erika..."

No reason to answer. *Adele. You could have made me laugh through this.*

No. Not even Adele.

She turned from him, because there was nothing that could be said. Sick, disgraced, Kal followed her inside, followed her up the stairs of his childhood home to see Hiialo sleeping in his old bed. As Erika covered her, he felt the enormity of his error.

Of not letting go of the dead.

It had cost him the living.

Without meeting his eyes, she walked past him to the door, and he tried the plea of the unfaithful. Grabbing her arm. "Erika. It doesn't mean anything. It's death. It's just death."

The room was dark, but her brown eyes were the eyes of Pele, the goddess of volcanos, who could turn men to ashes. With a steely strength he'd never known she possessed, she said, "Don't ever lie to me again."

And when she had gone downstairs without him, he stood frozen, leaning against the doorjamb, half clinging to it. He had lied.

And she had known.

His fear, the enormity of the knowledge between them, made him want to sink to the floor, to cover his head with his hands, to pray for it to be undone. How could he have been so stupid? Clinging to Maka was pointless. She was gone. She was utterly gone and would not comfort him and did not care.

Erika, alive—Erika, his lover...

Oh, shit. Oh, shit. He tore his hand through his hair, thinking he would go mad.

His breath grew weak, imperiled by recollection of his face against her thighs, of her cries, of their intense promises of devotion. *I love you so much. I'll never leave you.*

The hideous part was, he knew she wouldn't. She would stay.

For Hiialo.

Because she would never hurt his child.

WHEN HE CAME DOWNSTAIRS, she stood in the living room with his parents. Kin explored at the end of the leash in her hand as Kal's father remarked, "It's still *bon-odori.*"

Erika had seen Kal in the arch at the edge of the room. She ignored him.

Bon-odori. Adele. Skye. If she could deal with the deaths, if she could put them somewhere, she would find a way to go on. Oh, she couldn't think about Kal now. She had to go to California. The funeral. Horror returned.

Obon would end sometime in early August. She asked King, "Does it take long to learn the *bon* dances?"

"Well, there are lots of them. But I could teach you a few. Mom and I have done them many times. So has Kal."

From the arch, Kal saw his father's eyes. King's were saying, *You messed up, son. Hope you can make it right. Better start now.*

His stomach felt wrenched, and he remembered that once he'd had an ulcer. Without her. Before her.

Erika tried to think through her numbness. "Could I learn enough to participate? I'll be in California a few days. Maybe longer. But when I come back..."

"Weekend after next is the last, I think," said Mary Helen. "You could certainly learn some dances by then. I have a kimono you can borrow. You'll need one. But oh, mine will be short on you."

Kal ventured into the room and took Kin's leash from her hand. Relinquishing it without a glance, Erika said, "I'd like to learn the dances. I haven't made a plane reservation yet. But maybe I could come over tomorrow morning?"

"Sure," said King. He squinted at Kal. "You'll be at work, won't you?"

Kal stiffened inside, knowing the price his father thought he should pay. Because they'd practiced the dances together the summer after Iniki, after Maka had died. But when *obon* came, he couldn't face it.

Coldly, resenting the interference, he said, "Yes. I have to work."

A short time later, he and Erika left in the rain. She limped in silence, and he didn't try again to explain. He was shamed. And when they went to bed, she turned away from his love, from his hands touching her, needing her. He begged, pleaded for forgiveness without confessing his crime. But no longer denying it. "Please. I love you. You're here. Erika, I need you."

Her body was something he craved, and he'd never known before that she was his nourishment, that he would grow sick without her. "Please. Erika, I love you so much."

His voice reached her ears, and she had never heard a voice like that before. Even when René had begged forgiveness, she could perceive his falseness, that though he was sincere, he was also fickle.

With Kal it wasn't like that.

Wind banged the blinds gently in the windows as she turned to him. Her heart vacillated between hurt and distrust and the dreadful fear that, if she didn't forgive him, it would be over. That he would not come to her like this again.

She had forgiven in the past. But Kal mattered to her too much. How little she knew his character. How deeply she believed in it. She staked her heart on that faith and she told him, "Sorry isn't good enough."

They did not make love.

He got up and went outside with the Gibson, which he couldn't play. He slept on the lawn, rolled up in the quilt his grandmother had made before he was born. And when he came home from work the next day, Hiialo was at his parents' house and Erika was gone.

HE BROUGHT HIIALO HOME and slept alone in his and Erika's bed, her scent all around him, making him crazy with pain. He tried to lose himself in his music, and on Saturday he called Jakka and Danny to come over and practice. While Hiialo played with Kin, Kal poured his mind into the Stratocaster, forgetting everything until Jakka remarked, "Hey, where's the *keiki?*"

"Hiialo?" In the front room, where they'd been playing, Kal unfastened his guitar strap and set down the instrument. "Hey, Hiialo."

They all three began wandering through the house, and it was an eerie echo of the past. He and his two friends and a little girl. No mother. Hiialo wasn't inside, so Kal went out on the lanai and called for her.

She didn't come.

He searched the yard and the shed where the washer and dryer were. The dog was missing, too, so he called for them both. There was no response, and in his mind were Erika's worries about all the dangers he had said would never find Hiialo. He was scared, ready to call 911.

But first he jogged down the driveway to the beach, and there they were, Hiialo teaching the puppy to lie down.

Kal spent a long time catching his breath before he spoke. Even then, he yelled. She cried, threw a tantrum, reminding Kal of how it had been before Erika. It had been a long time since Hiialo had thrown a tantrum.

Kin comforted her and growled at Kal, behavior Kal had to discipline aggressively. They couldn't have an Akita who growled at them.

Band practice was over for the day.

He needed antacids, and he took them.

When Hiialo was in bed, Kal went into his old room, put Pink Floyd's *The Dark Side of the Moon,* side two, on the turntable.

The night was lonelier than before Erika had come.

He went into the room where they slept together and stared at the watercolors on her wall. In his mind he saw her hands and how she looked when she painted. Missing her, wanting just to see things that brought her closer, he opened one of the drawers under the bed and looked at her clothes neatly folded there. She folded his clothes perfectly after she washed them. Much better than he ever had.

From the next room he heard a bittersweet tribute to the passage of time, to late starts and missed chances.

He shut the drawer with his knee and fell on the bed, his head in his arms. *Sorry isn't good enough.*

Maybe it would have been, if not for the way things had begun between them. With the ad. And his letter.

Recollection gnawed at him.

Oh, God, that letter.

Did she still have it?

He sat up, scanned the room.

She must have it somewhere. Erika didn't throw things out, especially anything he or Hiialo had given her. There were dried *leis* hanging on the wall and all kinds of little paper things from Hiialo.

Possessed, he got up from the bed and began hunting, turning the room upside down in search of that fateful epistle he'd sent her. The first letter.

He felt no sense that he was violating her, because everywhere he looked he had a greater sense of Erika, a greater knowledge that she had made herself his completely.

As he should have made himself hers.

He found his letters on her art table, in a mahogany box he discovered also held ribbons from art shows. He read all the ribbons, all the things she'd won. His heart whispered, *I love you. I love you. Erika, I can't lose you.*

The letters were underneath, and he took them out and went to the first one. He knew it because it was addressed to Ms. Aloha, instead of to Erika Blade.

When he pulled it from the envelope, something fell out, and he remembered the cropped Christmas-card photo. Sweet Maka's arm.

He looked like a kid.

You wouldn't know me, Maka. Things have happened without you.

A hurricane happened.

And Erika, who had let him lick mango juice from her body, who had shown him a happiness that took him higher than he'd gone before. Higher. Deeper.

He unfolded the letter and read it.

. . . If you are still interested in Hiialo and me, please write back. But understand that even if a permanent domestic arrangement is possible, your relationship with me would be platonic. Maka and I were married for seven years, and no one can replace her in my heart. I want no other lover, and I would prefer to live alone, if not for Hiialo. Please understand this, because, as you said, we all need to be kind....

She had been kind.

She had saved his life.

And she still had this letter, in which he'd written that no one could replace Maka in his heart, which was true.

He hadn't known there was so much room in his heart.

He read the other letters he'd sent her, too. He looked at all the photos. When he was done, he put them away and went back to his old room and fell to his knees on the floor. Burying his head in his arms, beside the instruments on which he released his finest gifts, he begged and vowed to be a better man.

THE NEXT DAY was Sunday, and he made some bread and took Hiialo and Kin and the loaf to his parents' house for breakfast. His father was out walking Raiden, but Niau had come up, and Kal and Hiialo ate breakfast with her and his mother.

Afterward Kal caught his mother when she was alone in the kitchen. "Mom, would you mind watching Hiialo for an hour or so? I have something I want to do."

Her eyes were curious, but she didn't ask. "That's fine. If you're looking for your dad, he walked Raiden down to Ke'e."

Kal was not looking for his dad. However, he could keep King off his back—with a confession, via Mary Helen. It was a system that always worked for averting those father-son top-dog confrontations. "I'm going next door."

Her eyes fluttered. "Oh." After a beat, "I'm not sure they're home."

Kal shrugged as though it didn't matter, as though he just hoped for a cup of tea.

The day was hot and muggy, hurricane weather, and he shook the damp cotton of his T-shirt from his body as he walked down the drive to a slot between the flame trees, a path to the property next door, a secret passage from childhood.

They're probably not home.

Next week was the Floating Lantern Festival. They'd probably been asked to dance at the Judo Mission in Haleiwa, on Oahu.

But he saw the glint of the Akanas' silver-blue Buick, and as he scanned the tangle of flowers, the riotous garden in front of their graceful sprawling home, he caught sight of a man amid the ginger. Mr. Akana straightened, staring at Kal from beneath thick white eyebrows. Then he smiled and waved.

Brushing an insect from his neck, Kal made his way through the flower beds. When he reached the old man, Mr. Akana was removing his gardening gloves. "Good morning. Nice surprise."

"Good morning. Your flowers look good."

"Thank you. You want to come inside and see June? Where your little girl?"

"She's next door. I'll go get her," Kal offered. He made a motion of departure, but then he stopped. "Actually I'd like to ask a favor." Awkwardly he faced the man who seven decades before had sent across the sea for a bride he'd never met.

In halting words, as courteously as he knew how, he asked for what he wanted.

Mr. Akana leaned on his hoe, wearing the sober face of a veteran of the Second World War, of one of the bravest and most decorated Allied regiments. He said, "In Japan, we have belief called *giri*. I do you favor, you owe me."

"Yes. I understand that."

"I old. What you going to do for me?"

"I'll dance for you, sir."

Mr. Akana laughed, clapped him on the back. "Ah, good. Go get little Hiialo, though. We want to see her."

NERVOUSLY ERIKA WATCHED the shrubs rush past as the plane descended to the airfield. It felt like a lifetime since she'd first landed in Lihue two months before. How could things have seemed simpler then?

Oh, Kal.

She missed him.

The funeral had been depressing, and she had felt helpless to do anything for Kurt and Jason, who had lost the sun of their world. She had longed for Hawaii, for the quality of light in the morning, for the scents of pikake and gardenias and the advance of rain. For shave ice and mangoes and long rice. She wanted Kal and Hiialo and to forget that drizzling night, to forget Kal sobbing on the lawn.

Far away in California, where she could not hold his body, it had seemed unimportant, her reaction overblown.

It was going to be okay. They'd talked briefly the night before to arrange for him to pick her up at the airport. She'd heard his heart in his voice. *I really miss you,* he'd told her. *We've got to talk when you get home.*

Before she left, sorry wasn't enough. But into the phone she'd said, *It doesn't matter. I love you, Kal.*

He was there, right inside the door, when she stepped into the terminal. He grabbed her in his arms, and they held each other as though there had been no hurt between them.

"I love you," he said. "I love you, Erika."

But they did not kiss.

On the way to the car, carrying her garment bag, his free hand in hers, he explained that Hiialo had gone to watch a hula festival in Princeville with his mother. Anxiously he unlocked her door and let her in, and when he'd put her garment bag in the trunk, he came around and got in, too.

Erika gazed at him in the hot interior of the car. "I'm sorry," she said.

"I am." From the back seat, he brought forward a gift-wrapped box. The paper was oriental, like a bamboo-screen design.

There was no card.

Erika knew about conscience gifts. This wasn't one. She unwrapped the paper and lifted the lid on the box. Folding back the tissue inside, she saw silk.

It was a kimono.

For *obon*.

Kal said softly, "I bought a *happi* coat for me."

Erika saw and felt his hands cover hers, hold them tight.

"And I've been practicing the dances."

The box was crushed in their embrace.

MARY HELEN AND HIIALO had returned from the hula festival by the time Kal and Erika reached Hanalei. They picked up Hiialo and Kin at the gallery, and Mary Helen showed them two oil paintings of Erika's that she'd framed while Erika was gone. *Shave Ice* and *Talk Story,* which was a picture of two local women smoking cigarettes and gabbing at a table in the Haena Store. "I really want you to think about a show, Erika," said Mary Helen. "To celebrate your new style. And we really have to get some of your work into shows in Honolulu, too."

Erika liked the idea of a show of her own in Hanalei, surrounded by her *ohana*.

When they left the gallery, they took Hiialo for shave ice, then headed home. As the familiar drive came into sight, Erika's heart beat irregularly, and she experienced what she never had before.

This was her home.

But time had passed. There was a pungent tangy smell in the air, oversweet, almost like garbage. She sniffed.

"Rotting mangoes," said Kal. Mango season was *pau*, finished.

Heat hung in the air.

They went up on the lanai, Hiialo dripping shave ice. Kicking off his slippers at the door, Kal asked, "Want to go swimming?"

"Hooray!" shouted Hiialo, taking her melting treat inside.

But Kal paused suddenly on the porch and took Erika's hand. She followed his gentle lead into the house. Carrying her bag, he led her toward the hall but paused at the door of his room.

"Come in here a minute."

The beads clattered around their bodies. Kal set her garment bag on the floor. "I moved the stereo out into the front room," he said. "And I cleaned out the closet. I thought you might want to store some of your paintings in here."

The closet stood empty and he said, "I put my clothes with yours. I'm kind of a slob," he warned her.

Erika hugged herself. *Yes. But you're mine.*

THEY WEREN'T QUICK about putting on their swimsuits, though they had got them on and were lying on the bed kissing when Hiialo bounded into their room in her neon green suit, jumping up and down. "Come on, come on," she said. "It's time to go swimming!"

Kal and Erika got up, and they all went out onto the lanai.

"Let's go, Kin," Hiialo said. She climbed around the porch railing so she could jump over the heliconia to the lawn.

Slinging a faded towel over his shoulder, Kal slid his fingers into the back of Erika's swimsuit, stroking her skin. They took their time crossing the lawn while Kin watered the traveler's palm and the autograph tree.

In the shade of that tree, Kal paused to scratch one of the leaves with a twig: I LOVE ERIKA.

"Come on, Kin! Let's go swimming!" yelled Hiialo, skipping ahead down the driveway.

Erika followed her with her eyes, welcoming the familiar sight of the ocean at the end of the drive. Turquoise and green, teal like Kal's eyes. Kal walked beside her, holding her hand. He dropped it to retrieve Kin's Frisbee from the shrubs growing alongside the blue house. Erika waited.

Hiialo had disappeared.

Kal whistled for the dog, ready to throw the Frisbee.

Kin didn't come.

"Kin!" called Erika.

A moment later the Akita ran up the driveway from the beach, barking.

Kal threw the Frisbee.

Kin ignored it. He barked, then turned and ran back toward the water.

Intuition made Erika hurry down the driveway.

But Hiialo was fine. She was waiting for them before going in the water. "Hurry up, Erika! Eduardo and I want you to come swimming!"

Still barking urgently, Kin ran into the froth at the edge of the water. He stood between Hiialo and the sea.

"Go away, Kin," Hiialo ordered.

The puppy continued to bark.

Kal trudged across the sand to get the Frisbee the dog had ignored. It had landed at the high-tide line.

"Kin, be quiet," said Erika. "Come."

He did not respond at once.

"Kin. Come."

Taking advantage of the puppy's distraction, Hiialo bounded around him and into the surf. She dove and came up splashing. "Come on in, Mommy!"

Mommy. Erika stared, her eyes stinging.

Yards away down the beach, Kal watched her till she looked at him. He smiled, blew her a small kiss. Hiialo had asked him if she could call Erika that.

Bending over, he scooped up Kin's Frisbee and started to straighten up. Then he looked down again.

Within the circular imprint the disc had left was a fist-sized blob, whitish-clear except for the sand clinging to it. Kal straightened up, scanned the wet shore.

"Hey, Hiialo! Get out of the water."

Her scream tore through the sounds of the wind and tide, and he ran, easily dodging all the box jellyfish washed up on the beach. The fleet was in.

Erika, limping, was already in the surf, where Hiialo was screaming hysterically, brushing at lines of red welts on her chest, where jellyfish tentacles still clung. "Daddy!"

Knowing what had to be done and what would happen to her from doing it, Erika pulled the tentacles off Hiialo's skin. Burning shot through her fingers, weakening her legs, clenching her stomach. Some of the tentacles remained stuck to Hiialo, some to her own hand, causing the most excruciating sensations she'd ever known. Moving on autopilot, she put that hand in the water and tried to wash the rest of the tentacles off Hiialo, holding the shrieking child with her other hand.

Her hand was burning.

Hiialo's little face contorted. Her limbs went strangely rigid. As a wave washed her little body forward against Erika's legs, Kal's arms came down to gather her up. "I've got you. I've got you."

Erika staggered after them out of the water, trying to think beyond the agonizing fire in her hand.

Hiialo convulsed, fighting Kal's arms. He had to set her down, and she lay on the sand going rigid, doing strange back bends, terrifying him.

"Call 911!" said Erika. "I'll stay with her."

He ran.

Kin circled Hiialo, whining in concern.

Helplessly watching her convulsions, Erika didn't even realize that she could turn from Hiialo and put her burning hand in the ocean to try to cool the pain. There was only this child, her child, *and nothing she could do to help her.* "Hiialo, I'm right here. Your dad went to call the doctor. I love you, Hiialo." *Oh, make my hand stop hurting, make it stop.* She wanted to scream. The world seemed fuzzy, tilting unreal, and she wanted to throw up.

After an eternity Hiialo's spasms slowed. Ceased.

"Hiialo, can you hear me?"

She lay motionless, and Erika scooted toward her on her knees. With her left hand, she felt for the pulse in Hiialo's carotid artery, so close to those blazing red-and-purple welts. She could not find it.

And Hiialo's small chest neither rose nor fell with breath.

CHAPTER SEVENTEEN

IT HAD BEEN YEARS since Erika had taken a CPR class. She couldn't remember anything about resuscitating children.

Airway, breathing, circulation.

Airway. Airway.

Erika tilted the small head back and used her left hand to open Hiialo's mouth to clear her airway, move her tongue. *Mommy...*

Oh, God, don't do this. Don't do this.

She didn't know she was gasping from the pain in her hand.

Kal skidded onto his knees in the sand beside her, and Erika moved out of the way, watched him do the things she had begun. Watched him start CPR on his daughter.

They heard sirens immediately. Erika sat motionless, breathing raggedly, holding Kin's collar with her left hand, sick from the pain in her right, praying and watching Kal's steady movements.

He was still working when Erika saw the lights of the ambulance.

She started to sing softly, sing away her own fear. Sing about Puff.

"Yeah, yeah, do that," said Kal, still counting.

He felt Hiialo's chest stir beneath him.

She gave a small cough.

He picked up the words from Erika, sang about the dragon who'd lived where they did.

She was breathing.

She was breathing.

Erika released Kin's collar without thinking, and the puppy went and sat down beside Hiialo, watching her face, waiting for her to open her eyes.

"YOU CAN'T DRIVE," said Erika. "Get in the passenger side."

Kal didn't argue. He walked around the Thunderbird and got in, but when Erika reached past the steering wheel with her left hand to start the car, he said, "What's wrong with your hand? Erika!" He pushed open the door again and ran into the house, emerging seconds later with some gauze pads and three bottles. He opened the driver's door. "Move over."

She unfastened her seat belt and slid over. Kal got behind the steering wheel. The welts on her hand crossed the insides and backs of three fingers and her thumb. Painting hand. Turning sideways in the seat, Kal laid her hand, palm up, across his knee. He made a paste of meat tenderizer and vinegar and used the gauze to apply it to her wounds. In his mind he saw the welts on Hiialo. There would be scars.

Stupid, Kal. You're stupid.

"Better, baby? Not yet. I know." He opened the bottle of Tylenol and handed her three. There was a water bottle on the floor of the car, and he fished it out and uncapped it.

Erika swallowed the pain relievers, drank some water. She felt as if she'd lost quarts of fluid. She tried to go away from the pain, to fly out over the ocean. "I'm fine. Let's go to Lihue."

To see Hiialo.

THE HOSPITAL LET THEM spend the night in Hiialo's room. Kal couldn't sleep, so Erika lay on the extra bed. A doctor in the emergency room had prescribed codeine for her hand and she fell asleep, and Kal sat in the dark listening to the night sounds of the hospital, looking at small Hiialo in the dark, with the IV in her arm.

She had woken up crying in the ambulance, he'd heard, and he'd listened to her wail in the emergency room. It was a long time before they'd moved her to a regular room, longer still before she'd gone to sleep.

He couldn't stand being inside his own mind.

If he'd told Hiialo to check for jellyfish on the beach...

But there hardly ever were jellyfish on the beach.

He wasn't a worrier.

Maybe he'd worried some when she was a baby, about her smothering at night, things like that. But after Maka's accident...

You just can't stand to think in what-ifs, Kal.

Erika shifted on the bed, turning over.

Kal wished they were all at home, that he was in bed with Erika where he could hold her close.

CPR. Counting. Hiialo not breathing. *Can't lose her...*

If he hadn't spent the last two years working as a tour guide, renewing his CPR and advanced first-aid certifications every year, she would be dead.

Deep breath. Take a deep breath.

The electronic equipment on her IV pole made intermittent beeps.

A nurse came into the room on silent shoes. She touched Kal's shoulder. Her voice reminded him of Maka's. "You can curl up with your wife on that bed if you want. You don't have to sleep in a chair."

"I'm fine. Thanks."

She smiled and moved around Hiialo's bed, switched on the light. Hiialo didn't stir, and Kal checked again to make sure he could see her chest rise and fall under the white bandages. Erika had pulled the tentacles off. Brave Erika. Christopher Blade's daughter must have known better.

The nurse tried to take Hiialo's vitals without waking her, but her eyes opened and she began to cry, trying to rub them, befuddled by the tube coming from her arm.

He stood up and went to her side. "It's all right, Ti-leaf. I'm here."

"Daddy, I want Pincushion and Fluff...."

Kal found Pincushion wedged against the bed rail and tucked him in Hiialo's arms. Fluff was under the covers. His parents had come to the hospital earlier bringing clothes for all of them, and Pincushion and Fluff and Hiialo's blanket.

Kal stroked Hiialo's hair. "Go to sleep, *keiki*."

In her bed Erika grew restless as sound and sensation penetrated her mind. Her hand was stuck to a hot skillet on the stove. She couldn't pull it off....

With a moan she opened her eyes and saw Kal standing over her. She glanced at Hiialo's bed to see a nurse switching out the light. As the young woman left the room, Erika said, "Kal?"

Hiialo had gone back to sleep.

"Here, baby." Kal gave Erika a glass of water and two of the pills from the bottle he'd stuffed into the pocket of his shorts. Erika wasn't a hospital patient, just a visitor, like him. Parent of a sick little girl.

Erika took the pills and lay down, and Kal kicked off his slippers and got onto the single bed with her. "Hi." She lifted the sheets to welcome him, and soon his arms were around her, holding her. He wouldn't go to sleep. Had to be awake for Hiialo.

Had to stay awake.

Waiting for the hurt in her hand to lessen, Erika clutched Kal's big hand, his musician's hand, which lay across her opposite arm. His fingers wound with hers, and he pulled her closer, hugging her tight.

"Erika," he said softly, drowsily.

A few minutes later, she felt him drift off to sleep.

SATURDAY NIGHT was the last night of *obon*, and there would be a Floating Lantern Festival at the temple in Waimea. Hiialo had been home from the hospital for three days, and by that afternoon she was well enough to visit her grandparents.

As Erika and he kissed her goodbye in the Johnsons's den before setting out for the south side of the island, Kal eyed the welts that reached up above the neck of Hiialo's T-shirt. There would be scars, though not as bad as he'd feared, thanks to Erika's pulling the tentacles off so quickly. But he knew he'd never forgive himself.

He would never again take the same attitude about Hiialo's safety—that mishaps could not be prevented. He hated that he had learned the lesson at her expense. A kind of sickness held him, death sickness.

Tonight he would take the cure.

He was ready—to let Maka go.

And he felt a strange relief that tonight's event was leading him back to Waimea, which had been their home.

THE HILLTOP CEMETERY in Waimea, which was largely Buddhist, showed the care relatives had taken of the deceased during *obon*. Many of the graves were freshly swept and bedecked with floral arrangements. Throughout the cemetery, the plumeria trees were blooming, sending off their sticky-sweet heady fragrance.

Kal parked the Thunderbird under a tree with cerise blossoms. The Waimea sky was brushed with faint white clouds, and he didn't bother to roll up his window, just looked over at Erika in her jungle green silk dress, the dress he loved on her. Her kimono and his *happi* coat, protected by a plastic dry-cleaner's bag, dangled from hangers in the back window. "You come with me, yeah?"

Their eyes met with the certainty of love, and she nodded.

He leaned across her to open her door, because of her hand. Gathering up the flowers from the seat between them, he opened his own door, and they both got out. As the trade winds blasted their hair, he went around the car and shifted the bouquets to his left hand to hold Erika's uninjured one with his right.

"It's up this way." He remembered the layout of the cemetery. Sometimes, when Hiialo spent the night with his folks, he had driven down to Waimea in the middle of the night and sat on the lawn on the hill and played his guitar for her.

Now he came in daylight, like a sane man. With Erika.

They reached the headstone, the piece of granite with her name and the dates with not even three decades' gap between them.

MAKANOE-PALI KEKAHUNA JOHNSON
MEA ALOHA

My beloved.

Kal knelt beside Maka's grave, fit the bouquets into the two places set for them in the ground. *Miss you,* he thought. *Won't ever stop missing you. Won't ever forget the way you laughed.*

Erika touched his hair and he felt her moving away, drifting off to look at other places, to leave him alone.

He sat by the grave and tried to talk to Maka, tried to believe she could hear. *You used to dance for me. Tonight I'll dance for you.*

He closed his eyes and remembered her face and the way she moved, and he opened them and saw the letters etched in the stone. The engraved evidence of the permanence of death.

He could not have her and had learned it was wrong to want her.

The only right thing was to let her go and to dance with joy for the good life she had lived and for her right to let her soul part from him and go to a sweeter place.

THEY PARKED three blocks from the temple in front of an empty lot. The sun had set, and the sky was lavender with fiery stripes.

Standing outside the car, Kal put on his *happi* coat and Erika her kimono.

He told her, "Maka and I lived on this street."

"Where?" She looked about.

"We'll walk past. The house is gone. Someone has a trailer there now."

He took her hand, and they crunched along the gravel street in their slippers. They could smell the food already.

But it was eerie to walk past the trailer where someone else lived and remember when a white house had stood there.

Erika put her arm around him.

"The hurricane wiped it all away. Like we have no history."

"I know. I know."

It hurt. But this wasn't the guilty hurt of lying on his parents' lawn, sobbing over ugly longings. This was grief, in the open presence and with the blessing of his beloved.

But it was so intense he had to stop in the street he'd strolled with Maka and hold his head back, tip his face toward the dimming sky, to make the tears flow back into his eyes. After a moment he started walking again, his arm around Erika. They passed the places that hadn't changed, the laundromat where he and Maka had washed clothes and the gas station where they'd bought shave ice.

The lost past.

In the next block, as they turned at the main road and walked on the cracked and chipped sidewalk, Erika saw the first of the food stands and the people in kimonos and the bright paper-ball lanterns hanging around the perimeter of the temple grounds. The lanterns cast a white glow against the sky, luminescent as sparklers on the Fourth of July.

Kal heard instruments playing from the *yagura,* the musicians' tower. He heard the *taiko* drums and the gongs, and they resonated inside him so that his flesh and his breath became notes, too. His heart beat music, instead of blood, and *bon-odori* spoke the language he understood, which was song.

Erika's first impression was that all the people at the festival were Japanese. But then she saw the *haole* faces in the crowd and those of other races, as well. She glanced at Kal beside her. His teal eyes alert, taking in this world that was part of his childhood.

"Let's eat something," he said, and Erika knew the words meant more than, *Are you hungry?* Kal meant, *Let's be here. Let's live.*

They had passed a shave-ice booth, and Erika saw another which sold sushi. "That's what I want."

"Say please." He put his arm around her.

The faces were bright with smiles, voices laughing and talking in English and Japanese and pidgin. Erika and Kal stood in line together and bought sushi with something mysterious inside and devoured it and moved on and bought teriyaki sticks, saimin and *mochi.* Kal loved to hear Erika's voice, her good manners. *Please* and *Thank you* and *Wow, that looks good.*

The people serving the food smiled at her and liked her, and Kal stayed close to her. She was as precious to him as song.

As the sky grew dark, the lanterns glowed brighter. The *yagura,* the red-and-white-striped square tower where the musicians played, dominated the center of the open temple grounds, and the round lanterns reached out from the ornate oriental roof with its up-curved edges. The glow they cast matched the music as the *bon* dancing began. He and Erika joined the other dancers, who had formed several concentric circles around the *yagura*. Kal felt the slow beat of the music inside him.

Oh, Maka...

Beside him, Erika forgot his presence. The dance was Yagi Bushi, from the Fukushima prefecture in Japan, which had once been the Akanas's home. She found she could follow the steps, and she remembered Adele, her friend, and felt joy in her heart, felt Adele's joy.

Then darker thoughts came, and with them came Skye. Erika made the apologies and vows of her heart, and the mystery of a mutual forgiveness enveloped her.

There was only the music, the dance for the souls who had left the pain of earth and also its joys. The smells and the tastes and the sounds.

The tone of the gongs vibrated in Kal's veins, and he was with Maka as he had never been since her death. Her voice spoke inside him and her smile reached behind his eyes as he moved, as he manipulated the *tenugui,* the small hand towel, lifting it over his head, sliding it behind his neck.

Kal, we're not in the same place anymore. You must let go.

Maka...

You'll be fine. You'll be so happy. I want you to be happy. I like her, your picture bride. You love her and enjoy many mango seasons, yeah? And don't forget the sweet plums in Kokee; they should be ripe now. It's already August, so wiki-wiki, Kalahiki.

He cried.

Remember what you tell her, Kal? Give...

The struggle raged inside him, separate from the joyful faces around him. He was a wrong element, out of sync.

Another dance. Fukushima Ondo.

Give... Let go. He separated himself from Maka, tried to look at her from far away, and she was smiling in the way that would never leave him. And with that gift from him, the first step of separation, he knew the first glimmer of her joy.

The dancing went on for hours. He and Erika knew only three dances, and there were many, some of them old. Bound by invisible silken threads, husband and wife, they stood together watching and eating more until the time of the service to honor the deceased.

They went into the temple then, to a ceremony that was otherworldly but of his world, too, of Hawaii. Buddhist incense filled Kal's head, and the gong purified him, clearing away all other music. He took Erika's hand and held it tightly. She was alive—and his.

THE NIGHT AIR on the beach, the ocean's own, was a welcome bath on their skin. Erika inhaled deeply as she carried the candlelit lantern down the hard wet sand to the shore. The lights floating on the sea would guide the spirits back to the netherworld.

Nearby she saw men and women filling a straw boat with food and other articles. Already lanterns were setting out on the ocean.

Erika waded into the water, remembering the stings on her hand, remembering the jellyfish. She set the floating lantern on the water and pushed it out, away from her. *Goodbye, Adele. I love you!*

Goodbye, Skye...

Her eyes leaked, crying at the beautiful sight, the lights reflected against the water, bobbing their way toward Niihau, the Forbidden Island, and beyond, to the Paradise of the Western Regions.

When she glanced over to where she'd seen Kal before, he was crouched at the water's edge, the legs of his long white pants dragging wet in the sand. He looked beautiful with the glow of that one candle lighting up his face. Erika knew the gift that single light, that Maka, had given her

by being loved and making love with Kal and bearing sweet
Hiialo.

Thank you, Maka, she thought. *I love them so
much.*

Kal's eyes were on the candle, the light inside the lantern, casting its glow onto his hands and the water and the
sand. Holding what represented Maka's soul, he stood up
and waded deeper into the sea.

Maka, I can't say goodbye. I can't say goodbye....

Kal, you know what to say.

The candle blurred with the water, with all the lanterns
everywhere, the loved and lost, the ancestral spirits, the
souls who had left the living behind. He set the lantern on
the surface of the water. It floated well, and he nudged it
away from him, pushed it farther away.

"Aloha, *ipo,*" he whispered. "Aloha."

He watched it drift till the current caught it and pulled
it away from him. Then he turned his back on the lantern
and waded out of the summer water to Erika, who was
holding their slippers. Her arms went around him, all
warm, and they turned away from the temple and walked
back along the beach to their car parked on the street
where he had lived and loved with Maka.

And she was really gone.

THAT NIGHT in their bedroom, they made love in the
comfort of cool darkness, and each knew the reassurance
of the other's body, of heartbeat and breath and the trust
of love.

"I needed you," he whispered. "You must have known
when you read that first letter, the letter I wrote when you
answered my ad."

"I guess that's true. It made me cry."

"*That* doesn't surprise me."

"I needed you, too, Kal. You know, I used to tell myself that only desperate people have anything to do with personal ads."

Their eyes met. Simultaneous laughter. *Who could have been more desperate than us?*

Kal's arms could have broken her with their embrace. He remembered something they'd talked about on the way home from Waimea, a surprise for Hiialo. "She's really going to make us crazy."

Erika smiled against him in anticipation of Hiialo's joy.

THEY'D BEEN INVITED to breakfast at his parents' house. Hiialo was awake when they arrived. She ran out into the foyer to see them, and when she saw the flat package wrapped in Cinderella paper, which Erika carried under her arm, her eyes grew big.

Kal smiled. "Come on in the living room, Hiialo. Where are Grandma and Grandpa?"

"Right here!" Armed with a camera, Mary Helen found a place beside the plate-glass windows while King leaned forward in his easy chair, petting Raiden. Kal had called to warn them that morning.

He and Erika sat down on the couch on each side of Hiialo.

"It's not my birthday," she said, clearly excited nonetheless. And she was already opening the envelope that held the card.

"Look, it's Kin!" She held up the card to show her grandparents. "Mommy painted Kin for me."

Then she unwrapped the package and turned over the special teal blue frame flecked with black and green.

"Oooh," she said. "Oh, Mommy, look what you made me." She hugged the picture, frame and all.

The camera flashed.

Everyone laughed.

"Look, Daddy! It's you and Eduardo."

The *mo'o's* head, neck and front feet were emerging from the dark water in the Blue Room. In the watercolor, Kal leaned forward from the ledge where he sat, as though listening for wisdom from the giant black lizard, whose tail just showed above the surface of the pool.

"I love this picture. I want it right by my bed."

"Hiialo," said Erika softly. "Your daddy and I talked about this. If you want, my publisher—" Her voice caught. Just Kurt was her publisher now. "We can make that picture into prints to sell and use the money for you to go to a *halau hula* when you're bigger, if you'd like."

"And I can be a hula dancer?" Hiialo asked, eyes wide.

Erika nodded.

"Oh, Mommy." Hiialo cuddled against her, gazing at the watercolor. "But would I have to give away my picture?"

"No, no, no. They make something called a plate and use the plate to make pictures like yours. Then other people can enjoy your daddy and Eduardo, too."

"Okay." Hiialo smiled big and kicked her feet on the couch. "I love my picture. It's the best picture you ever painted. And it's a good thing it's of Eduardo, because now I can remember what he looks like."

Kal stilled. Erika looked at him.

He gazed down at his daughter. "What do you mean, Hiialo?" A strange feeling crept up his spine, and he felt his parents—his father who'd never known anything but Hawaii and his mother who loved all things Hawaiian—staring, too. They all understood the same things. They all knew about *mo'os*.

Hiialo smiled happily at her picture. "Oh, he left. Last night."

The four adults in the room exchanged glances.

King reclined in his chair and levered the handle to pull out the footrest. His hand on Raiden's head, he observed, "I think that's probably a good thing."

Shifting her back against Erika, asking to be hugged, Hiialo said, "I don't need a *mo'o,* anymore. Now I have a mommy."

Kal caught Erika's eyes. He said, "We all have each other."

EPILOGUE

Two years later

"IT'S GOOD TO PLAY for a local crowd."

The revelers in the gym yelled back.

They were, as he'd said, mostly locals, from all the islands. But others in the audience were from the mainland. One listener was a producer from a growing independent label based in Seattle, a man who made his second home in Haena. Ever since he'd landed in Kauai for his annual two-week vacation, he'd been hearing the same voice on the radio. He was hearing it again, and he saw that the voice went with good looks and charisma. With star quality.

"We had to come back to Hanalei, because my wife, she *hapai*."

The crowd roared enthusiastically at this personal news.

In the back of the gymnasium Niau touched Erika's rounded stomach. "He obviously wanted to tell everyone that."

Erika thought the shaking on the floor was going to start her labor. "I think I need some air."

"I'm supposed to get him if you go into labor," Niau reminded her.

"No, I'm fine. I'll be back in a while." She made her way to the rear door and slipped out into the evening to look at the painted sky and the mist-laden *pali*. The night was warm. She could hear the music perfectly, and she lay down on the lawn on her side, putting her hand on her stomach against the cotton of her oversize T-shirt.

On the front of the T-shirt was a stylized reproduction of the cover art of Kai Nui's first CD, *Mo'o*. The picture was a reprint of the watercolor she'd given Hiialo two years before, *Blue Room Meeting*. Her father-in-law liked to joke that Hiialo could start her own *halau hula* with the money from that one picture. Two hundred and fifty lithographs had sold out, and a new poster series was in production. The *Mo'o* CD was gaining popularity in Los Angeles and San Diego; in Hawaii, it was first on the pop charts. Disc jockeys throughout the islands were spinning "Picture Bride" and "Mo'o" every hour. Everyone loved Kal. He was a *kamaaina,* a child of the land, one of their own.

On the lawn Erika listened to the music drifting from the gym, to his haunting voice, to what his fingers could do to a guitar. She lay on the grass through the whole first set. When she knew they were taking a break, she got up and went to the door behind the stage. It opened, and Jakka came out with his cigarettes. He smiled broadly at Erika, "Howzit?" He stuck his head back inside. "Eh, brah!"

Kal came outside, drenched with sweat.

He grabbed Erika and hugged her, adjusting his body to her shape. "You okay?"

"Fine. I just want to kiss you."

His lips covered hers before the words were out.

They spent the break together in the privacy of the Thunderbird. When it was time for the next set, Erika said, "I'm not going back in the gym, Kal. I can hear fine outside. It's too hot in there."

"Okay."

Welcoming the solitude, knowing such moments would be increasingly rare in the future, she lay down on the lawn again, listening to the songs she knew so well. The second set crept on. They played "Kona" and "Lanterns."

Then came "Picture Bride," and it sent shivers up her spine.

Shivers . . .

Cramps.

She sat up and got to her feet, limped barefoot over the warm lawn. Lihue was an hour away.

ERIKA HAD WAITED till the end of the second set to go into labor, but now Kal wanted to get away, to be with her. He left through the closest door of the gym and found her outside, with his mom and dad and Hiialo. Niau had called his parents on the phone. Everybody wanted to go to the hospital. Keale had promised to come from the Big Island as soon as the baby was born, and Leo was down in Poipu already, seeing a girlfriend. Even Jean and David and Chris and toddler Cecily were expected soon, coming by ship from Australia.

Couldn't have a baby without the whole *ohana*.

"Kalahiki," said a voice behind him.

Kal glanced back. A man had come out the door after him. A *malihini* in an aloha shirt. Expensive wristwatch. Big smile.

"I know you're in a hurry, but here's my card. I'll be in Haena for a couple of weeks. Give me a call."

Kal took the business card and pocketed it without looking at it. "My wife's having a baby. I have to go." He was already reaching for Erika's hand, and his dad was getting behind the wheel of his parents' new Land Rover, where Kin was looking out the window.

Danny peered out the door of the gym, grinning. "Eh, brah, we see you at da hospital, yeah?"

Kal returned his grin.

The man who had given him the business card waved. "Aloha."

NOON SUNLIGHT shone through the window of the birthing room.

"Look at her, Hiialo." Though at six she was getting too heavy to carry, Kal held Hiialo against his hip, reassuring her while they gazed down at Ano, his infant daughter in Erika's arms.

"You can both sit on the bed," said Erika. "I'm really fine." She scarcely noticed that her bottom was sore. She'd almost forgotten fifteen hours of labor in the happiness of holding Ano.

Kal set Hiialo on her feet, and she climbed up on one side of the bed. He walked around and sat gently on the other. He kissed Erika, touched her hair. "I love you. You're amazing."

Erika asked Hiialo, "Do you want to hold your sister?"

"Okay." Hiialo bit her lips together uncertainly.

"Now, don't let her head fall back. She can't hold it up on her own." Erika carefully moved the baby to Hiialo's arms and helped settle her. The baby winced, then shifted in her sleep. Erika hugged Hiialo and whispered, "I love you, Hiialo."

She felt Hiialo's body relax. Afraid of being supplanted by the baby. Hiialo said, "I love you, Mommy." Like a person making a decision, she said, "I love Ano, too. Oh, look. She's making a face. I think her nose is cute. Look at her cute nose, Mommy. Her hands are so small."

"I haven't even seen her eyes open yet," said Kal, one arm around Erika, the other hand on her leg. "Have you?"

Erika shook her head. She hoped they would be blue, like his.

King, Mary Helen, Leo and Niau all crowded in the door, looking in.

Niau said to her parents, "Hiialo's turn, I guess."

"Yes," said Hiialo. "I'm holding my sister."

The others went out, and after a while Hiialo yawned and said, "Is it Daddy's turn?"

"Are you done, Ti-leaf?"

"For now. I'll get to hold Ano lots."

Kal lifted his arms for the baby. Hiialo got down off the bed and went out into the hall. Erika heard her exclaim, "Danny! Is that a present for the baby? I got to hold her."

Kal held Ano, infatuated with her, seeing features that might have come from Erika or from him. It took him a moment to remember something he'd wanted to do when he and Erika were alone.

"I have a present for you." He glanced at Erika, then bent his head to nip at the shoulder of her hospital nightgown. When she lovingly nipped him back, he said, "It's in my shirt pocket. You've got to get it out."

Something they'd talked about before. She wanted it, too. He *hoped* she still wanted it.

Erika reached across, touching his chest, feeling his heart, before she dug into his shirt pocket and pulled out a key on a ring she had seen many times before, a key ring with a plastic pineapple on it.

It was just the key to the blue beach house, the key they gave David or Jean or whomever when they came to visit Kauai.

Erika started to reach into his pocket again.

Kal laughed, and the baby opened her eyes. "Look! Her eyes are going to be blue." He prodded Erika very gently. "Like our house."

"Kal!" She slid her arms around his neck and hugged him and kissed him.

Mary Helen and King looked in the door again, and Erika saw Hiialo beyond them in the hallway performing *hula kahiko* for an audience of aunt and uncles. She rested against Kal's shoulder and closed her eyes, embraced in the fold of her family.